Roger Ormerod is the author of over thirty novels.

He was born in 1920 and left school at seventeen to join the Civil Service in which he had spent most of his working life. He retired in 1970 and later worked as a postman and in the production control department of a heavy industry factory. He lives in Wolverhampton.

THIRD TIME FATAL

Philipa Lowe's school friend, Heather, is at last taking the plunge, and Philipa is attending the wedding with her friend Oliver. When the groom, Martin, doesn't turn up, they go to discover the cause of the delay. Though Martin is reported to have returned to his bed the previous night, he is not there now. But someone else is — a woman who is not merely naked but also dead. Is Martin as guilty as he seems, and what happened to the dead woman's clothes?

Books by Roger Ormerod
Published by The House of Ulverscroft:

A GLIMPSE OF DEATH
TIME TO KILL
FULL FURY
A SPOONFUL OF LUGER
SEALED WITH A LOVING KILL
THE COLOUR OF FEAR
DOUBLE TAKE
A DIP INTO MURDER
THE WEIGHT OF EVIDENCE
ONE DEATHLESS HOUR
TOO LATE FOR THE FUNERAL
CART BEFORE THE HEARSE
PARTING SHOT
FAREWELL GESTURE
THE SEVEN RAZORS OF OCKAM
FINE TUNE
FINAL TOLL
SHAME THE DEVIL

ROGER ORMEROD

THIRD TIME FATAL

Complete and Unabridged

ULVERSCROFT
Leicester

First published in Great Britain in 1992

First Large Print Edition
published 2003

British Library CIP Data

Ormerod, Roger, *1920 –*
    Third time fatal.—Large print ed.—
    Ulverscroft large print series: mystery
    1. Detective and mystery stories
    2. Large type books
    I. Title
    823.9'14 [F]

    ISBN 0–7089–4712–3

Published by
F. A. Thorpe (Publishing)
Anstey, Leicestershire
Set by Words & Graphics Ltd.
Anstey, Leicestershire
Printed and bound in Great Britain by
T. J. International Ltd., Padstow, Cornwall

This book is printed on acid-free paper

Dedicated with gratitude to Dorene for her invaluable advice on various aspects of the sex scene in Chapter Four.

R.O.

1

We were going to a wedding. Not ours, more's the pity, because Oliver was still stupidly concerned about marrying my money, as he called it, but nevertheless a wedding. I'd had the vague idea that it would give him romantic ideas, but so far I'd seen no sign of them.

Already, only fifty miles towards our objective, I knew we were going to be late, in spite of the fact that we'd started out early. He had assumed — almost insisted — that he would be doing the driving, and he was naturally taking it steadily. I couldn't blame him for that, as his right arm was recovering only slowly and was clearly giving him pain. I wasn't supposed to notice that. Oh — why do we have to stroke their egos so carefully?

Eventually my nerves wouldn't allow me just to sit there, staring at the dashboard clock.

'I'll take over if you like,' I offered, even managing to sound casual.

'Now, Phil . . . you know I've got to use my arm as much as I can, and the car's lovely to drive.'

1

I grimaced to myself, and settled deeper into my seat. That was the reason I'd bought it: easy to drive. It was a BMW 735 with an auto box and power-assisted steering, all of which I had hoped would ease the effort for him. But oh dear me, I'd even had to be careful over that. One wrong move and I'd have had him developing an inferiority complex.

Yet I had intended that I would be doing most of the driving. It was mine, after all, but it was significant that his reservations about sharing my income were not present when it came to driving my car.

'We're going to be late,' I said quietly.

'Nonsense!' He flicked me a distorted grin. 'You women — fuss, fuss. No need for hurry. It's only a wedding.'

Only! But it was the wedding of my special girlhood friend, Heather Payne, poor, repressed and unassertive Heather, who at school had needed me as a friend, as a buffer against life's agonies. To Heather, everything had been a painful obstacle to clamber over; everywhere confronting her were problems over which she would pessimistically brood herself into depression. No wonder she'd been so long getting herself married, in finding a man, the right man. But she had never possessed one iota of self-confidence, and I couldn't expect any improvement now. She would need me. She would quiver into hysteria if I wasn't there. And on time.

Ten miles further on I was beginning to work myself into a state of nerves. Still over a hundred miles to go, and Oliver was simply sitting back and enjoying the drive.

'Shall we stop for coffee?' I asked. 'The first place we come to.'

'I thought you were in a hurry.'

'All the same . . . '

Then, sitting opposite him with a table between us, I could observe what I had guessed, that his face was pale with tension and his lips down-drawn against the pain.

'You're overdoing it,' I told him.

'I can still drive — '

'The keys,' I demanded, holding out my hand. He hesitated. I insisted. 'After all, it's my car, and you won't let me get my hands on it. The keys, please.'

Then he smiled, and things happened to Oliver when he smiled, gloriously intimate things that caught at my heart. I knew he realized I was sparing him from having to admit that the effort had almost beaten him. He placed the keys in my palm.

'It's got a bit of understeer unless you accelerate round the corners,' he told me.

'I'll watch it.'

'And don't forget it's not run in yet.'

'I'll not forget.'

What I wasn't forgetting was that we had a little over two hours in which to reach the church, which was about ninety miles away, and there was no motorway to which we could easily resort. And Heather would be a quaking mess if I wasn't there on time.

'Didn't I tell you,' said Oliver ten minutes later, when I clipped a grass verge on a fast corner.

I said nothing. The car was a dream to drive fast, and the engine refused to feel or sound over-stressed. I relaxed and gave it its head.

One of the difficulties was that we were driving into unknown territory. Neither of us knew Somerset, and we had only the simple instructions that St Asaph's was twenty miles inland from the north coast. Head for Lynton, had been my instruction over the phone. Then Oliver, who was a better driver than navigator, gave me a seemingly wrong direction, and in five minutes we could see glimpses of the sea ahead, and we hadn't passed a church for miles.

'Hell!' I said.

'Next left,' he told me.

'How d'you know that?'

'I took the precaution of looking it up in a

church directory, my love. Somehow, I guessed we'd get lost.'

I said nothing, but took the next left. The clock on the dash already indicated that we were late. Poor Heather!

It was a tiny church on the edge of a village that had never developed into anything resolute, little bits of it exploring side lanes and baulking at the hills that surrounded it. It had no centre, just a few houses clustering about the church, where a stream trickled along beside the road, and another few visible around the bend further along. In front of the lich-gate was parked a very smart Mercedes sports coupé, and no other car. Leaning against the gate was a bored, dark-haired man who looked about forty but was probably less. The best man? If so, why wasn't he with the groom? Or was this the groom himself? No — he couldn't be. No groom could look so bored. Impatient, perhaps, if the bride was late, but surely not bored.

Then I saw that the bride was not in fact late, as she walked into sight from inside the churchyard. And oh, how she had changed! Plumper, even slightly podgy now, her hair no longer the bright cascade of gold I could recall, but an indeterminate straw with shades of grey, and in a blue going-away costume that did nothing for her figure. She was clearly under stress, unable, it seemed, even to stand without great effort.

It was the groom who was late. Wasn't it part of the best man's duties, to get the groom there on time?

She recognized me at once, clattering forward on high heels, her arms wide.

'Oh, Philipa! Phillie!'

Then she was shaking against me, sobbing, ruining her makeup but not caring for anything now. Because he hadn't arrived.

I thrust her away from me a little, sufficient to be able to consider her face. As I recalled her, still she had that petulant, pouting expression of a child deprived of something she wanted and had to have. There had always been a point when she had been able to resort to a reserve of stubborn and inflexible purpose, and if the desire was strong enough she would go to extreme lengths to satisfy it. What she currently desired was marriage to this particular specimen of manhood, even though he lacked the grace to be on time, and by heaven she intended to get him.

But he hadn't turned up to be got.

Beyond her, I could see that Oliver was having a few words with the bored and clearly hung-over man, who had to be the best man. I made comforting sounds, and when I felt

6

that very soon she was going to collapse in my arms I led Heather to my BMW and got her seated inside, sliding in beside her.

By now a few of the guests, or perhaps all of them, had followed to see what was going on. Or not. It was going to be a quiet wedding if it ever got going. That would be typical of Heather, always so introverted and never one for show. There were two hovering ladies, one in pink and one in green, who were clearly her maids-of-honour, but they hovered at a discreet distance, looking pained at Heather's distress but not intending to become closely involved. Was I Heather's only real friend? I tried my best to justify the responsibility.

'That's the best man?' I asked her.

'Yes. It's his friend, Jeff Carter.'

'I don't even know your . . . your man's name.'

'It's Martin. Martin Reade. With an 'e' on the end.'

'And what does Jeff Carter say about him?'

'They had a party . . . '

'Oh yes, they would. Stewed to the eyeballs, I'll bet. And didn't his friend see him home?'

'I don't know,' she whispered. 'I don't know anything.'

'Then we'll have to find out.'

7

I got out of the car and went over to Oliver, who was looking very annoyed. 'Like getting blood out of a stone,' he told me, clipping the words.

I took a more careful look at Jeff Carter. He was a thin, angular man, dark and sullen with grey, piercing eyes, very much bloodshot now. He was untidily dressed for a wedding, in a crumpled suit he seemed unused to. Quite definitely he'd been drunk the previous night. If he'd had a shave that morning, he had forgotten to put a blade in his razor. He wouldn't raise his eyes to mine after the first glance.

'He doesn't remember getting home,' said Oliver. 'Says he walked. The party was at The Rolling Stone, a pub in the next village.'

'Hasn't Jeff got a car? How did he get here this morning?'

'He's got a car,' said Oliver patiently. 'A black Fiesta. But it's not in running order. Got a lift from a mate who was coming this way.'

'Hasn't he tried to contact him, this Martin Reade?'

'Take it easy, Phil,' said Oliver quietly. We had been talking about Jeff as though he wasn't there. Strictly speaking, he wasn't. Certainly, his mind was somewhere else, groping for its way to the present.

8

'He could have phoned,' I said stubbornly. 'Done something, anyway, instead of just standing here.'

'He's phoned, from that box along there, by the little bridge. Several times — but there was no answer.'

'Right,' I said. 'Then it's obvious. We'll have to go and dig him out.'

'Exactly,' agreed Oliver gently. He'd already decided that.

I went back to Heather, who had crunched herself into a compact ball of misery in the passenger seat, and told her what we'd decided to do. There was some difficulty in getting her to understand, but in the end we got her into the Mercedes, which was her own I gathered, and in which they had intended to drive to Heathrow Airport for a plane to New York, on their honeymoon.

'Now don't worry,' I said. 'He's probably hung-over, but we'll get him here somehow. Now, tell me how to reach his place.'

She looked at me for a moment with empty swimming blue eyes, making an effort to understand what I'd said. Then she got it, and gave me the directions. Martin Reade had a garage, where he dispensed petrol, sold second-hand cars, and did repairs to local vehicles. It was eight miles away. Straight through this bit of a village, turn left at the

9

crossroad, and it would be on our right. Couldn't miss it. There was just one detail I nearly forgot. I turned back to Heather. How would we know if we passed him on his way here? It was easy, she said. Martin ran a bright yellow Triumph Dolomite, which he used for rallies. We would be able to tell it by the dents, I gathered.

Once again I drove. Oliver was silent. I glanced at him and he sensed my mood.

'Sheer hell, these weddings,' he said.

'They wouldn't be if you stupid men didn't have wild stag parties on the night before.'

'There're hen parties, too.'

'It's not the same.'

'Who can say? Who's ever been to both?'

We passed no yellow car coming the other way. We saw only two vehicles, one of those a farm tractor. And, with eight miles on the mileometer, there was his garage, just this side of another village, but a more sizeable one than Heather's.

Reade's Rapid Repairs, indicated the sign. Crypton tuning. The repair shed was corrugated iron, a little back from the forecourt, which had four pumps and a small kiosk. We drew on to one side of the forecourt. At the far side of it there was a line of six cars, all of them with price stickers on the windows. Nothing was over £2,000.

There was no sign of a battered yellow Triumph Dolomite.

As we hadn't drawn up beside the pumps, the shadowy figure in the kiosk made no sign of life. We got out of the car and approached. Oliver opened the kiosk door. It was a young man, his head lowered over a magazine, flowing hair draping forward to mask the nudes.

'Is Martin Reade around?' asked Oliver.

'Doubt it. Gone on his honeymoon, he has.' The head was lowered dismissively. For a moment, dark eyes had flicked over us with rejection.

'Did you see him leave?'

'Nah. He'd have gone before I got here. I'm in charge. For a fortnight I am, anyway.'

'Where does he live when he's here?' Oliver was being carefully patient.

'Got a place behind the repair shed.'

'Thank you,' said Oliver. 'Much obliged.'

We walked round to the rear. The surface here was untreated soil, very much cut into channels, but now hard and difficult to walk on. It was June, hot already at ten in the morning, the sun baking every surface. It seemed to bounce back at us from the half-cylinder of the corrugated iron repair shed. It was an army surplus Quonset hut from the last war, rusting itself away, with

11

windows set half-way up its curved sides. A smell of oil and fumes and hot rubber assailed us as we passed the sliding door at one end, which was half open. It appeared that it had been in this position for a number of years, as the bottom edge was not in its rails.

Walking past this opening, I glanced inside. The yellow Dolomite was there, six feet off the ground on a hydraulic hoist. I had no difficulty in recognizing it, as my father had owned a Dolomite when I was very young. What seemed to be its engine was on the bench to one side, beneath one of the windows. Its tappet cover was off. I could see the word Triumph cast in the aluminium cover.

Martin Reade seemed to be fairly well equipped. I'd been inside repair bays before, and knew an electronic tuning set-up when I saw one, recognized the air-pressure tank, and knew that the circular table was for stripping tyres from their rims.

We paused only a moment. Oliver had been keeping his attention all around him, as befitted an ex-police inspector, and said, 'Let's go and have a look at his cottage.'

It was thirty feet further back, this again a relic from the war, a pre-fab house set on a concrete base, designed for quick and easy erection and not expected to last for this length of time. But so many are still standing sturdily, and happily occupied by people who like a compact home.

All the curtains were drawn, as though the last occupation had been in darkness. Oliver tried the front door, set centrally in the side facing us. It opened. He grunted at that, and led the way in.

One living-room, one bedroom, a small kitchen. The bathroom was so tiny that it demanded a shower. Its door was open. No shower; just a hand basin and a toilet unit.

'Anybody home?' Oliver called out.

There was silence, a silence seemingly deeper than a simple lack of sound. He tried a door from the narrow hall. It opened into a living-room. The light was still burning, a central unit in the ceiling. We hadn't noticed this from outside. Instinctively, my hand moved towards the switch, but he said quickly, 'No.'

It was then, my attention drawn to him, that I realized he had changed. There was something tense about him, concentrated. His gaze was moving slowly round the room, absorbing and memorizing what he saw. I had to suppose it was instinct. He must have been aware, from tiny facets of the situation carefully dovetailed into his consciousness,

13

that there was something here out of order.

To me, it was simply an untidy room with an ancient settee which had collapsing unholstery and looked as though a suddenly lowered bottom would raise a cloud of dust. There was a TV set, small, which had a suit of filthy overalls thrown over it. Even in here, the stench of oil and rubber predominated. There was one easy chair, also with its stuffing escaping on to the worn carpet, one upright chair, and a small table. Those completed the contents of the room.

Oliver backed out. Our eyes were now accommodating to the low light level, after the blaze of the sun outside. It was possible to see that the door opposite was open an inch or two. He urged it further with the end of a ballpoint pen, and took one pace inside.

A bedroom. There was a single bed beneath the window opposite us, which was draped with a thin, tenuous curtain. The light was just good enough to reveal details. A green metal vertical cupboard, which would have looked more at home in the repair shed, was being used as a wardrobe. Its doors were open, and there was very little in it. A simple chest of drawers was against another wall. The only floor covering was a car carpet, thin, worn and blue.

On the bed, beneath a single sheet, with

dark hair splashed against a dirty pillow, there was somebody lying very still, as though the alcohol fumes still held sway. Oliver crossed to the bed in three quick strides. His finger hooked under the edge of the sheet, and he lifted it clear of the face. I couldn't see anything from where I was standing.

'It isn't him,' he said softly. 'It's a woman. Stay where you are, Phil, and don't touch a thing.'

I drew in a quick breath. He lifted the sheet higher, peering beneath, and I caught just a whiff of perfume, something resembling cedar, and not normally a woman's scent.

'And she's naked,' he murmured.

'It's not polite . . . ' I protested.

'She won't mind.' He shook his head, a sad and weary gesture. 'She's dead, Phil. Dead.'

He must have sensed a death the moment we'd entered beneath the roof. Police experience, I had to suppose. I was unable to imagine how he could be so calm and undisturbed about it, when cold sweat was trickling down my back. And how could he bear to touch her, even though it was only with the back of his hand to her cheek? Twice, he touched her, first the cheek, then with one exploratory finger beneath her hair, behind the ear.

'Where are her clothes?' I asked. To me, my

15

voice sounded distant and cold.

'What? Clothes? How do I know?'

'I don't see any about,' I persisted.

'Put away in the cupboards,' he said impatiently, anxious to get away from there as fast as possible.

'Oh, use your imagination, Oliver, please. What d'you think we've got here? A woman for him on his last night of freedom . . . she'd strip off and toss her clothes — little enough of them, I'd guess — any old where. So where are they?'

'It's not for us to speculate.' He seemed annoyed. His anger dismissed Martin Reade from his mind as an acceptable male — he who would take a woman to his bed on the night before his wedding. But what surprised me was his lack of curiosity. A woman was dead in Martin Reade's bed, and he hadn't turned up for his wedding . . . and Oliver was all cool practicality.

'Let's get out of here,' he said abruptly. 'There ought to be a phone in that kiosk.'

'A phone? Who d'you want to call — the vicar?'

'Philipa . . . ' He sighed. 'He didn't simply leave a dead woman in his bed, he left a murdered one. There's an abrasion behind her ear and blood in her hair.'

'But you can't . . . it can't be!'

I was completely thrown off my balance, my concern not for this anonymous dead woman, not for the missing Martin Reade, but for my poor dear Heather, waiting there. Waiting.

Oliver was ushering me into the open, anxious to get out of the house. 'I'll have to report it to the police, Phil. Surely you can see that. And you — '

I halted him. 'Now wait a minute. Don't be so damned cold and official about it. Are you implying that this Martin Reade — whom we've never met, so we know nothing about him — that he'd not only have a woman in his bed and kill her, but would do it on the night before his own wedding, and then take all her clothes away? It makes no sense.'

He now seemed impatient with me. 'Let's leave it to the police, Phil. Shall we?'

'But her clothes . . . '

'Damn it, he might think it would hide her identity to take them away. He might've thought anything.'

'Rubbish. She's probably a local girl — in a country district. Of course she'll be missed.'

'The important thing is not what you think, Phil. Not what I might think, either. It's what *he* might have thought. And we don't know that. Now be sensible. I'll call the police, and wait for them, and you . . . ' He looked into my eyes, all sympathy now for me and my predicament. 'Sorry, but it's got to be done — you drive to St Asaph's . . . ' He leaned forward and kissed me on the cheek. 'Let's get it over, shall we!'

I was trapped, and there was no point in struggling. Miserable now, my mind racing, I walked beside him back to the kiosk, my ankles turning on the hard-packed ruts.

Oliver opened the kiosk door. There had been no change inside. The young man turned bored eyes on us.

'Have you seen him this morning?' Oliver asked.

'Not seen him since yesterday mornin'. Told you that. I'm here on me own. The amount we've bin selling, we might just as well not open.'

'He's left it to you for . . . how long?'

'A fortnight,' he said. 'I told you that as well. He's gonna call from the US if they decide to stay on. So he said. Don't ask me. What gives, anyway?'

Plainly, he knew nothing of any relevance. Oliver glanced at me. 'Better get going,' he said. 'I'll have to hang on here, I expect.' He leaned past the youth's shoulder and read out the number on the phone. 'You might be able to contact me here, Phil.'

I nodded. He was the complete professional now, back in a routine that had been his life, before a shotgun had nearly robbed him of his right arm. 'I'll be in touch.'

Then I went back to the BMW, at last in full and sole control of my own car, and I was not looking forward to the trip at all. It had to have an ending, when I must confront Heather. And what the hell would I say?

Logically I should have driven slowly, rehearsing my announcement, but I found myself driving on the very limit allowed by the winding lanes. I was anxious to get it over, rushing to get it done before my nerve failed, and all the while my anger was growing against this man, the first Heather had found for herself. He had barely entered her life before he'd ruined it.

The Mercedes was no longer parked outside the church, and there was no sign of guests or best man. So perhaps she had driven back to her home, the location of which I didn't know, almost too blinded by tears to be able to drive. I stopped. The vicar was just closing the gate. I got out of the car.

'I'm too late.'

'You are, young lady, and a very happy occasion it has been.'

I realized I was standing on a sprinkling of

flower petals. 'Has it?' I asked emptily, my mind groping.

'They had to leave in a hurry, to catch a plane I understand. Such a handsome couple, I must say, though I did think the groom might have had a shave and changed out of a suit he could well have slept in.' But his grimace was one of amusement. It had still been a happy occasion. He inclined his head, and slowly moved away.

For two solid minutes I stood there like a fool, wondering what to do. Could I simply back away from the responsibility, allowing Heather at least the delight of her honeymoon before she returned to . . . well, to what? But that would mean a whole fortnight for her with a man I knew nothing about, except that he was possibly a murderer. Or should I chase after them, and perhaps catch them before their departure and . . . well, do what? Warn her? Warn him? Try to persuade them to return?

But, damn it, I was wasting time. Responsiblities have to be faced, or your inadequacy will surely undermine you. I began to run towards the phone booth by the little bridge, repeating over and over in my head the number of that kiosk, in case I lost it in the last second.

It was answered at the first ring. 'Hello.

20

Who is this, please, and who do you wish to speak to?' I knew that official tone. Oliver had dutifully called the police, and they were on the job. Now I dared not say a word. I simply hung up.

There remained no alternative but to go alone after Heather and her new husband. I didn't know what flight they were on, nor how much time I had. They had started late themselves, so I would have to drive hard to make it.

A quick glance at my map indicated that I could pick up the M5 at Taunton and the M4 at Junction 20 and straight along there to Heathrow. It would be over 150 miles of motorway driving. I got settled into my seat and started to reduce that distance.

I have to admit that I drove like a maniac. The car even encouraged it, seeming to be happier at speed. But I was running the risk of police intervention because I was rarely out of the overtaking lane, as I overtook everything. Every minute I expected a police car on my tail or a police trap for me ahead. But I got through and reached Heathrow just two and a quarter hours from St Asaph's.

I had never been to Heathrow, not as a visitor from outside it, and the directions are confusing. I had to watch the signs anxiously, assuming that International was what I wanted, and when I reached it I was clearly in a limited parking area. But to hell with that. I left the car and ran into the reception hall.

It was chaos. Mid-June, and everybody wanted to be in some other country but their own. I was looking for Heather's blue going-away costume, and I could barely see twenty yards ahead, and that was with jumping up and down. And what airline was I looking for? Pan Am? Aer Lingus? Air India? British Airways?

Then I saw them. They had already checked in their luggage and were turning away from the desk. Heather was pointing upwards, where the steps led to the departure lounge. The tall, slim and seemingly placid man beside her was allowing her to take the lead. Maybe it was no more than courtesy, but he would have to learn that Heather required, even demanded, to be taken care of, to be reassured, to be cosseted.

I tried to run towards her, but a man and a woman were before me. They closed in on Heather's man, on Martin Reade. I saw the male partner of the duo plunge a hand into his inside pocket and show both Heather and Martin something. A few words were spoken, then a heavy hand was rested on Martin's forearm. Martin was flapping with his free hand, protesting, throwing back his protests to Heather, who was standing lost and confused and unable to move. Before following her partner, the female officer paused for a few words with Heather, and to offer a smile, which did nothing to reassure my poor lost friend.

Then the group of three was lost in the crush, and around Heather there was a clear space, as though a plague had descended on her.

Into that space I stepped.

2

She stared at me with huge and furious blue eyes. The anger quenched the tears for now, and left her quivering with a hard and implacable determination that I'd seen only once before.

Heather had always cherished a passion for fairness. Life was supposed to be fair — wasn't it? I'd told her often that life wasn't at all fair, and she was expecting too much. Yet she always did expect it, depended on it. Life wasn't fair to Heather because she expected, all too often wrongly, to be carried through its difficulties. And if the unfairness became too blatantly cast against her, she would weep. If it passed a certain point of harshness, then, and only then, would she explode into fury and action. She had once been given an imposition for something she had not done. Stubbornly, she had written a hundred lines of Virgil, taken them to her house mistress, and torn them to shreds before her eyes. And only then had she collapsed into a weeping mess.

That fury was gripping her now. Could anything be less fair? I knew I had to step in quickly before she began to scream, and tear something else. Such as my hair.

'They can't do this,' I said, before she could. 'We're not going to let them get away with it. Oh no. I'll throw the best lawyers into — '

'*You will?*' she demanded. 'Indeed! I'll do the throwing, thank you, Philipa. I'll get damages for wrongful arrest . . . '

'It was an arrest, was it?'

'What the hell did it look like?' she stabbed at me. 'I don't know . . . understand . . . Oh, Phillie, what am I going to do?'

So we'd got past the aggressive stage and re-entered the more usual pitifully inadequate attitude. I'd taken the edge off it.

'Let's try to find a bar,' I said. 'We can't talk here.' We were being jostled, and the apologies were becoming less sincere. 'I could do with something. What about you, Heather?'

She allowed me to take her arm, glanced quickly at my face, and said, 'But they've taken him *away!*' It was a muted wail.

I found the bar, bought us two brandies, and settled her at a table behind hers. Then I excused myself and left her brooding over it, but quiet, menacingly quiet. The first thing was to move my car. I was due for a bit of luck, and there it was. It hadn't been ticketed, towed away, or clamped. I drove it to a short-stay park, returned, and headed for where I'd seen the rank of telephones. I dialled that kiosk number again, and this time I was lucky. Oliver answered it.

'Of all the dirty, rotten tricks!' I shouted, before he could say a word. 'I could kill you, Oliver. Kill you.'

'Phil? What's wrong? Where the devil have you got to?'

'Don't you change the subject, Oliver Simpson. I'm at Heathrow, and they've just arrested Martin Reade. Dragged him off under Heather's nose. And who else could've tipped them off but you?'

There was a slight pause. I heard him sigh. 'I've told them nothing, Phil, nothing except the basic facts leading to how we came to find the body. Now relax, and tell me what's happened. The Scene of Crime team's still working here, but they've hardly troubled me. Tell me why you're at Heathrow.'

He was speaking in a quiet, controlled voice, which I supposed was a professional trick, used to calm hysterical women. Had I sounded like that? Clearly, it must have seemed so, for how could I have expected Oliver to guess that Heather and Martin had travelled to Heathrow as planned? So I drew a deep breath and began again more sensibly.

I told him what had happened, how he and I seemed to have missed Martin Reade on his way to the church, that they were married — and the police had picked him up in the main concourse.

'It all sounds ridiculous to me,' he said in a puzzled voice. 'There's no way they could have operated so quickly, and from what I can gather there's nothing yet sufficiently positive to warrant an arrest, his or anybody else's.'

'From what you can gather?' I asked sceptically. They wouldn't confide in Oliver.

'The officer in charge of the team seems to be a sergeant, and he's friendly enough. As long as I keep away from that pre-fab, he doesn't care what I do. I've told him he can find me at The Rolling Stone, which is just along the road from here. As you can, Phil, when you get back here. I suppose you *are* coming back?'

'I've got to, haven't I? If only to pick you up. And I'll have to see that Heather gets home all right. Is there any identification yet, Oliver? The dead woman.'

'No. There was comment on her missing clothes . . . your point, as I remember. Otherwise, nothing. I'll see you here, then?'

'Yes. Certainly. But I'm trying to handle a woman who's on the brink of something, and she might leap either way. She's changed since I knew her. I mean, really changed. Still the poor lost soul in need of support, but there's something harder now behind it. I can't stand here talking, though. Must get back to her. I'll see you later . . . some time.'

'Look after yourself.' Then he hung up.

I hurried back to Heather, and only just in time, it seemed. She had finished her brandy and had nearly finished mine.

'Hey, take it easy,' I said. 'You've got to do some driving, you know.'

She seemed dazed. 'Driving?'

'Your car's here, somewhere. You'll have to drive it back home. I'll tag along in mine.'

'I suppose.' All impetus had flowed from her.

'Where else is there to go?' I asked.

'I don't want to be *anywhere*.'

'Of course you do. He'll need to know where to go when they release him.'

'To me?' she asked hollowly.

'Of course. I expect they've taken him in — somewhere — for questioning. Nothing worse than that. When they let him free, where else would he go but to his wife?'

'Don't call me his wife,' she said dully.

I attempted a laugh, but I knew this mood. The shock had taken her back to her childhood. 'Come on, Heather, you can't disown him simply because he's been picked up for questioning.'

She glared at me. Her fingers were white round my brandy glass. I half expected it to shatter in her hand. 'Disown!' she said bitterly. 'I don't disown him. He's mine. I want him. I love him, Phil. Lord, how I love him! You just can't imagine. It's agony. I can't live without him and they've dragged him away.'

'But not for ever,' I said comfortingly. Heavens, it was going to be hard work. Had I got to explain that if it came to the worst, even a life sentence these days need not mean more than six years? Six years to Heather would seem like an eternity, just at this moment.

'For ever and ever,' she whispered.

'Nonsense. I wouldn't be surprised if you get home to find him waiting on your doorstep. *His* doorstep, now.' I felt it did no harm to stretch the possibilities at this time.

'It's not his home. I'm not his. He's not mine.' Her eyes were raised to my face at last, puffy and pathetic and with a wild look in them. 'Can't you get it into your thick head, Philipa, that he can't ever be mine? He's already married.'

'Already . . . ' I couldn't think how to go on with that.

'What d'you think they arrested him for,

you fool? They distinctly used the word: bigamy.'

I saw that she was caught between a quivering fury at Martin, for deceiving her, and a moaning outburst at the infamy of life in general. I had to get her out of there before she began throwing things.

'Come along,' I said briskly. 'On your feet. Home for you, my girl, and no arguing. We've got to sort this thing out, and the sooner the better. There's something all wrong here, I'm sure. Very wrong.'

A little unsteadily, she got to her feet. I put a hand to her arm. She walked with me like a child, led, trusting and lost. Pressing through the crowd in the concourse, I suddenly thought of something.

'Oh heavens, your luggage. It'll be on its way.'

'Luggage? Damn the luggage. Where're you taking me?'

To my car, that was where, because it was now quite clear that she couldn't be trusted behind a steering wheel. Another problem. For once, she didn't take it to herself and brood about it. She hadn't realized it.

'Where's your Mercedes?' I asked.

'In the long-stay park. Somewhere. Martin was driving and I didn't really notice.'

'Then it'll have to remain there for now.

30

Come on — I'm parked over this way.'

She dragged, hesitated, then abruptly broke into a trot, stopped, hid her face in her hands, and had to be urged onwards. As I got her seated in the BMW she said, 'I'll kill him if it's true.'

I didn't know what she meant, so I said nothing. There had been no conviction in it. I drove us out of there, and found my way back to the M4. Steadily, we headed westwards.

I still hadn't decided what to tell her. That Martin had been arrested for bigamy in consequence of his marriage to Heather was quite unacceptable. I didn't know much about the law on bigamy, but I did know something about police procedures, my father having been a chief superintendent. And I was certain that the police didn't look on bigamy, these days, as a terrible crime against the populace. No — for the police to become involved would require a long and tedious process, probably initiated by the injured party. It was impossible for Heather's marriage to Martin to have become involved in this. There just hadn't been enough time.

I asked her for fuller details, in a tentative way, but there was no response. When I glanced at her I saw she was asleep, perhaps from the brandy, but more likely because of emotional exhaustion. It had been a day she

31

would never forget, probably that I would not forget, either.

Yet still I had not told her about the naked and dead woman in Martin's bed. I dreaded the thought. She would probably fall apart altogether.

On this trip I took it easy. There was a certain amount of urgency involved, but not enough to risk being picked up. Heather remained asleep, an exhausted sleep with her mouth fallen open. I was abruptly seized by a feeling of such tender sympathy that for a moment tears blinded my vision. But I had to be practical. There was no time for emotion. She had to be told, and it would be better if it was settled before I had to face Oliver with her by my side. He would plunge in, assuming she had already heard the worst.

I drew in at the service area just beyond Junction 17. She awoke to the stillness of the car. 'Where? What?'

'A cup of tea, Heather. A bite to eat, perhaps.'

'I couldn't touch a thing.'

No? I got her to a table and fetched us two of everything in sight. I was ravenous and when it came to it so was she. She seemed to have dismissed her problems from her mind. She loved Martin, was certain he loved her, so it all had to be a mistake. My nerve went.

I couldn't tell her at that table.

We sat in the car. She turned in her seat to face me. 'Are we just going to sit here? Why aren't we moving?'

'There's something more that you've got to know, Heather.'

'More? How can there be more?'

'Something you don't know. Oliver and I didn't see Martin heading past us for the church. His yellow Dolomite was in his repair shed when we got there. I don't know how we missed him — how he got to the church.'

'Oh, I know that.' She flipped it away with an undulation of her palm, a minor distraction. 'He told me. He'd got his friend Jeff's Fiesta in for some work on the brakes. He'd promised to let him have the car back before he . . . before we went away, and yes, he was drunk last night. They got him back to his place, and he remembered Jeff's car. He's like that, Martin is. He'll go to extremes so's not to let down a friend. You'll see. You'll meet him. Everybody likes him.'

Every woman on whom he cast an eye? 'I'm sure you're right. And yes, I'll have to meet him.'

'Yes.' She nodded. 'How could anything horrible happen . . . ' She put her hand to her eyes, lowered it, took a deep breath, and went on. 'He'd done the work, see. All it needed was a test run. So — he took it out on the road.'

'At night? Drunk?'

'He's done rally driving, Phil. He knows how far he can go, or not. He was out — oh, ten miles away — and he told me he felt sleepy. So sleepy. He didn't dare to drive like that, so he pulled into a lay-by and had a nap. And he didn't wake up until ten minutes before he was supposed to be at the church. That's why he looked so terrible and scruffy. Poor dear! But he got there, so everything was . . . was all right.' Her voice went wobbly just there.

'But it wasn't all right,' I told her gently.

'Don't I know it! Perhaps . . . perhaps it's all some stupid joke his mates played on him. Having him arrested.' She brightened at this obscure thought. 'You know what they're like . . . men. Anything for a laugh, and if they're drunk enough . . . '

She turned to me, her face shining at this treasured rationalization.

'I don't think it was a joke, Heather. No, don't toss your head. You've got to listen very carefully. Martin's in trouble, real trouble, and it's not over bigamy. Bigamy's no big deal, nowadays. But there's been a death, Heather.' I stopped there, waiting for her to absorb each detail separately. She'd never been very astute, always struggling to understand. Slowly, take it slowly.

'A death? You don't mean . . . Oh, I see. Out with Jeff's car — don't tell me Martin knocked somebody down. Killed them! How terrible.'

'No. Not that. When we got to Martin's garage this morning . . . that's my friend and I. Oliver Simpson. You'll like him. When we got there, we went to that little pre-fab of his — '

'Isn't it horrible!' she cried. 'I just *had* to rescue the poor dear from that.'

'When we got there, we tried the pre-fab to see if he was there.'

'Of course he wasn't. He was sleeping in Jeff's car. Somewhere in the lanes. Or just about waking up.'

'I know that, Heather. Now, I do. We didn't know it then, so we went inside to look, and there was somebody in his bed.'

'Then it wasn't Martin.' She nodded, certain of that.

'It was a woman.'

'In his bed! You're lying. He wouldn't. He was testing Jeff's brakes.'

'He wasn't in the pre-fab, anyway, when we got there.'

'I've told you, over and over. He was asleep in Jeff's car . . . '

'So all right,' I conceded heavily. 'But this woman was there — '

'I know what it is,' she burst in, flapping a palm on her knee, over and over, faster and heavier. A core of distress was building up. She had matured; she now used anger to boost her, in lieu of sympathy and encouragement. 'You're trying to make me hate him, so that I shan't regret losing him. My God, Philipa, you always were devious, but you're going too far now. I'm warning you — you're going too far.'

'There was a woman in his bed,' I repeated quietly. 'And a lot of people are going to be able to confirm that. Official people, Heather. Such as the police. So accept it, please. I'm just trying to put you in the picture.'

'Well, thank you! Police? What the hell are you talking about? As though he'd have a woman in his bed the night before . . . the night before . . .'

'She was dead, Heather. Dead. And the indications were that it wasn't natural. She'd been struck a blow — '

'Let me get out of this car!'

I reached over for her arm. She stared down at my fingers, too tight no doubt. 'Don't be stupid, Heather. Listen to me. We're in this together.'

She stared into my eyes, the fear and the

fury and the distress distorting her face. I tried to smile. Then she shrugged me off.

'Together?' she asked suspiciously.

'If you want it like that.'

'All right. Tell me the worst. Get it over.'

'She'd been killed, Heather, by a blow behind the ear, with something hard and heavy. And Heather . . . she was naked.'

'Oh dear Lord!' she whispered.

'That's nearly the lot. You know what we're up against now.'

'But they said . . . well, bigamy.'

'They did? You're sure of that?' I was still doubtful. 'Think, Heather. It might be important.'

Her eyes were wild. 'Think! How can I think?'

'Try to remember. What was said?'

She pressed her fingers to her temples. 'All formal,' she said, mumbling it. 'Something like: Martin Reade, you did bigamously marry . . . ' She stopped.

'Not you, surely! That couldn't be.'

'No, no. Don't be an idiot.'

'Then who?'

'It was Scottish. Mac something. McBride, that was it. Bride, you see, and *I* was the bride. That's how I remember. Jean . . . no, June McBride. This month. I remember that, too. That you did bigamously marry June

McBride. The man said that. His very words. Who the devil's June McBride? That's what I'd like to know.' She glared at me, as though I'd have the answer.

I stared back, unable to tie down a whole string of contradictory thoughts. If there was a charge of bigamously marrying this June McBride, that had to mean there had been another wife before her. At least one. Had this Martin Reade left behind him a whole string of deserted wives? And where did that leave poor Heather? Her own marriage would be void, useless, a nothing ceremony. Not simply voidable, which meant a marriage that could be annulled, but a marriage that did not exist.

Now I felt desperate. Could I try to load on Heather another complication? Could I expect her to appreciate it? Fortunately, she found her own answer.

'Perhaps,' she suggested in a flat voice, 'this June McBride is the dead one in his bed. So if she died in the night, then he didn't marry *me* bigamously. Then *that's* all right.'

How wonderful is the brain, sorting out its own pressures and providing a soothing release!

'Perhaps so,' I murmured, though what she'd said was quite ridiculous.

'Come on, Phil,' she said. 'Let's not sit

here. We've got to get back and settle it all. Then I'll book another couple of seats on a flight to New York. Or should we try somewhere else, d'you think? The Bahamas, say. Now, that's a good idea.' Then in a discursive and vague flood of words, as though they might suppress what her mind didn't want to consider, she muttered herself finally to silence.

But I was already driving. Let her lull herself into a false sense of security, it would calm her. I didn't want to be around when the full enormity of this Martin Reade's prior behaviour was revealed. There are men who deliberately prey on women for their money, trying to persuade them to part with a portion of it, then they disappear. But this wasn't like that. One had a mental image of suave gentlemen in dinner jackets, haunting the gaming clubs of the Côte d'Azur and with nothing further from their minds than marriage. It didn't fit the Martin Reade I'd been hearing about, he of the greasy hands and the soiled overalls, he of the stripped rally car he'd left behind for a fortnight. And he who, apparently, didn't baulk at marriage at all. On the contrary. I couldn't wait to meet him.

When we were well into Somerset, Heather, who had been very silent for so long, suddenly spoke up in a decisive voice that sounded strange from her.

'Take me directly home, please, Philipa.' It was said with dignity.

'You'll be alone. That's no good.'

'I have a housekeeper.'

'Goody for you. But you wouldn't want to weep on your housekeeper's shoulder. Undignified.' I tried to make a joke of it.

'I don't intend to weep on anybody's, thank you.' But she didn't sound certain about that. The nearer we came to her district, the nearer we came to a possible meeting with Martin. And she wasn't yet certain how to handle that.

'We'll drive to The Rolling Stone. I expect my friend will have booked us in there.'

'Please yourself. I'd like to meet him. Oliver, was it? Yes. *Then* you can take me home.'

I nodded, but I didn't think she was looking.

We drove past St Asaph's. She averted her eyes. I knew the way to Reade's Rapid Repairs, and headed there. I wondered how rapidly he would be able to repair this mess.

There was very little activity on the forecourt, though a police car was parked by the pumps. It was nearly six o'clock, and I'd had enough of driving for one day. There was nobody manning the kiosk, and police ribbons cordoned off the approach to the repair bay.

'Straight on,' said Heather in a tiny voice. 'It's on your left.'

I could already see the pub. Though this place was somewhat larger than Heather's own village, which probably didn't even rate a name, I could have driven right through it in two minutes. It was large enough to boast a signboard, though. Hellyspool, it was called. They rated a sub-post office, also selling bits of confectionery, The Rolling Stone pub, a general store, and a haberdasher's. No church of their own, though. St Asaph's probably drew in a congregation from miles around.

Oliver came walking out as we arrived. He must have been sitting by a window. We got out, somewhat stiffly, and I made the introductions. Heather fumbled the task of shaking hands with him, so he bent forward and kissed her cheek. She blushed. The blushing bride at last. There was no kiss for me.

'A fine mess we've got here,' he said.

I nodded. 'And you don't know half of it yet.'

'We must talk.'

'We must,' I agreed. 'Any news?'

He glanced at Heather. 'Later.'

I nodded. It had to mean that what he had found out was not for Heather's ears, not until he knew how much she could take, anyway.

He was ushering us inside the bar. There was a corner table empty, though the place was quite full. It seemed that he had established a presence. 'What can I get you?' he asked, as he edged us towards the table.

'Nothing for me, thank you,' said Heather petulantly. She had taken Oliver's measure, his bulk and his poise, and his craggy but usually placid features. I felt her envy of me. It irked her that his most intimate smile had been reserved for me, and only a formal one for herself.

'White wine for me,' I said. 'Bring the same for Heather, Oliver, please.' She'd had both the brandies, so I'd drink her wine if necessary.

He was known at the bar. He didn't ask for his draught bitter, but it slid towards his hand. We sat waiting, Heather and I, she tense, her hands in her lap, her lower lip jutting in a way that had always preceded a quiver. Now it seemed to indicate an impatience, a determination.

'I want to get home,' she whispered.

Oliver returned with the tray in his one

good hand. He placed it down, sat opposite us, and beamed from face to face in appreciation. 'Nice beer they've got here,' he said. 'No juke box, thank heaven, and the customers have all been regulars. Except two of us.'

'Two?' I asked.

'Don't make it obvious, but when you get a chance take a look at that man with a paper, the one in the grey suit on the bench to your left. He's not reading it. He's been here all day. Watching me.'

'Reckon he's a reporter?'

'Too soon. They'll be here any time now, I wouldn't be surprised.'

Of course, Heather had to turn and look, leaning forward and making it all too obvious. She jerked her head back and groaned, whether at the sight of him or at the publicity I didn't know.

'I've booked us a room here,' said Oliver placidly, ignoring Heather's reaction.

'A room?'

'It was all they'd got. The bed's a bit narrow, but — '

'I know him,' said Heather, tight-lipped. 'He's been up to the house.'

'Doing what?' asked Oliver gently.

She hesitated, fumbling. 'Well . . . he said he was selling encyclopaedias, but he hadn't got one to show me. I didn't let him get past the door.'

'But asking questions?' Oliver pressed softly.

'Oh yes. What you'd expect. Name, date of birth . . . '

'Marital status?' he suggested.

'It was mentioned.'

'Hmm!' Oliver was sceptical. 'He's got all the trappings of a private investigator. God knows what he could be working on, but he's certainly been hanging around. Earning his fee, no doubt. Hold on!'

He must have possessed instincts I hadn't suspected, as he wasn't looking in that direction. The man had come to his feet and was folding his paper. He headed towards a door that led to the rear. When he opened it, I saw the sunlight blazing on the yard at the back.

'Oliver . . . I . . . '

Oliver was already on his way out to the street.

'Stay here,' I said to Heather briskly.

'Don't leave me — '

But I'd already moved, following the man the shortest way. For one moment I was blinded by the glare. Then I saw that he was taking rapid strides to the opposite side of the yard, where a dun-coloured VW Golf was parked. Oliver, coming round the building, was intercepting, not running but moving rapidly. As the man inserted his key in the door lock, Oliver's left hand fell on his arm.

There was no abrupt or aggressive reaction. The man turned. He was as tall as Oliver, dark, his tightly curled hair low over his forehead. Black, arched eyebrows reached up to his hair. The eyes were narrow, brown. His grey suit was tight at the waist, where he was growing out of the waistband. The paunch projected above it.

'Yes?' he asked, his voice low but contained. 'You wanted something?'

'I'd like to know your business.'

He laughed harshly. 'Likewise, feller. Take you hand off me.'

Oliver obliged. He smiled. 'You've been asking questions around here. I just won-dered why.'

'I sell encyclopaedias.'

'And not one sample to show?'

'Get out of my way, friend. I can see you've got a dicky arm, and I don't like hitting handicapped people.' His lips were thin. They did not smile easily. It was more a grimace.

'I think we ought to get together.'

'You do, huh?' His eyes moved to take in every inch of Oliver. 'And who are you?'

'My name's Simpson. Oliver. Ex-police

— the arm injury threw me out. And I have a personal interest in what's going on around here.'

The dark eyes almost disappeared behind the hair. 'Something going on, is there?'

Oliver beamed at him. 'I've seen you around all day, and if you don't know what's going on by now, then you're not much good at it.'

'At what?'

'I think you're a private eye. Care to tell me the name of your client?'

The man leaned back against the car, relaxed, flapping his folded newspaper against the roof. He showed us a lousy set of teeth. 'If you want to tell me yours.'

'I haven't got one. Call it a personal interest. You know that a woman is dead. You must know that. Perhaps *she* was your client?'

The dark eyes were now bright, his interest captured. The thin lips parted as he licked them. 'You'd know better than me. Did you see her, this dead woman?'

'I found her. You can see, I've got a reason for hanging around here. The police don't want me to leave.'

'Describe her.' There was command in the voice now.

'Slim. I didn't see much. Perhaps just over five feet. Black hair. That's all I saw.'

46

'Then she's not my client.' Relief showed in his voice.

'So who is?'

He shook his head.

'Then perhaps you'd better tell me your own name. Better still, let me have your card. I might have work for you.'

Still the man hesitated. He was suspicious — one ex-copper recognizing the other. Then he reached inside his jacket, produced a card case, and offered his card. The suit was made of a shiny grey material. In the sun it gleamed like silver as his hand disturbed it.

'May I make a suggestion?' I asked.

They both turned and stared at me. They had been so absorbed in each other that they hadn't been aware of my presence. It was not a woman's business. I tried to smile into their blank and unresponsive faces

'Does the name of June McBride ring a bell?' I asked meekly, enjoying it.

His eyebrows flicked; his eyes narrowed. It meant a lot. He turned away, sliding the key into its lock.

'And may I suggest', I went on, 'that it was you who tipped off the police that Martin Reade was leaving the country from Heathrow?'

He didn't turn back, but I saw his shoulders stiffen. Then he slid into the driving seat, started the engine, and drove out of the yard without another word.

Oliver turned to me and shrugged his good shoulder. 'Was that a wild guess, my love?'

'Not exactly wild. I haven't had time to tell you yet, but Martin was picked up by the police for bigamy. Not for murder. And the name of June McBride was mentioned.'

'Clever girl.' I could've hit him. 'Let's get back to your friend, if she hasn't run away.' He glanced at the card. 'His name's Victor Peel. Private Investigator, working out of Birmingham. So we know where to start looking for June McBride.'

'You think we'll need to?'

'Definitely. Oh, most definitely.'

So he had decided we were going to get ourselves involved. I was a little surprised, but said nothing.

We went back to Heather, only just in time because she seemed poised for flight.

'Where have you *been*? You left me here . . . '

Oliver said firmly, 'It turns out he's a private detective, Heather. Name of Victor Peel. That was what he was doing at your house, detecting. Maybe he was feeling out the situation. I mean, if we're talking about bigamy here, there could be no end of wives

48

Martin's left scattered around. Perhaps Peel had traced Martin to this place. Yes — that must be it. Somebody must've tipped off the police that Martin was just about to do it again, and that he was going to leave the country . . . '

'Oliver . . . ' I said warningly.

He's usually very good at this sort of thing, being able to impart terrible news in a light and humorous way, wildly exaggerating it in an attempt to imply that it wasn't very serious after all — nothing that couldn't be tidied away neatly. Carry it a little further, and he might even convince you that it was almost too absurd to be accepted as real.

But he didn't know Heather.

'No!' she whispered entreatingly.

He missed it. 'And I wouldn't be surprised if he's been collecting fees from all Martin's wives. 'Where's he got to?' they'd ask. 'I'll let you know for a small consideration,' he would say. If he asked you for money, Heather, then I've guessed right. He'd make a big deal out of mere bigamy.'

But Heather's mind didn't move fast enough to keep up with Oliver's fantasies. I could see her lips still fumbling to protest at the 'mere' that had preceded 'bigamy'.

'But it's you the police'll bring him back to, Heather,' he said reassuringly. 'In this sort of thing, it's last come who get served best.'

Then she screamed, a high-pitched and tearing scream that cut through the clamour around us, and she threw the remains of my white wine in his face.

3

I overtook her half-way along the main street, and caught at her arm. She shrugged me off.

'Leave me alone.'

'I'll take you home in the car.'

'Not with that horrible man, you won't. Where did you find him!'

By now Oliver was at her other shoulder, feebly protesting. 'I apologize. I'm sorry. I didn't realize. I was exaggerating wildly, just to show you how farcical it can get if you let your imagination — '

'I know what you were trying to do. Frighten me, that's what.'

But she had drifted to a halt. Heather was never much of a walker. I handed Oliver the car keys, saying nothing because he knew what it meant. But really, it was perhaps a good thing that she should begin to realize just what kind of a man she had linked herself with. From what I was hearing, Martin Reade certainly wasn't a great catch, even if anybody could catch him, and the present likelihood was that Heather wasn't legally married to him at all. The sooner she accepted it, the better.

But I couldn't wait to meet Martin Reade.

'It's just not fair!' she cried.

'We all make mistakes.'

We were standing in the road, me watching Oliver back the car around.

'It wasn't a mistake,' she said stubbornly, that lip creeping out again. 'I love him, and I want him, and I'm going to have him.'

'It might be better to wait on events.'

'I'm not going to wait on any events. The poor dear, he must be feeling terrible. What's the time? Oh . . . look at the time! I'll never get hold of my solicitor now. Oh Phillie, what am I going to do?'

'Wait,' I said, not with much expectation. 'Wait patiently.'

'Perhaps they'll let me see him.'

'If we could find out where they're holding him, then we could try.'

I was, I'll admit, beginning to lose patience with her. She had never been able to look things squarely in the face. Fortunately, Oliver drew up beside us. I got Heather in the back and slid in beside her. Oliver said, 'Which way?'

'I don't want to go home,' she decided, close to tears. 'I want to go to Martin, Phillie. To Martin!'

'We don't know where he is. Home, Heather. You'll need some rest.'

'Home!' she said in disgust, as though it couldn't be home without him. 'Oh — very well. Go back past the church, and take the first left.' She was staring straight ahead, her chin raised with pathetic defiance. But her hand crept into mine. 'You'll both stay with me, I hope.'

I wasn't sure whether this was a plea or a demand, and therefore compromised by answering, 'Of course, Heather.'

It amused me that Oliver's shoulders twitched. He had, after all, booked a room for us at The Rolling Stone. It was part of a game — or a contest, rather — between us, and all based on his reluctance to settle it once and for all positively by marrying me. He didn't want anybody, including himself, to think he would be marrying me for my money.

'Marriage is a contract, Phil,' he had declared solemnly. 'What's mine is yours and what's yours is mine, and yours is a lot more than mine. It wouldn't be fair.' Reminiscences of Heather. Fair! Who the hell cared? So I had been playing Oliver's game against him, as he wanted us to live together without benefit of clergy or Registrar, and I was holding him at arm's length. Which, if he had only known it, was more strain on me than on him, really. But I wanted him. I wanted him tied to me, with nothing stupid like money between us.

Neither of us had weakened yet — but he was trying every trick in the book. The room at The Rolling Stone had been one of them.

'The drive entrance is just round the next corner,' said Heather, her voice now more confident. She was about to enter her own four walls. Safety would wrap around her.

There were two stone gateposts with no gates, but there was a sign on one of them: Hellyspool Hall. The drive was gravelled. It swept up and round, through and under trees in their full complement of leaves at this time, trees that needed surgery, as the approach was like a tunnel with the lower branches rustling against the top of the car. We came out on a half-circle of gravel with the Hall before us, modest as halls go, but probably better for that in so far as a larger one would have meant a huge financial drain for maintenance, with the consequent involvement of the National Trust. Square, uncompromising, grey stone and green creepers, mullioned windows, tall and stolid chimneys — I could have wished to live there. Now . . . *that* was a good idea: expend most of my modest fortune on such a house, then we could live on Oliver's pension. And that would satisfy his ridiculous male ego, even if we starved.

I'd been so involved with this idea that I

hadn't realized we were inside the hall until a woman, a comely and buxom woman in her sixties, I guessed, came bustling in from the rear. Her hair was flying about because she'd obviously just washed it and hadn't got to the setting stage.

'Why . . . why . . . Miss, er . . . Ma'am, I didn't expect you. Haven't you left?' She clamped a hand to her chest. 'Oh, I don't know what I'm saying. Isn't he with you? And who are these . . . ' Her face puckered. The situation quite over-bore her.

'Oh, Kathie! I'm so sorry to land on you like this. It's all gone wrong. I can't explain. I'm married and I'm not married — I don't know *what* I am, or where I am. And my poor Martin . . . they've arrested him for just about everything you could think of, and there was a dead woman in his bed — and how many other wives he's got I don't know. I just don't know!'

She was flapping her arms, and Kathie seemed undecided whether or not to clasp her to that ample bosom. She lifted her plump chin, braced herself, and said, 'Now you go into the drawing-room, my dear, and I'll bring you a pot of tea. That'll settle you.' She grimaced bleak sympathy at me.

'Thank you, Kathie. And these are my friends, Philipa — I told you about

Philipa — and Oliver. Will you prepare the green room for them, please?'

'Of course.' She smiled at us.

Oliver caught my eye, and winked. I dare you! But how could I speak up and demand two singles?

We followed Heather into her drawing-room. 'Bring your cases in later,' she tossed over her shoulder. She was in her own home now, and she was a changed woman. 'I know you didn't expect to stay more than one night, but I do hope . . . oh Phillie, I'd be so grateful if you would stay longer. I'll need help. And you're so strong . . . '

What the devil did she mean, strong? 'Oliver's ex-police,' I told her. 'He'll know a lot of things that could help.'

'Oh yes.' She was twisting her lips, lowering herself on to one end of a settee. 'He seemed to have the situation completely in hand.' Then she tried to smile in his direction. Oliver had been hovering, circling the room in a very professional manner. He paused to smile back.

'We'll be pleased to do what we can,' he told her.

'But Heather,' I said. 'We didn't expect even to stay overnight. We've brought no cases or even a change of clothes.'

'Oh dear. Never mind. It's going to be a

hot night, so you won't need night things. And I can lend you — give you — some of my stuff. Oliver . . . ' Again she flicked him an uneasy smile, still not certain whether he was really on her side. 'Oliver will have to manage.'

'I can do that.' He beamed at me. 'As long as Phil doesn't mind if I don't shave. In a couple of days' time I'll look like . . . ' He brightened. 'Like a film star, all rough and craggy and downbeat. you'll like that, Phil.'

I didn't get a chance to comment. Brush, soap and a razor went at the top of a mental list I'd begun to assemble. Or an electric one. Yes, perhaps that. As I reached this decision, Kathie came in with a tray of tea things, and tiny sandwiches she'd somehow managed to assemble in such a short time. It seemed to me that these two women were much more intimate than the initial formality, for our benefit, had suggested. Kathie had probably been Heather's nanny. She seemed to be the fussy and protective type who would shelter her young charge from the harsh realities to be expected later, thereby spoiling her from a very early age, robbing her of her natural defences when she had eventually been forced to leave the nest. We were close, Kathie and I, if that had been the case, as I'd taken over at the boarding school and continued the shielding process.

'There now,' said Kathie, putting down the tray on an inlaid low table. 'You can relax now, my dear. It'll all come right in the end.'

Then, sweeping a complacent smile round the room, she went out and left us to it.

As Heather didn't seem to be taking her hostess's duties seriously, but was now prowling backwards and forwards in front of the Adam fireplace, I poured the tea. Oliver was watching Heather with concentration, watching her walking with one elbow cupped in her other palm so that she could pluck at her lower lip. He was concerned. I was beginning to understand Oliver. He presented a flip and casual attitude as though ashamed of a personal emotional involvement he wouldn't be able to control. But inside he was completely serious.

'Wouldn't it be a good idea to phone your solicitor?' he suggested to her.

'What!' She stopped in mid-pace. 'At this time?'

'It's what they're for. He won't mind.'

I smiled to myself at that. My own solicitor, Harvey Remington, would have rushed to my side in a similiar situation. His bill would later reflect his attentiveness.

'He'll be at home,' she protested.

'Phone him,' said Oliver, this time a firm

instruction. 'This thing's going to be a great tangle of law and legal procedures. I can sense it.'

She stared at him for a couple more seconds, then she threw herself into a chair alongside the fireplace, facing the phone, which waited on a little table. I noted that she dialled the number without reference to a directory. She had worried him at home before, perhaps many times. That sounded typical of Heather, the paltry deceit, the reaching for advice.

Oliver and I sat side by side on the settee, drinking tea and nibbling at sandwiches, hearing only one end of the conversation. Heather seemed to wander now and again from the factual truth, in an attempt to exaggerate her plight. That probably came naturally. I was itching to take the phone from her and state the exact situation, shortly and precisely, but Oliver touched my arm and shook his head. We gathered that her solicitor's name was Rupert. Probably his family had served hers through several generations.

She hung up, and turned a flushed and glowing face to us. Then she came to sit primly on a seat facing us across the table, her eyes now bright and her attitude relaxed, even mildly excited. 'He'll be half an hour,' she told us. 'Isn't he a dear? He always comes when I ask.'

'I thought he might,' said Oliver blandly.

'You'll like him. Rupert Anderson. I could never understand why he's not married. You wait and see, Phillie. You'll fall for him like a flash.'

I looked down at my cup. Oliver said, 'It'll take more like an hour. You'll see. If he knows his job he'll be phoning around for any information he can get, before he faces you, Heather.'

'With encouraging news,' I said. 'If I'm not mistaken.'

But now Heather was restless at the prospect of Rupert arriving. She barely finished her tea, but bounced to her feet.

'I must go and see how Kathie's fixed for food. I was anticipating . . . ' She paused, and flung her arms around. 'Something different,' she finished miserably. Then she rushed out of the room.

'Encouraging news?' asked Oliver quietly. 'Such as what? In this situation, with a man such as Martin Reade involved — what on earth could be encouraging? It seems to me he's been leaving cart-loads of trouble and distress behind him for years. Now it's all catching up with him.'

'He probably never *meant* any harm.' For

now, I had to give Martin the benefit of any doubt that there might be available.

'No,' he said. 'They never mean harm. Lord, Phil, you ought to have had a spell in the police.'

'I as good as did.'

'Your father? Oh sure. Chief Superintendent Lowe. I'm sure he used to come home, and you'd sit and listen, fascinated by his experiences. But wasn't he deliberately priming you? No . . . couldn't have been . . . priming you for what, that's the point? Naming you Philipa Lowe because he was a Chandler fan — now, that's far-out if anything ever was. Did he expect to train you as a tough private eye, walking the mean streets where a man must go? Philip Marlowe, but without the mister! You're not a man, Phillie, thank heaven. But your father was a wild romantic. I can't imagine how he ever got the rank of Chief Super. But he always thought of you as a boy. And he sat there and talked to you, and he saw he was talking to a girl, so his romantic mind polished it all off nice and clean and hygienic. It wasn't the truth that you heard, Phil. He trained *you* into a romantic, too.'

'You're talking a load of rubbish.' I turned a shoulder towards him.

'You're as bad as this Heather friend of yours. Didn't mean any harm, indeed! The truth is that they're completely selfish, these men immersed in their own desires and ambitions, and they give no thought to anybody but themselves. Martin Reade! We're guessing right now that there have been three women involved. Three at least. And do you imagine he's given any passing thought for any of them, or even regretted for one moment the misery he's strewn around in his wake?'

'It might not be like that,' I said quietly. Oliver was being brisk and severe. He was annoyed with me. 'You must give him a chance. Innocent until proved guilty.'

'Hah!' he said. It was a kind of laugh. 'What's the betting you can't wait to meet him, and see what this man can be like, who seems to attract women like a magnet. Trusting women, Phil, probably all of them as guileless and innocent as Heather. They fall for him like rocks down a hillside. And you can't wait to see him, and get your mind working on some way of getting him out of all this.'

'For Heather,' I whispered.

'Don't you think she'd be better off without him?'

'Certainly not,' said Heather from the

doorway. 'I feel better already with Rupert on his way.'

So fortunately she'd heard no more than Oliver's last sentence.

Oliver came to his feet. 'I was thinking . . . if he runs a family practice, this Rupert of yours might be unused to criminal procedures.'

'Rupert knows everything.'

Which seemed a good line on which to close the present subject and make the conversation more general. It appeared that Kathie wasn't so poorly stocked as Heather had feared, and something would be ready later.

'I've been choosing the wine,' said Heather.

So we were in a celebratory mood, perhaps because Rupert was coming, because Rupert was rushing to her side. It occurred to me that he might not have approved of her marriage to Martin Reade. Solicitors see more of life and people than one would expect, as the mental image is of them shut away in their offices, surrounded by dry and rustling paper. Rupert Anderson might well have seen right through Martin, and would bring his own suffering with him, if he was to be expected to rescue Heather's man from the clutches of the law.

We ate — I can't remember what — in the

dining-room, with the table beautifully set with expensive china, silverware and crystal glasses, and drank a splendid burgundy that Heather's father or grandfather had laid down. And still Rupert had not arrived.

Fortified in her trust in him, Heather said, 'He'll be along. I'll show you your room while we're waiting.'

We followed her, not speaking and not even glancing at each other, up the staircase, which hugged each side of the hall to a half-landing before continuing directly upwards from the centre. The green room was clearly kept always ready for visitors. A stripped-down room could not have been made ready in the spare time Kathie had had. She'd needed only to change the sheets. The top of the sash window was open. Beyond it, the sky was a deep, heavy green, with some light still caught in it. The air was sultry.

The bed was huge. It must at one time have been a four-poster, but the posts were gone. The rest of the furnishings were of massive, solid oak, probably bearing a famous name. We had nothing to put away in the drawers, nothing to hang in the wardrobes.

'The bathroom's just down the hall,' said Heather. 'To your right as you go out. Kathie's put on a sheet and a thin cover. Frankly, I shan't sleep, weather or not. We might get a storm. D'you think we could get a storm?'

'It's a beautiful room,' I told her.

'Yes.' She glanced at Oliver, having belatedly become aware that his right arm was somewhat disabled. 'Shall you be able to manage?'

He smiled and nodded. 'We'll manage,' I said for him.

He seemed to manage alone in the flat he still kept in Penley. I had returned to my cottage in Lower Streetly, unpleasant memories or not.

It was then that we heard the front door bell, and Kathie had let Rupert in by the time we reached the half-landing. He stood in the hall, looking up. Fifty-ish, I thought, and smiling at us — at Heather — almost laughing, though that would have been unprofessional. But he was pleased to see her. It was as simple as that. We followed her down to the hall. She almost ran the last half-dozen stairs to Rupert, who was holding out both hands so that he could take hers and stand back and eye her with his head tilted, still with that twisted smile, like an uncle who hadn't met his niece for ages.

'Oh Heather, Heather!' he said. 'What have you been doing to that poor man?'

From Oliver she'd not been able to accept

this inverted form of humour; from Rupert Anderson she could. It flowed into her, relaxing her. She even managed a tiny giggle.

'So good of you to come, Rupert.' Trying to keep it formal.

'I'd have come . . . any time. You know that.'

'Yes. I know.'

He released her hands. She stepped back. 'This is Rupert,' she introduced. 'My friend, Philipa Lowe, and Oliver . . . I'm sorry, I've forgotten.'

'Oliver Simpson,' said Oliver.

They shook hands, weighing each other up. Then Rupert switched hands and took mine, and instead of shaking it he raised it to his lips. When his eyes lifted to mine there was something mocking in them, fine grey eyes that told me in that second that when he entered this house he entered centuries of inherited service, that he was an old family heirloom come to do his duty. All this in spite of the fact that he was fit and slim and completely alert, that he was hard pressed to present an image of age and wisdom. And it told me he was in love with her, that he knew it was obvious to everybody but Heather, and he'd kill me if I told her. The stupid creature that she was.

He had been carrying no briefcase. I liked

that. He had it all in his head, and he came as a friend. There was a grave dignity about him, a formal grace that went well with his six feet and his wide shoulders. Put him in court, and he would be listened to; he carried that authority with him. No briefcase, just his dignity and awareness.

Heather sat him down. Then she took a seat opposite him, demurely, knees together, as solemn as a witness in the box. He produced a pipe but didn't light it. He used it to employ his fingers, as something with which to gesture.

'I've done some phoning,' he told her. 'It's been difficult, with so many police areas involved. But they'll have him back in this district tomorrow, Heather, and you'll be able to see him. They'll probably even release him, as it's only for questioning they want him at this stage, and that's in respect of the dead woman.'

He was making it sound so very easy and straightforward. I wasn't sure it was the correct approach with Heather, but he probably knew her, as she was at this time, better than I did.

'Of course,' he went on, 'there's the question of the bigamy. You know about that. You mentioned it. He was picked up at Heathrow on that charge. Quite frankly, that

67

surprises me. The police aren't much interested in bigamy these days, unless it's linked with something more serious. Such as fraud or wrongful conversion. I gather there's something like that, but not, I'd have thought, anything requiring them to take him into custody before he left the country. After all, he was going to be away only a fortnight.'

'Our honeymoon,' whispered Heather.

'Yes. Your honeymoon.' He stared at the pipe in his hands for a moment. It was shaking a little. In spite of his calm voice, he wasn't finding this pleasant. 'Tell me, Heather . . . whose idea was it to choose New York? Isn't your own country good enough?'

'Well . . . Martin's idea. He said he'd always wanted . . . what do you mean?'

'It did occur to me,' he admitted, and now there were lines down his cheeks, 'that if there's bigamy involved, and that bigamy was committed when he married a woman called June McBride eight years ago, then there must have been another wife before her. He's an expert at running away from wives. Sorry, Heather.'

'It's been explained to me,' she said numbly. 'They must have been terrible to him — that's all I can think. Both of them. Martin's not *like* that. Wouldn't hurt a fly.'

Rupert touched his tie. He seemed to wish

he might loosen it without detracting from his dignity. 'It's occurred to me that he might have wished to get out of the country. Heather — you know there was a dead woman in his bed this morning. You mentioned that.'

'She wasn't there when they booked the trip,' I cut in sharply.

He turned to look at me, his eyes for a moment empty of expression. I'd broken into his line of thought. Then he smiled. We were both on the same side — hers. When he smiled the cheeks puckered up beneath his eyes, which half closed. He inclined his head fractionally. Such a noble head, with wide brows. Leave it, his eyes told me. I know what I'm doing.

'I'm aware of that,' he said to me gently. 'But at the time the trip was booked he might have been aware that efforts to trace him were being made, and that they'd been successful. So it would be necessary for him to have to calculate on getting out of the country.'

Heather was shaking her head. It was too difficult for her. 'But you said . . . you did, Rupert . . . you said that bigamy isn't all that serious — even if there was something, fraud or whatever, involved. Money, you mean. I've got money . . . I can't . . . ' She flung her head about, disturbing her hair. 'I *am* married to him. Tell me I am, Rupert.'

'I can't tell you that. Sorry, Heather.'

'Why can't you? Why not?'

'I explained. If he committed bigamy by marrying June McBride, then he also did so by marrying you. Any marriage after the first, unless that one was terminated by divorce or death before the later marriage, would be void. Wouldn't exist, Heather.'

I could pity him. His profession demanded that his client should hear the truth, in a legal sense. And he was hating every second of it. To sit there and torture her . . . and there was more to come. I knew there was more.

'I don't understand what you're saying, Rupert,' she said pitifully, twisting her hands together.

'There was a dead woman in his bed, Heather,' he reminded her gently

'I know. He'd got nothing to do with that. He was in his friend's car, asleep all night, somewhere in the lanes. And he'd got no reason . . .'

'I'm sure he was. But it looks bad for him. You'll have to admit that.'

'I don't admit anything of the sort. It's ridiculous. Martin couldn't *kill* anybody. I want you to get him free, Rupert. I don't care what it costs. Find that woman, June something, and pay *her* off. I want him home here. He's my husband. I want him here. Bride. That was it. June McBride.'

At the end her voice had been flying around all over the place. Rupert tried to get comfort from his pipe again. He was twisting it so violently I expected it to snap in two.

'But I've explained, Heather,' he said very gently, very patiently. 'The odds are that he isn't your husband. In only one way could he be. Only one. And I just don't want to contemplate that.'

There was a silence while she thought about it. She already knew, but had thrust the thought into the waste bin at the back of her mind. Then it refused to be rejected any longer, and burst to the front. She turned in her chair and thrust out her arm and pointed at Oliver. '*He* said that!' she cried. 'Oh — you're all against me.'

Then she was out of that chair and rushing to the door blindly, but not so blindly that she missed the doorknob. She left the door swinging behind her. We heard her feet pattering up the stairs.

'But I only ... it was only wild conjecture ... ' Oliver was protesting.

Rupert got to his feet stiffly. He'd been using physical tension to prevent himself from betraying the emotional one. 'Not your fault,' he said quietly.

'Has the dead woman been identified?' I asked.

'No. They said not. But I got the impression they know where to enquire.' He sighed. 'Sometimes I feel like putting her over my knee and spanking her.'

'Perhaps you should have done,' I told him.

He raised his eyebrows, then understood. 'Perhaps I will.'

'I'll have to go to her,' I said, not even knowing which was her room.

But Kathie was standing in the open doorway. 'I'll go, if you don't mind. I know what to do. I've been doing it since she was a baby.' Then she turned on her heel and hurried up the stairs.

Rupert gave me a rueful smile. 'I'll have to leave the spanking until later.'

We saw him out. He said he would be in touch. We closed and locked the front door.

'And so to bed,' said Oliver, too abruptly I thought.

4

I was standing in front of the tall cheval mirror in our room, down to my briefs and bra, which was as far as I intended to go. Just checking. Not really bad at all, I decided. Reflected, I could see Oliver, standing at the sash window with the top still open, getting what cool breeze there might be available. But the air was still and breathless. He was staring out at the night, wearing boxer shorts, not Y-fronts, I noticed.

I couldn't think of anything to say but the obvious. 'We're going to get a storm.'

'I love storms. What about you?' He turned for my answer. 'They clear the air,' he explained.

'Yes,' I agreed, my eyes sliding to the bed, which now seemed very much less wide than when I'd seen it first.

He read my mind. 'I'll sleep in the wing chair,' he told me encouragingly, though without any noticeable enthusiasm. It was not, I thought, very flattering that the decision had come after he'd turned round.

'Oh no you won't,' I told him, thinking of his arm. 'I'll try the chair.'

'I don't see why either of us . . . ' He said it with his eyes judging the width of the bed, and no doubt seeing it wider than I did.

'Did they say anything about the murder weapon?' I asked. 'Have they found it?'

'What?' He walked to the foot of the bed, measuring it with his eyes. 'Oh yes, they found it.'

'And?'

'At least, they seemed to think it was the weapon.'

He turned, his eyes measuring me, in relation to the bed no doubt. For a moment the sky behind him flickered with light. The rumble was distant. I reached up to ruffle my hair, which crackled.

'Yes,' he said vaguely. 'The weapon.' But he didn't pursue the subject.

It had occurred to me that, having regard to the fact that it was his right arm that gave him pain, he would naturally sleep on his left side. Which meant that if he slept on the left-hand side of the bed he would by lying with his back to me if I was on the other side, perched on the far side, perhaps with the bolster lengthways between us . . .

'It's ridiculous talking about the chair,' he decided, dismissing it from his calculations. 'The bed's a mile wide, and if I take the left-hand side . . . ' He made a wide,

74

measuring gesture with both hands spread, though, as his right arm wouldn't extend fully, it didn't present a telling argument from where I was standing. He was eyeing me with his head tilted in consideration, and with a strange, mocking smile on his silly face.

'Yes, I realized that,' I conceded.

He rubbed a hand over his chin. 'My face is already like sandpaper. You wouldn't want to come in contact with it.'

'Most certainly not.'

It seemed that he considered this had settled the matter, and he returned his attention to the bed. 'I think we'd better lie on the cover. It's too hot for even one sheet.'

'If the storm breaks, it'll go cool,' I said tentatively.

'Perhaps we wouldn't notice.' He turned, and raised one eyebrow at me. When I didn't allow myself to respond, he amplified, 'The window would be on my side, and I'd act as a kind of windbreak.'

'Thank you.'

'It's nice to think I'd be of some service to you.'

'I'm sure it is,' I assured him. 'Shall we have the light off?'

'Yes. Suits me. You'd think they'd have a bedside light.'

There was only a clock and an extension phone on the small table between the window and the left side of the bed. 'In a place like this,' I agreed.

I walked over to the door and put off the light, aware of his eyes on me as I moved. Why did I find myself walking stiffly? As I turned, the sky glowed and faded. The rumble was closer, sharper in its outline. 'And what was it?' I asked.

'What was what?'

'The weapon.'

'Oh . . . ' He sat on the left-hand side of the bed, his shape silhouetted against a background of fluttering blue. 'That! It was a spanner, if you really must know. An adjustable one. I gathered they thought they'd found what they wanted. There was blood on it, it seems.'

'Then that sounds a reasonable supposition.'

I watched as he swung his legs up, almost continuously outlined now against the sky. He balanced on his left arm.

'Can you manage all right?' I asked anxiously.

'I usually do. I just shuffle further towards the middle. Like this.' He managed barely a foot.

'Your arm all right?'

'I'll just let it lie here.'

'No pain?'

'Quite comfortable, thank you.'

'Then I'll go round the other side.'

'Yes,' he said, one eye peering sideways at me. 'You do that.'

I pattered round to the side behind him, pursued by more-purposeful claps of thunder, blue light reflected from my arms. The bed was caught in harsh outline. I sat on my side and swung up my legs, so that I was facing his back. Damn it, I'd forgotten about the bolster. There was a brief period of silence.

'It's strange, really, when you come to think about it,' I commented to the night.

'What is?' It was a mumble, though he didn't seem sleepy.

The bulk of him was too far away to shield me completely from the now rapidly cooling air. I shuffled a little closer.

'The fact that the clothes were removed,' I said, 'but the weapon wasn't taken away. Now . . . if it'd been — '

'It's all right,' he interrupted, 'if you just rest your hand on my arm.'

He had detected that I wasn't comfortable with my left hand trapped beneath me and my right wandering around for somewhere to settle.

'If you don't mind.'

'Not at all.' He said it with no apparent reluctance.

'Just rest my hand on it.'

'That'll be quite acceptable,' he admitted.

'The other way round, now, that would be more sensible.'

He spent a moment or two thinking about it. 'You mean, me resting my hand — '

'No, no. I meant: the weapon taken away and the clothes left. It'd have been much the most sensible thing.'

'Ah!' he said, a trifle coolly I thought. Gently, I rested my hand on his arm. He was so big, and so distant, that it was as far as I could reach, though it would certainly have been less painful and more comforting, I thought, if I could reach beneath his arm and rest my hand on his chest.

'You didn't tell me where it was found,' I reminded him.

The lightning suddenly lashed at the window, the thunder almost immediately following.

'Where what — '

'The weapon. Where it was found.' I raised my voice, but the thunder buried the last word.

'It was . . . ' he began. But the thunder buried his last word, too.

78

'I can't go on shouting at your back,' I shouted.

'Then come round the other side.'

'Shall I?'

'Why not?'

'If you can just slide across a bit more, while I just trot round . . . '

'I'll do that . . . with pleasure.'

I slipped off the bed and ran round, lightning chasing me. His face was alight with it, the thunder pressing from behind me.

'You're sure you'll not be hurting your arm?' I asked anxiously.

'Not at all.'

I sat on the edge and swung up my legs. He hadn't moved far, not as far as I'd have wished, towards the centre, but I felt I couldn't really point that out, the effort having been so great for him to have reached as far as he had. But it meant we were too intimately close. How was I going to relax?

'So where *was* it?' I asked.

In the blue light I saw that he was smiling gently, teasingly. I'd expected impatience, but for some obscure reason I amused him.

'The blasted spanner?' he asked, in a period of silence into which the roar of the rain barely intruded. 'On the bench, in his repair shed. Happy now? Is that all clear?'

'Thank you, Oliver, yes.'

'So we can relax.'

'If you say so.'

His right arm now lay uncomfortably between us. He seemed to be an ungainly lump. I suggested, 'If you'd find it better, rested on my hip . . .'

'It's all right.' He dismissed my hip.

'No, it isn't. Don't be stubborn. Here . . .' I reached over, picked up his hand, and placed it on my hip. 'There — isn't that better?' My voice wasn't steady, yet I'd never been afraid of storms.

'Most certainly better,' he conceded.

A blue glow spread over his face. The smile was there, so very tender. My heart was racing. I reached out and touched his cheek with my fingers. It had a masculine, hard bite to it, a velvet aroused and erect. It clung to my palm, grasping it, never to let go. I had to drag my hand away; the lightning was a spark crackling between us.

'You might last another day, Oliver,' I said softly, meaning his beard.

'I'll be happy if I can last through the night.'

I moved his hand a little. The flesh was hot beneath it. A perfect gentleman, he was, not having moved it himself. Damn him, he was luring me into making the moves myself. Bless him, he was not urging.

80

'With one hand,' I whispered, 'you can't undo my bra.'

'My most disabling incapacity,' he murmured. 'But you . . . '

'Like this.' I demonstrated.

'Or slip anything off,' he amplified.

'If you feel that anything more needs to be slipped,' I murmured, my voice strangely husky.

'I think it must.'

I rectified that situation in a few seconds, for both of us. A blown gust of rain prickled my bare back.

'I'm afraid,' he said gently, 'I'll have to leave it all to you, Phil.'

I kissed him gently on the lips, partly to silence him. I'd made the same decision.

'Like being married to money,' he grumbled vaguely.

'What is?' I ran my hands down his chest.

'You're in charge. The boss. Oh, all right. Do it your way.' It was a gracious concession.

I lowered myself towards him, gently, slowly, and his right arm discovered a new flexibility, a strong and persuasive right arm, as the storm broke, crashing about us, pitching us into a tense darkness and then into blinding light. The rain lashed down. Somebody moaned. I whispered, 'Oliver,' and the phone on the table behind me rang. I was poised, tensed, but it rang and rang, with the urgency phones can produce when you don't want to hear from anybody, when there's nobody else in the world.

It couldn't be for us. Couldn't.

'Oh hell,' said Oliver.

The spell was broken. Groaning, I rolled over, forgetting I was so close to my edge and nearly falling to the floor. I snatched at it angrily, in that second when it stopped ringing, and I heard Heather's voice cry out, 'Yes, yes. What is it?' A tight voice, it was, a voice that craved news, and dreaded it.

'Heather! Heather, is that you? It's Martin, my darling. Martin.'

I rolled back on to the bed, the phone to my ear. Oliver knew what was my intention. He clasped me to him, cupped in the curve of him, so that his chin rested from behind on my bare shoulder, and I had to move the phone only half an inch from my ear for him to get it all. His beard rasped at my skin. He did it deliberately.

'Martin!' she screamed. 'Where are you?'

'They've got me at Taunton. All over the country, we've been, one place to the next. Nobody wanted me . . . or everybody did. There was a lot of argy-bargy, then off again, me between two coppers on the back seat of their car. You'd never believe it! You'd think it was a matter of rape, or something serious like that. Are you there, sweetheart?'

'I'm here,' she said breathlessly as though it had been she who'd gabbled it all out.

It was private and it was personal, and we shouldn't have been listening to it — but there was bigamy and there was murder. We listened, concentrated every nerve on listening, though Oliver distracted me by cupping my right breast in his hand. His poor arm!

'A rotten shame, it's been,' Martin complained. 'Off on our honeymoon, and they had to come and snatch me. It could've waited.'

'It's bigamy, lover.' A pause. 'They said it was bigamy,' she went on almost pleading for a denial.

'Oh . . . that! I can explain all that. Listen, precious. They've let me have this one call, so I phoned you.' He said it as though he was handing out an award. 'And they're probably listening on an extension.'

As we were. I lifted Oliver's hand, but he simply transferred it to the other one.

'You should've got a solicitor right away,' she told him, suddenly taking charge.

'I knew *you* would, my darling. You have, haven't you?'

'Yes, yes. Rupert Anderson.'

'Oh . . . him. Bit of a wet, isn't he?'

'You mustn't say things like that,' she reproved him gently. 'When are they letting you come home? They can't keep a husband from his wife.'

There was a minimal pause. Then, 'There might be a difficulty there.'

'Never mind that,' she said. 'Come straight here, Martin. Do you understand? I want you with me.'

'There's a possibility I might not be.'

'Might not be able to?' she cried in distress.

'No. Might not be your husband,' he admitted glumly.

'Don't worry about that. D'you hear me? We'll sort it out. You'll see. And we can always do it again.'

'Do what?'

'The marrying, silly.' And she giggled.

'Yes. I suppose so. It won't be long, anyway. They only want me for questioning. A lot of twaddle, that is. Dear old Rupert can come and dig me out.'

'He isn't old. Now talk sense, Martin, please. They'll want to know all sorts of things, I expect.'

'About a dead woman, they said. What woman? I asked. They don't know what woman. I don't know anything about any woman.'

Heather was silent for a few moments. I

could hear her taking deep, shuddering breaths. Then she said, 'She was dead, and in your own bed, Martin. And she hadn't got any clothes on. The night before . . . *Last* night,' she realized with a bit of a shock.

'Then I wouldn't know, would I! They're taking me to see her tomorrow. Today, I suppose. The morgue. Yuk! Cripes, it's nearly two o'clock. Did I wake you, lover?'

'You can wake me any time.' She giggled. 'Now Martin, just you behave. Just answer their questions, and they'll let you come back to me. And if necessary, we'll do it again.'

'What?' he demanded.

'Get married again. If necessary. I *told* you that.'

'There's a kind of — '

'Just come to me, darling. Please. As fast as you can.' Then, on a sob, she hung up.

Not once had he asked her how she was, how she was managing, whether she was distressed. Slowly, I drew away from Oliver and replaced the phone. Beyond it, the rain hammered down, making a solid roar of it as it pounded into the trees. I fluffed up my hair.

'That's that, then.'

'Yes,' he agreed. 'That was it.'

Then the door burst open. I should have expected it, but Heather caught us both naked.

85

'He's phoned, he's phoned!' she cried, half-way between tears and joy. Their conversation had hardly been that inspiring, I thought.

Oliver reached back for a pillow and placed it against my front as I sat up. He managed to cover himself decorously now with one hand.

I tried my best to act innocent. 'Who's phoned, Heather?'

'Martin.'

'And what did he say?'

'That he's coming back to me. It's all been a mistake. He didn't do anything.' Then she seemed to realize we were in the dark, apart from the times when the night was split apart, and she switched on the light. She padded across to the window and slammed it up. 'Really, Phillie! The carpet will be soaked.'

'Sorry. We . . . '

'Oh,' she said. 'Were you two . . . '

'It's all right.'

'I'll leave you to get on with it, then.' She moved towards the door, paused, and turned. 'Do you want the light off again?'

'It doesn't matter.'

She put it off anyway. From the darkness she said, 'It'll all be sorted out tomorrow. You'll see. I *knew* it would be all right.'

Then she closed the door, and was gone.

'I'd better go to her,' I said.

'Nonsense.'

'All that dignity and restraint,' I explained. 'That took every bit of her resolution. She'll be a mess in a couple of minutes. Her pillow will be wetter than our carpet.'

'Phil,' he said, 'if you leave me now, I'll divorce you.'

'We're not married.'

'Makes it so much easier. Haven't I explained the benefits of not marrying?'

'Better perhaps than marrying too often. You and Martin ought to get together. He's got it worked out to a fine art. Between you, you ought to be able to come to a compromise.'

'I refuse,' he said, 'to be compared with Martin.'

'You wouldn't leave a dead woman in your bed?' I asked.

'Not unless she died of ecstasy.'

'There's modesty for you!'

'I didn't get a chance — '

'And now it's gone.'

'Not for me . . . '

But I kissed him to silence, raised my face far enough to whisper, 'For me it has. Another time . . . '

It had been an aberration, a moment when my emotions had sought relief, when I'd relaxed to a point where love didn't relate to marriage. And now I wanted him more and more, to have and to hold, and tied by the farce of a wedding. An illusion, that was marriage, but an illusion into which I wanted to relax.

'I'll go round the other side,' I said.

'If you must.'

'With the window shut, there'll be no draught.'

'But close, Phil, please. Close, or we'll get cold.'

'Close,' I promised.

As it was, cupped together, with my hand beneath his arm and resting on his chest.

By the time we got down to breakfast, not even knowing what time it was to be offered, nor whether there would be anything, I was feeling very scruffy, and Oliver's beard looked dreadful.

'We'll have to get to the shops,' I said.

'We must.'

We peered into the dining-room. Nothing. Then Kathie was behind us. 'If you wouldn't mind . . . I've laid breakfast in the kitchen.'

'Thank you.' I smiled at her. She seemed very bright and perky. As we went with her I asked, 'And how is she this morning?'

'Isn't it marvellous!' she said, beaming over her shoulder. 'Everything's going to be all right. He'll be home today.'

'Not today, Kathie. Surely not. You mustn't expect too much.'

'It's all been a mistake,' she assured me.

Whether she believed it or not, she had to accept what Heather told her, and glory in the fact that there would be an interval of peace for us all. I couldn't bring myself to shatter that.

'I'm sure it has,' I agreed, the mistake I had in mind being Heather marrying Martin in the first place.

The breakfast Kathie offered us was ham and eggs and gallons of tea. It was the best ham I'd ever tasted. Half-way through, Heather came down. She was no longer wearing her going-away costume, but nevertheless had on a very smart two-piece. She was bright and chirpy. The mood was still with her.

'I don't think I could eat a thing,' she said. 'Yes, perhaps I could. I think I might, Kathie.'

Kathie was very pleased. Fondly she watched her little girl tucking in. The telephone rang when Heather's fork was close to her lips. It clattered down on the plate as she plunged across the kitchen. She had phone extensions everywhere. The one here was on the wall. Kathie would be a recipient of all her secrets — as she had probably always been.

'Rupert!' she cried. 'Is that you? Where are you? Where? Oh . . . Taunton. Yes . . . yes, I heard. He's there. No, no, I don't think so, but as you're there . . . all right. I'll come over . . . no, it's no good arguing. I'll come. It's all right, Rupert . . . no, no, you've got things all wrong. Yes . . . didn't I say . . . he phoned. It's all a mistake. Very well, you be all stroppy, if you like . . . but I'm telling you it's a mistake. Yes . . . yes. Goodbye, then.'

She put down the phone heavily. When she came back to the table she was frowning. 'Solicitors can be so difficult. All legal this and legal that. Ordinary common sense gets nowhere with them.'

Heather's brand of common sense certainly wouldn't.

'He's being difficult, then?'

She shrugged. 'He's being stupid, if you ask me. He says they're unlikely to release him today. Have you ever heard such nonsense! I'll be there to make sure they do.'

'We'll go along with you,' I put in quickly.

'No, no.' She put a hand on my forearm. 'You good people will want to make an early start for home.'

'We'll take you to Taunton.'

'I can drive myself.'

'No, you can't, Heather. You car's at Heathrow. Remember?'

She clamped a hand over her mouth, then removed it. 'Oh heavens, yes.'

'We can do some shopping in Taunton while you — '

'But it wouldn't work.'

'What wouldn't?' I realized that her mind was flitting around from place to place.

'It would be out of your way to bring us back here. Martin and me,' she explained.

'We'll risk that, Heather.' I was certain he wouldn't be coming back today, anyway.

Then of course, being Heather, she had to decide that the costume she was wearing was perhaps not suitable. A little severe, she thought, for mid-June, though it was still cool after the storm. She insisted that I should go up and help her choose. What *did* one wear for bailing out a lover? Cheque book, that was all it needed. But she had loads of stuff in her wardrobe, which occupied a whole wall in her bedroom, too much to make the choice easy.

'What about jeans and a T-shirt?' I asked impatiently.

'Oh, I've got none of those,' she assured me gravely.

She finished up in a light two-piece, still not really suitable, but it did serve her figure better.

'Ready now,' she said.

We went out to the front, Kathie standing

in the open doorway to see us off. As we watched, a very sleek Jaguar saloon came from beneath the trees. It swept in an arc on the gravel and stopped behind my BMW.

Three people alighted, one of whom we knew. It was Victor Peel, the private eye from Birmingham, who'd been by himself in the back. He seemed to be a minor character in the trio, as he nipped round quickly to open the front door so that the driver could get out. This was another woman driver who insisted on driving her own car. I, too, wouldn't have trusted a Jaguar to Peel, and the small, inadequate-looking man who'd been travelling beside her would probably have been unable to see over the wheel.

But it was the woman who immediately attracted attention. She would do so anywhere, with that svelte look imparted by her personal *couturière*, the confident toss of the head, the severe style in which she had her brown hair, and the eyebrows low over the dark and brooding eyes. This was a woman who knew what she wanted, and to hell with anything or anybody who got in her way. She was tall too — around five feet eleven.

Beside her now, having hurried to her side clutching a briefcase under his arm, her fellow traveller looked meagre, weak, a dry stick that might snap any second. His hair was sparse, his face lean, and there was something about his eyes I didn't like. No yes man, this, and she was a woman who would not expect to be opposed — a dry, wrinkly man who bristled with an awareness of his excellence in his own field. I'd have said, at a glance, a lawyer.

Victor Peel seemed uneasy. He remained in the background, staring at us from beneath lowered eyebrows, his shoulders hunched. Physical trouble he could handle. This was trouble, clearly, in which he had become involved, and of which he disapproved. But he was uncertain of his own position and of his part in what was about to happen.

We stood and watched them approach the steps.

'You're Heather Payne,' said the woman. It was almost a condemnation. 'I want a word with you.' Without hesitation she had chosen the correct person.

'Heather Reade,' said Heather, but it was weakly stated. 'Mrs Heather Reade.'

'I think not. We've got some talking to do, you and I.'

'We were just on our way out.'

This seemed not to influence our visitor. 'It can wait. He's not available, anyway.' She made a dismissive gesture. Her tone indicated that the 'he' she spoke about was perhaps fortunate to be elsewhere.

'Who isn't?' asked Heather. 'Oh, Phillie — who *is* this? What's she talking about?' She stared fixedly, imploringly at our visitor.

Who seemed prepared to explain, but, 'Inside,' she said. 'We can't discuss it here. And I'm talking about Martin Reade, in whom I have a particular interest.' She made a small, strange grimace as she said this, a sourly humorous comment to herself. 'My name is June McBride.'

So this was the woman who had so drastically imposed herself into Heather's life, whose bigamy charge had led to Martin being plucked from Heather's side.

I felt Heather shaking beside me. I took her arm. 'We'd better see what this is all about,' I told her quietly. 'Before we leave.'

'I want to go to Martin.'

'Better not,' I advised. 'We ought to know what this woman wants, first. Don't you think? It's the sensible thing.'

There had been a harsh aggressiveness about June McBride, the sort of approach that so easily reduced Heather to tears. But we had to know what this was all about, and my friend in tears in front of this woman was not likely to help Heather's cause.

'You'd better come inside,' I said quietly, as though it was my house, and Heather meekly

94

complied, turning back to where Kathie still stood, hesitant in the doorway.

They trooped in, Victor Peel beside the small man, towering above him. Yet strangely there was no mistaking the fact this was a lawyer who was in charge.

The law held sway. We had to bow to its demands.

5

We used the drawing-room again. Kathie hovered for a moment, uncertain whether she ought to provide refreshment. But this was hard and cold business. I shook my head, seeing that Heather was too involved with premonitions, and Kathie withdrew, not from the room but, after closing the door, to a far corner. Heather took a seat in one of her wing back set of chairs and leaned forward tensely, knees together, fingers entwined on her lap. I stood at her shoulder, and Oliver went to lean against the fireplace. Victor Peel retired into the background, choosing an upright chair by the window. The lawyer sat beside his client on a settee, which he'd carefully moved so that they faced Heather directly.

But June McBride wasn't the type to sit. On her feet, she was more commanding, and she intended to waste no time on social trivialities. She sat, yes, but she was on her feet at once.

'You know who I am. Oh yes, I'm sure you've all heard by now. June McBride. This is my solicitor, Mr Raeburn. I'm Martin Reade's second wife. We suppose. There could have been a whole team of them for all we know.'

Raeburn cleared his throat. His voice when he spoke was remarkably clear and resonant. 'There's no need to assume there was any wife prior to Amanda Tulliver. She's the only one to claim legally to be Mrs Reade.'

'All right, Raeburn,' June McBride said. 'Leave this to me, will you please? You stick to your law. All right?'

He raised his eyebrows. Wrinkles scored his wide forehead and he pouted. 'As you wish. But I reserve the right to intervene.'

'Intervene if you like!' She meant 'dare'. Returning her attention to Heather, she began pacing backwards and forwards, three steps one way, three the other, hands cupping her elbows and arms, across her chest. 'I employed Peel, over there, to trace my precious Martin, when he left me, which was eight years ago. When he left me.'

'It's taken me six months,' put in Peel, unwilling to have it assumed he'd been eight years on it.

'Six whole months!' she said sharply, stabbing at him with her eyes. 'I've never known such ... anyway, he traced him. Reade Rapid Repairs. But at least he didn't waste the whole of the six months. He discovered that our darling Martin was already married to a woman called Amanda Tulliver. That marriage was three years before he went through a farcical ceremony with me. She's refused to divorce him and still uses his name. Mrs Amanda Reade. What the devil she's been thinking about, I don't know. I'd have divorced him like that.' She snapped her fingers derisively. 'Desertion! If that isn't grounds for divorce, I don't know what is. She'd at least got *that*. Me — I couldn't even divorce him. I didn't have that satisfaction.'

'I've explained — ' began Raeburn in a dry, exhausted voice.

'Oh, you have. Over and over. But it still doesn't seem right to me.'

'Your marriage was void, Miss McBride.' He appeared slightly to emphasize the 'Miss'. It seemed they didn't share the same Christian name familiarity as did Heather and Rupert. 'It never existed.'

'And I'm to let it go at that?' she demanded, turning to him.

He twisted his dry lips. 'You couldn't even let it go, because there wasn't anything to hold.'

As they stared at each other — not an ideal solicitor/client relationship — Heather, bless her, put in a quiet word.

'Does any of this affect me?' she asked. Foremost in her mind was the fact that she was being delayed in getting to Martin. His past history was of no concern to her.

June McBride turned back to her. 'Of course it affects you. You're in the same boat.'

'Your marriage is void, too, young lady,' said Raeburn. He said this with cool, dispassionate precision.

'What do I care about that?' Heather demanded, quite firmly for her. She could see no problem involved. 'We will simply live together, married or not. Everybody's doing it now.'

'You don't seem to understand,' said June McBride, irritated by anybody who didn't carefully follow her reasoning and then agree with her. 'He can't live with you if he's in prison, can he?'

'My solicitor will soon put that to rights,' Heather told her.

It was simply that she had a blind faith in Rupert. She had long ago put behind her any hope or intention of ever understanding the legal ramifications. Rupert would sort it out, and she could take Martin to her marital bed without any of the fuss of actual marriage. Rupert was going to bring that about.

'He's going to have a job wriggling out of a murder charge,' said Peel morosely. 'A dead, naked woman in his bed!' He lifted his head, having been speaking to his feet. 'Hah!' he added.

Then Raeburn spoke up quietly and acidly. It was a voice he would use in court. Never raise the level of your tone, then everybody strains to hear. He intended now to be heard, and we all concentrated on him.

'If you will please sit down, Miss McBride,' he said, gesturing with a hand that was like a piece of parchment caught in the wind. 'And you remain silent, Peel.' Without glancing round. 'I would like to explain the legal situation in which Martin Reade finds himself. Then perhaps we can get to the reason we have come here.'

'We're waiting to hear that,' I said, Heather having relapsed into a sulky silence.

'Very well.' He leaned forward, knees apart, elbows resting on them. 'My client, Miss McBride, having heard from Peel that Martin Reade was living and working in this district, instructed me to institute proceedings against him for bigamy. You will understand that bigamy is not an offence of much magnitude these days. Though it is a criminal offence, the police would be reluctant to act on that alone. We have a growing group of immigrants in this country for whom multiple marriages are a tradition, and in fact is part of their beliefs — '

100

'Oh, get on with it,' cut in June McBride. She was now sitting beside him, but poised and impatient.

He shrugged minimally. Ten guineas had just been added to his bill. 'Fortunately.' He bared his teeth at this fortune. 'Fortunately, my client could also level at him a charge of wrongful conversion of funds she had entrusted to him. That made it more serious. I was able to take out a private summons, and he was made to attend court, where he was committed for trial. He failed to appear for that second hearing, and a warrant for his arrest was issued. That warrant was executed at Heathrow Airport on information laid by myself based on the facts of another void marriage about to take place, and a trip to America being contemplated. Do I make myself clear?'

He paused, looking round. I wouldn't have said he was smiling, but he was pleased with his own phraseology. Beside me, Heather was breathing heavily with suppressed anger, panting. I put a hand on her shoulder. Nothing was sounding very pleasant to her. As there was no complaint that Raeburn wasn't making himself clear he went on, his voice still unaccented by any emotion whatsoever.

'You will understand that there was a

distinct possibility that Martin Reade had no intention of returning to this country, and of course it would be difficult to extradite him on such a minor charge as bigamy, even aggravated by fraud. In fact, the likelihood was that he'd planned to disappear, once in the USA, and that he was using yet another non-marriage to get him there — '

'No!' interrupted Heather violently.

'A possibility, dear lady. Only a possibility.' If that was his soothing voice, I didn't want to hear him when he became severe. 'But, as you probably know, he now has to face more serious charges. A dead woman was found in his bed. She had been struck behind the ear with a heavy spanner, which was found in his workplace. He is unable to account for his movements that night — the night before last — and it has to be assumed, at this stage, that he was in that bed with her at some time that night.'

'I'm not going to listen to this,' said Heather breathlessly, trying to get to her feet but her legs failing her.

'I thought I might be doing you a favour by outlining the facts,' he said, hurt and puzzled. It was beyond his comprehension that legal matters could invoke emotion. He was merely stating the facts.

'We'd better hear it all,' I told him.

102

'However painful.'

He frowned. It caused him no pain.

'Very well. The basic fact is that my client's charge against him will naturally take second place when he's faced with a murder charge. But he has not yet been charged. He claims he was elsewhere, and it could be difficult to prove it one way or the other. A good lawyer . . . ' He grimaced his apology that he was unable to assist in that way. 'A good man should be able to obtain his release, pending enquiries. On the murder aspect of it, that is. But Martin Reade must be held on the bigamy charge. There is a warrant outstanding for failing to appear in the Crown Court. He will now be held until his appearance there. The barrister I have instructed speaks of a minimum sentence of six years, on that charge, it being coupled with fraud. It's on this matter that my client wishes to consult you. I'll say this: I do not approve of what she has in mind . . . but I am under instructions.'

He gestured his resignation, and sat back. June McBride bounced to her feet.

'And I'm going to say it. I don't care a damn what the sod gets — six years or none. What's the good of that to me? Am I supposed to gloat over every day he spends in prison? A lot of use that is. No — he did me out of money, the rotten cheat. And I want it back. I trusted him, and he disappeared with it. I want it back.'

'I don't understand . . . ' Heather was always slow. It seemed very clear to me.

'I doubt he's still got it,' I said. 'Doubt it very much.'

'Hell, if I thought he had I wouldn't be here.' The dark eyes flashed. She turned to appeal to Raeburn, but he shook his head in something close to despair.

'I can't agree with this,' he murmured.

'Are you saying . . . ' Heather was getting there, if belatedly.

'If I get my money back, I don't care where it comes from. That's what I'm saying. And anybody can have *him*. Anybody!' She flung herself about, taking in the whole of our little group.

Heather murmured, 'How much?'

'You can't do this, Heather,' I whispered to her tersely. 'You just can't. It's ridiculous.'

'I can do what I like.' She tossed her head in defiance. Heather defiant was a rare sight.

'You'd be *buying* him,' I said, my lips close to her head, trying to keep my voice down when I felt like slapping her.

The eyes she turned on me were full of fury. Her cheeks were flaming. 'It's only like paying a fine. Keep out of this, Phil, for God's sake.'

Then she turned back to our visitor, whom I was beginning to regret we had ever allowed inside. She was stolidly standing there with her head back, waiting, but from the look in her eyes waiting with confidence.

'How much?' Heather demanded.

Raeburn cleared his throat, but Oliver, who had been very quiet, at last raised his voice. Not much; the silence in the room was tense.

'It'd be a good idea if it was made clear what's on offer here.'

Raeburn glanced across in annoyance. 'I was about to explain.' He was crackling with cold dignity, disapproval souring the line of his mouth. 'If I may . . . ' He was waiting for his client to resume her seat.

With a grimace, almost of contempt, she sat. 'Get on with it, then.'

Once more with elbows on spread knees, but now with his hands raised to each side of his face, he complied. Every word was a drip of acid.

'My client is willing to withdraw her summons on the bigamy charge. That's simple enough — a signature on a dotted line. But the fraud — the illegal conversion of my client's money — that is a different matter. Recovery of the money does not negate the fact that wrongful practice took place. Indeed, it was very close to theft. He did not produce the goods for which the money was intended.' He brought his fingertips together beneath his chin, and pouted above them. He was enjoying this, the chance to expound on the difficulties involved, whilst making sure it was understood that he could surmount them.

'If, however,' he went on, 'the goods on which my client's money was expended could be returned — even though they might not be exactly the goods for which the money was intended — then I might be able to put up a reasonable argument that the fraud, as well as the marriage, has been rendered void.'

'I don't know what you're talking about,' said Heather, pitifully left behind again. 'Simply tell me how much . . . ' She put her head in her hands. 'Tell him, Phil, for pity's sake. I just want to know how much.'

'She wants to know how much,' I told him.

He nodded. I'd swear his eyes glinted with a hint of amusement. 'The nitty-gritty,' he murmured, 'as I believe it's called. Very well — leave the technicalities to me. Now, let me see . . . ' He turned to his client. 'Wasn't it around £25,000?'

'You know damn well — '

But he cut right through her voice, speaking to me now. 'The original figure was about £25,000, give or take a little, in the form of a bank certified cheque, which Martin Reade converted to his own purposes. That was eight years ago. If we calculate an average interest rate on money lost at ten per cent, the figure would now be . . . let me see . . . say £54,000.' He said this as though he'd worked it out in his head. Instantly.

'I'll pay it. I'll pay it.' Heather was weeping now, but whether from joy or tension I couldn't say. 'I'll get my cheque book.'

He smiled. 'I'm afraid it would have to be another certified cheque.'

'All right. All *right*.' She reached down over her shoulder so that I could take her hand again, and Oliver seized the opportunity to interrupt once more.

'And can we be told for what the defrauded money was intended?'

'Of course.' Raeburn shuffled through the filing system between his ears. 'It was intended to purchase a car, a Mercedes Benz 500E, for which the purchase price was approximately £25,000 at that time.'

'Then,' said Oliver placidly, 'instead of attracting interest, the investment would have depreciated. Even a Merc, over eight years. I don't think she should be expected to pay interest.'

'You shut your mouth!' Heather screamed. 'Phil, tell him to stop. I'll pay it, I'll pay it.'

'Hush, hush,' I told her, shaking my head at Oliver, who merely flashed me a smile and cocked an eyebrow. 'It's all right, Heather. Do it as you wish.'

She straightened in her chair, trying to be dignified and businesslike. 'Prepare your legal papers, or whatever, and I'll sign them. And we can go to Taunton together and get you the wretched cheque. My bank manager has always been most obliging.'

'I'm sure he has,' said Raeburn. 'But there'll be nothing for you to sign.'

'Well, all right,' said Miss McBride, bouncing to her feet again. 'Let's get going, for Chrissake. All the morning'll be gone.'

Victor Peel heaved himself to his feet. His presence there had been unnecessary, unless he'd been a bodyguard. Had they expected physical attack?

'We were just about to leave, anyway,' said Heather. She too got to her feet, but I noticed she had to grip the chair back firmly. 'Oh, Phillie, isn't it marvellous!' she cried, her voice shaking.

I wasn't sure how marvellous it was. To me it all seemed wrong. It was like buying a slave. Did she expect undying gratitude from her Martin, undeviating obedience? If so, I guessed she was in for a bit of a shock.

In a procession, June McBride, Raeburn

108

and Victor Peel were heading for the door, but Kathie was there before them and jerked it open. Then, in the hall, she pushed past so that she could snatch at the front door, which, however, was heavy and ponderous so that she didn't get quite the effect she'd wanted, but there was a definite disapproval in her attitude. She couldn't wait to see the back of them. Even when Heather went hurrying after them, Kathie was not her usual self. For once, her precious Heather had done something of which Kathie did not approve, and at no time, even if only with a raised eyebrow, had Heather appealed to Kathie for help and advice.

They reached their car. Oliver was at my shoulder. He raised his voice, catching June McBride just before she stepped into her Jaguar to take the wheel.

'Oh — one more point,' Oliver said. 'Before we leave. In view of the fact that Heather will be repaying the wrongfully converted money, wouldn't it be correct to say that she ought to know what it was converted to? I mean — whatever it is, she'll own it.'

I knew that Oliver was trying to make the point that Heather's £54,000 wasn't buying Martin. She was entitled only, for that sum, to the remnants of Martin's indiscretions. I squeezed his arm.

It was Peel who answered, lifting his dark, shaggy head. 'You can go and pick it up yourself. It's that clapped-out yellow Dolomite Sprint in Reade's workshop.'

Then he smiled complacently before he ducked his head inside the rear of the Jaguar. It was the first time I'd heard it was the Sprint version of the Dolomite.

'There you are, Heather,' I said. 'Not only do you get Martin, but also his old wreck. Isn't that delightful?'

She didn't answer, but got into the back of my BMW, as June McBride leaned sideways in the driver's seat, a pleasant and relaxed woman now that she'd got her own way, and called past Raeburn's head, 'There are car-parks opposite the County Hall, in the Crescent. See you there.'

Then, with a defiant spray of gravel and a bit of a tail-slide, she swept round and dived her Jaguar into the tunnel beneath the trees.

'Do you know Taunton?' I asked Heather.

'Of course I do.'

'Then you'll have to guide us when we get there. And don't go to sleep,' I added, 'because we may need you to get us to Taunton.'

'I was only closing my eyes,' she said. She'd probably been assembling a mental image of

Martin, as she would shortly see him. 'And you can follow them, can't you?'

'I'm not going to make a race of it, Heather. We've got all day. You do realize, I hope, that it'll take a long while!'

'Not *too* long,' she pleaded, not to me but to fate. 'I couldn't stand that.'

Then she was silent, and when I glanced round, pausing at the entrance, she was asleep, probably catching up on what she'd lost the last two nights.

But I was well equipped with maps, including town plans, and Oliver guided me well. 'Should be straightforward,' he said. 'We'll be coming in from the north-west.'

'D'you think it's going to work?' I asked him quietly.

'I'd reckon that Raeburn will have tested out the temperature around Martin at this time,' he decided. 'I got the feeling he's probably discussed it with the police, and if I know superintendents they'll be only too pleased to see the back of a bigamy and fraud charge. Then they'll be able to concentrate on the murder aspect.'

I thought about that. There was a possibility that Heather could still be disappointed, and she wouldn't be able to bear that. Somehow, I felt responsible for her. She'd taken me right back to our schooldays, because really she was still the young girl I'd known.

'But they might keep him in for questioning, surely?' I asked. Let him out of one door and drag him back through another.

He was silent awhile, giving me instructions as we wound through the country lanes, until we picked up the B3224. Then he relaxed, and said, 'You'll pick up the A358 at Bishops Lydeard, then it's south-east directly into Taunton.'

I settled down to it. There was no sign of the Jaguar. 'You didn't answer my question.'

'I've been thinking. *Would* they hold him for questioning? It depends. There must be something unsatisfactory about their murder case, or they would've charged him with it by now. I mean, it's so obviously all against him. His little hut, his little bed, a naked woman in it and dead from a head wound, and what seems like the murder weapon lying on a bench in his workshop. And such a lousy alibi — asleep in a car in a lay-by! I ask you.'

'You ask me what?' I risked a smile at him. 'To comment? All right, I will. Why weren't there any of her clothes? And why *was* there a weapon hanging around?'

'I can't find you any answers, Phil. But it's a useless alibi he's got.'

'We don't know that.'

'But the police will know, pretty damn soon. If they get even a vague cross-check on a car in a lay-by, they'll ask themselves; why there? Did he drive there after the killing, perhaps to dispose of her clothing . . . '

'And forget to dispose of the weapon?' I asked with scorn.

'It could've been important to hide her identity.'

'Which he could've done by taking her out with him in the car he was using and dumping her body somewhere a long way away. Why didn't he do that?'

He laughed. 'You asked me a question. Why haven't they charged him? You've just answered it yourself. Every time you twist the facts around to assemble a bit of logic, it all comes up as nonsense again.'

'What would *you* do?'

'If I was in charge?' He waited for me to nod. 'I'd let him go, pending further enquiries — and watch what *he* would do.'

We were silent awhile. Then he ventured, 'You're on his side, aren't you?'

I shook my head. 'No. How could I be? But Oliver — I want to meet him first. He doesn't sound at all like a murderer, not from what we've heard so far. A villain, a heartless rogue, perhaps. Completely self-interested, yes. But violent . . . surely not.'

'We'll see. It looks bad for him, though. We're coming into the town now. We'll have to watch it carefully from now on.'

We did, Oliver barking out instructions, and Heather, who was now fully awake again, not helping at all. But we found the car-park, not only that but the correct one, there being two off the Crescent, and managed to park only a few cars away from the Jaguar.

Then there was a little trouble. Heather had the idea she was going with them, directly to sign for Martin, if she had to give a receipt for goods delivered, and that it was going to be a rapid transaction. Certainly we had to stay together for now, as Heather had to visit her bank. Raeburn was quick enough to remind her of that. And there, she was shut away with her friend the bank manager for twenty minutes before she emerged waving a certified cheque for £54,000, payable to June McBride. Raeburn took control of it.

I had thought I was wealthy, at least warmly comfortable, but I would not have been able to do that. Certainly not so quickly. There are degrees, though. Perhaps Oliver would realize that his marrying me would not be for my money, now that he'd seen what real money was, so abundant and so immediately available. And how many other women there were, so generously endowed,

114

who were looking round for a mate! I trusted he would learn from it, and realize that there were degrees, too, in the acquisitiveness involved in marrying for money, Martin being a prime example of the expert.

As Raeburn carefully placed the cheque in his wallet — it was the best way of making sure of his fee — he said, 'This is going to take a long while. Shall we meet at — say — four o'clock in the Old Market shopping centre? My client will have to accompany me, of course.'

It meant we had over six hours to get through.

In a town strange to me I like to search out the interesting by-ways, taking my time, relaxed. But the possibility of relaxing with Heather present was nil. We couldn't abandon her, though, but really she was quite dreadful, wanting to sit in the shopping centre all day in case Raeburn had miscalculated, and it was all settled in a few minutes. But Oliver and I had shopping to do, there clearly being no chance of our driving home to Shropshire that day — or maybe for quite a few days. And Heather did know the town, so we needed her, and we had to drag her along with us. She developed a distressing tendency to keep peering over her shoulder, or stopping altogether and looking round, as though *he* might be there, searching for her, thrusting and swerving through the crowds as he ran to her with open arms. All of which made our bit of shopping difficult.

It was a miserable day altogether. Heather perfected a technique of craftily guiding us back to that same shopping centre from wherever we'd managed to reach. I could list every shop in there, and detail the complete contents of their window displays. We ate lunch there. Oliver and I ate lunch — Heather pushed hers around and nibbled desolately. There was, as we came out, no sign of Raeburn and June McBride. No sign of Martin.

'It's only half-past one,' I said impatiently.

'I know . . . ' Her eyes were everywhere.

Two and a half hours to go. I felt desperate. 'There're supposed to be some nice walks by the river,' said Oliver, who'd been scanning a guidebook.

'Oh no . . . ' Heather moaned.

I didn't dare risk the river, anyway. The desire to push her in would have been irresistible.

But four o'clock came round. We had nearly reached a number of interesting places, but always Heather had turned back. Four o'clock with the crowds in the Old Market shopping centre slightly easier to walk through, and we did walk through. Twice. Raeburn hadn't said exactly whereabouts in the precinct. Heather nearly passed out with suspense.

Then there they were — June McBride and Raeburn. No support from Peel . . . and no Martin.

'Where is he? Where is he?'

'It's all right,' said Raeburn. 'Peel's with him. They're waiting by your car.'

'But it isn't *my* car!' cried Heather, quick to see every problem before it even lifted its tiny head. 'He won't know Philipa's.'

Raeburn twisted his lips. 'I realized that. But Peel knows it. That's why I sent him along.'

'Is everything satisfactory?' I asked him, trying to be practical.

'Certainly.' He smiled thinly. 'Bigamy charges dropped. There's uncertainty with the murder business, so they've let him go free.' He lowered his voice. 'For now.'

'Why aren't we going there?' Heather demanded.

'A second.' I was almost pleading, when I was seeking information on her behalf. 'He's free?' I asked. 'Fully?'

'I said I couldn't promise anything on the aspect of the murder.' Raeburn was even drier, his face almost crackling as he grimaced. 'He's not supposed to leave his district, and they'll want him for more questioning. Otherwise . . . '

'I could do with a drink,' said June McBride flatly. 'Come along, Raeburn.'

I wondered whether he would get her to pay for it, as we left them to find a bar. It was necessary to hurry to catch up with Heather and Oliver, who were disappearing into the crowd. I supposed he didn't want to touch her in order to restrain her, but she soon slowed to a walk. It'd been tiring on the legs, that long, long day.

Then there he was, Martin Reade. Or at least, I assumed it was he, as two men were standing by *my* BMW, one of them Peel. They were not speaking, but maintaining a distance from each other. And Martin was not keeping an eager watch for our arrival. He seemed repressed, the watching being in a hunted manner, from beneath lowered eyebrows.

Then he saw us . . . saw Heather. He came alive, as though a slow fuse had reached his charge, exploding into his personality. It seemed that he unwound to his full height, which was an inch over six feet, and it became a performance, a display, this being the Martin Reade he offered to his world,

118

which was mainly female. For one moment he had been repressed, his spirits low, now he emerged as gangling and untidy, glowing with life and energy — and pathetic.

This he offered to Heather. It wasn't that he ran, though his eagerness seemed uncontrollable — it was Heather who ran — but he certainly moved towards her, slowly, arms wide apart and with a great silent laugh illuminating his handsome but rather too pretty face. Then she was in those arms, and he was kissing her face all over, forehead, cheeks, chin, nose, and lips, which had been poised, puckered, from the start.

'Lover!' he said softly, holding her back from him to check it was indeed his Heather.

'Oh my poor darling!' she cried. 'What have they been doing to you?'

He looked beyond her and caught my eye. His blond hair was flying untidily, but his lack of a shave wasn't evident. The face was smooth, seeming ageless, though he would have been well into his forties. His brow was wide, his chin sharp, his nose an impudent snub. He met my eyes, and in that moment there was an awareness. I could see it in his smile, which wasn't for Heather. The laughter of delight had been for Heather. For me the smile, and abruptly I had to look away.

Peel would probably have told him that the

BMW was mine, and Martin would have been able to price it — exactly. It put me in a bracket, a marriageable bracket. So I had to look away because, damn it, in that second I had realized what three women had seen in him, and perhaps a hundred more. And I knew I was going to like him. Or worse.

Really, it would have been a good time to leave it all and drive with Oliver home. But we couldn't leave them there without transport, and by the time we reached Hellyspool Hall it was too late.

What Peel told us on the way back to Heather's made it too late — and what Martin had already told me with his eyes.

6

It was the difficulty involving the transport that brought it about. We had no way of guessing how long June McBride and Raeburn would be in returning for her Jaguar, and there was no assurance, anyway, that they would be prepared to run Peel back to his car, at The Rolling Stone. Peel was the snag, and we couldn't simply leave him there. In that district and with an isolated objective such as the village of Hellyspool, it might be well nigh impossible to make the journey by bus. And Peel was now in all ways surplus to requirements. His work for June McBride was completed, and he needed only to return to his home patch, Birmingham. Yet he was minus one car.

It was then that I spotted Rupert Anderson, who was just approaching with a document case under his arm, and who now stopped and stood with his feet apart, watching the tableau of Heather and Martin.

No thought had been given to Rupert for some considerable time, but it seemed clear to me that he must have been involved in the complexities surrounding Martin's release.

121

The grave face, the stance of poised disapproval, could well have resulted from Heather's actions — all taken without seeking his advice. But in the end he gathered together a smile and advanced, seeing that the two central figures had now completed their mutual welcome.

'Rupert!' she cried. 'Where were you? It's all been so exciting!'

'I've been intimately involved,' he said quietly. 'And Martin . . . ' He offered his hand. 'I'm so pleased to see you free.'

'It's all settled,' said Heather, who hadn't the slightest idea of how much wasn't. 'It's been so exciting,' she repeated.

Her memory was short, too. It had been a terrible day.

'I'll have to see you sometime, Martin,' said Rupert, smiling sadly and fondly at Heather. 'There's a lot to discuss.'

'I don't know what, then,' said Martin, his tone dismissive.

'You know very well. I'll be up to the house. Soon.'

'Oh . . . sure.'

It was clear to me now that Rupert would have to be persuaded to help out with the transport. Rupert wasn't going to be pleased if he got landed with Peel, and frankly I didn't think I'd be able to concentrate on my driving with Heather and Martin sitting behind me, he keeping up a steady stream of enthusiasm and platitudinous nonsense, and she lapping it up.

As I worked on this, Oliver had come to the same conclusion and added a reasonable argument. 'I want a word with Peel,' he told me quietly.

Rupert decided it. He must have realized our dilemma, and offered to take the loving couple home. After all, she was his client. He did it graciously, but there was a grim twist to his lips and his frown was heavy.

We watched them go. Then Peel was urged into the front passenger seat of my car. He had no alternative, though he must have realized it meant further interrogation. Oliver knew I would want to hear, and with the two of them in the back that would have been difficult.

So, before we even got out of the town, Oliver was leaning forward and talking between the two headrests.

'This'll be the end of it for you, I suppose?' he asked Peel.

'Seems like it.'

'Job done, account to be submitted. And that'll be that?'

'Something like it.' But Peel was unresponsive.

'That *was* the job, I take it? I mean, tracing Martin for Miss McBride.'

Silence. I glanced at Peel. He was surly and tense, on the defensive.

'Wasn't it?' Oliver insisted.

Peel contemplated the miles of road ahead of him. 'You heard Raeburn. That was the job.'

'But I seem to remember you went beyond that. You also traced an earlier wife. A first one. Was *that* part of the job?'

Peel twisted in his seat. 'Aw . . . come on. You follow up leads. They point you somewhere else. It grows. You ought to know that.'

'Yes. I can understand it. And there would always be the chance of a bit more cash arising from it?'

Oliver was speaking as though he might have been considering his own future career as a private investigator. He was interestedly requesting information. Was it all worth the effort? Was there anything to be made on the side?

'Such as what?' Peel demanded.

'I don't know. You tell me. Information's always valuable, either to give, or to be withheld.'

Peel pretended ignorance. 'Fancy words. But what the hell do they mean?'

Oliver poked his shoulder with a finger. He managed to sound jovial, one good feller talking to another good feller. He'd been in the same line of work, though not privately.

'Well, I don't know, really. But you'd get paid either way, it seems to me. I might try it myself, you see. So I'd like to know the ropes. I mean . . . there isn't all this twaddle, with a lawyer and a client, or a doctor and a patient. Confidentiality. Secrecy. Information could fetch more money from the one who wouldn't want it known than from the one who wants to know it.'

'Now you just wait . . . '

'No hurry, is there? Take your time. It's quite a decent run.'

'I'm not telling you — '

'The tricks of the trade? No, I wouldn't expect that. Not the tricks. But I mean . . . you traced Martin for the McBride woman. At one end, there she was. She would want to know, of course. You were going to get paid for it. All right — but there was also Martin. He'd be willing to pay for the information to be buried, I'd have thought.'

Peel calmly unveiled his principles. 'What . . . him! Since when did he have any hard cash?'

'You mean you put it to him?'

'No.'

'Why not?'

'He was broke. It was obvious.'

'Yes. It was. One sight of that garage set-up, and you'd walk away, shaking your head.'

'But surely', I interrupted, 'Mr Peel would discover that Martin was about to be married to money.'

Oliver murmured, 'Watch the road, Phil, for God's sake!' And I'd only swerved a little.

'Yes,' agreed Peel. 'You keep out of this, lady.'

When Oliver spoke again his voice was more cutting. 'Let's forget the chit-chat, Peel. You'd got Martin in your sights. He was soon going to marry money, and Martin had a reputation for acquiring some of it from his women . . . '

'Not the first wife, he didn't.'

'All the same, there was a good chance with this new one.'

'Now see here . . . ' Peel was furious — a dark and contained anger he had difficulty in controlling. He heaved himself round, unfastening his seat belt so that he could face Oliver squarely. 'D'you think I'd . . . ' Then he laughed harshly at a thought. 'In any event, if that great floppy weed Martin ever gets money out of her — and he will, he will, you mark my words — he'll just disappear again with it all in his own pocket. I ain't stupid.'

'Of course not.' Oliver sat back. 'You already knew he'd defrauded your client, Miss McBride. I was forgetting. But of course, there's still Heather herself. Now she — '

'What! Tell *her?*'

'Why not? You've seen her. You must have observed how things are with her. She's crazy over him. She'd have taken him, married or not. She *has.* And she'd have paid a lot to make that possible. She's done that, too. You ought to have gone to her. She'd have paid you to put in a nil return to your client — to tell her you couldn't trace him.'

'Tcha!' Peel said disgustedly.

'Heather wouldn't have cared that he was married,' I intervened. 'His real wife wouldn't have to be told that he'd taken on another.'

'June McBride wasn't his real wife,' he reminded me with a hint of triumph.

'I didn't mean that one. I meant Amanda Tulliver. She's the real one. Amanda Reade.'

'I've had enough of this,' said Peel. 'You haven't paid me for anything. I ain't saying another word.'

'The point,' said Oliver heavily, 'is that you took this case way past what you need to have

127

done. You traced Amanda — '

'Stop this car! I'm getting out.'

'All right,' I agreed. 'Please yourself.'

I caught Oliver's eye. Minimally, he inclined his head. The car rolled onwards smoothly until I saw a lay-by ahead. Into this I turned, stopped, and drew on the handbrake. Peel got out quickly, awkwardly, and at once turned to face the rear door. I'd tipped him off by using the handbrake, the gesture denoting more than a pause. Oliver was climbing out too.

I didn't like this. The big, shambling lout was larger than Oliver, heavier, more aggressive, and Oliver really had the full use of only one arm. Perhaps Oliver had wanted room to move around. Or perhaps I'd misinterpreted his inclination of the head. In any event, I reached under the dash for the heavy torch I kept there, and got out too. Then I went to stand just beside Peel, close enough to be able to reach the back of his head with a good, loose swing.

If Oliver saw the torch, he made no gesture or comment. They stood facing each other, Peel now more relaxed, easing his shoulders purposefully.

'Now,' said Oliver. 'Let's talk about Amanda . . . Tulliver, was it?'

'Talk away. I don't give information free.'

'Walk to the nearest phone box and call for a taxi — and see how free that is.'

'Funny!'

'Amanda . . . '

Peel shrugged. 'She's always called herself Reade. She was his real wife, his first. Does that help?'

'Not much. We already knew it. You met her, did you, and spoke to her? When you were nosing around — '

'Go to hell.' Peel now seemed more confident. He even grinned. His teeth were still as bad.

'I'm not going to believe you didn't try something,' Oliver said. 'There'd be money there, or Martin wouldn't have been interested in the first place.'

'Be fair, Oliver,' I put in. 'We don't know that. He could well have loved her.'

He darted me a startled look. 'Martin loves himself. *Was* there money, Peel? *Is* there money?'

'There wasn't then, but that's changed.'

'Changed?' I asked. 'Was it different when Martin married her? When *was* it, this first marriage, anyway?'

'Two questions,' said Oliver disapprovingly. 'One at a time, that's the way to do it.'

Peel jerked his head from one to the other of us. 'Do what?'

'Conduct an interrogation,' Oliver told him.

'I'm not listening to any interrogation. You can't make me —'

Oliver smiled placidly. It was his confidence, I think, that was irritating Peel. 'Of course I can't. There's no cell I can toss you into, and leave you to think about it. No . . . we're offering you a lift to your own car, for information. Interested?'

Peel shrugged. The huge shoulders moved. 'Say your piece.'

'When were they married?'

'Ten years ago. Maybe twelve.'

'Which?'

'Twelve, I think. But if so, she'd have been only in her teens. She's about thirty now. Females are daft at eighteen. She must have been — to marry him. Two years he gave her, then he was off.'

'Leaving her broken-hearted?' I put in a question Oliver would not have asked.

Peel turned to me, eyebrows crawling up to hide behind his lock of hair. 'Guess she was. My info is that she still was — two weeks ago, when I was around there.'

'You spoke to her?' Oliver asked.

'No. Never said a word to her. Asking around . . . you know.'

'Hmm!' said Oliver. 'Let's get back to the

money. Was there money when he married her?'

'No. Her father had money, but he wasn't going to part with it.'

'And she's an only child?'

'As far as I know. If it matters.'

'But the father was old — no? Fit and well? Hale and hearty?'

'At that time he was.' For some reason this seemed to amuse him.

I wasn't happy with Oliver's completely materialistic approach to this, but before I could interrupt, Peel went on, 'They were married for two years. Together for two years. She was twenty when Martin simply walked out on her. Well . . . I mean . . . he was a good bit older. Thirty-five or so to her eighteen, when they married. How he could stand her around him, the silly little creature . . . heavens, it's a miracle he stuck it that long.'

'Silly?' I asked, ignoring Oliver's obvious objection to my direction of approach. He knew I was more interested in Martin; he must have been aware. But silly! She was not necessarily so, simply because she might have glowed in his presence. 'Because she loved him?' I demanded of Peel.

His face bore the supercilious expression that is so infuriating when such questions arise. Love? It was a woman's word. To Peel it would be an aberration. He raised only one eyebrow this time. 'Call it what you like. She was still mad about him a fortnight ago, that's all I know. Or why hadn't she divorced him? Why hadn't she married again? You tell me that. There were plenty who'd have been glad to . . . ' Then he brightened. 'Tiny little thing. Five feet and a bit, and pretty as they come, and lively, when she'd had a drink or two and forgot for a while. Laughing. I saw her doing it in a pub, with a whole crowd of men around her. And only that big nerd Clive Garner trying to put the mockers on it. Sitting there like a ruddy great cloud, watching her every second. Used to be first in line as her future husband, I found out, and only waiting till she was eighteen. But Martin got in first.'

'Clive Garner . . . ' I began, but Peel was well launched now. A chatterer, this Victor Peel was, a gossiper, once the point at issue slid away from his professional interest.

'Still thought he'd got to look after her,' he went on. 'Like a bloody great brooding uncle. He's not her uncle, mind you. A cousin or something. He works the home farm. But you'd have thought he owned her. Still keeping his eye on her, he was, and you could tell she didn't like it.'

'She'd made one mistake,' I put forward as

132

an explanation. 'He wouldn't want to see her make another. But I suppose he'd have no say in it. Not now.'

'No.' He grinned. 'But he's got a great big knobbly fist, and that'd be a fair argument if it came to the put-to.'

'If it did.' Oliver seemed impatient, wanting to keep to the point. 'But it sounds as though she still had Martin on her mind.'

'Seemed like it to me, too,' Peel agreed amiably.

'So why,' I asked, having difficulty in controlling my voice, 'didn't you approach her for money? You could have told her where she could find Martin. Play one against the other. June McBride against Amanda. Or is it that she still hasn't got any money?'

Peel shrugged. 'I'd already got my client — Miss McBride.'

'Very honourable, I'm sure,' I said. 'So Amanda still hasn't got money?'

'Oh yes she has.' Peel drew himself up. He was probably tired of these insinuations as to his loyalty to a client. 'I wasn't about to ask her for any, and that's it.'

'She has money now?' asked Oliver, keeping to his line. 'You mean her father's dead?'

'Well, yes. Didn't I say?'

'You did not. When did he die?'

Peel licked his lips, making them more flexible for the horribly complacent beaming smile he produced. 'A month after Martin left her. Now, isn't that a shame! Tulliver went off the road in his car, down a steep bank. The police reckoned he was driven off.'

I drew a breath, a shuddering one. 'A month after?'

'And Martin had left.' Peel laughed harshly. 'What a pity.'

Driven off the road, he'd said. He meant by another driver. Another, more expert driver. But it couldn't have been Martin. No. Or Martin would have returned to her. In a contradictory way, heart dictating to the mind, I was pleased to come across an iniquity that Martin hadn't perpetrated, yet I had to remind myself that, where money was involved, I wouldn't have put it beyond him. Or would I? It was a thought to be hidden away, to be explored secretly later.

'It seems to me,' said Oliver heavily, 'that this little investigation of yours has laid you open to collect large sums of money from several people. Are you saying you haven't?'

'Don't be a damned fool. If I had, they'd all have intervened in some way. It's only my client who has.' Then his mind stumbled over a thought. 'I think.' And he blinked rapidly several times.

'And what does *that* mean?' Oliver demanded.

'If you people want to get on, do it. And I'll start walking.'

'No.' Oliver was suddenly tense. 'Say it — whatever it is.'

Again Peel licked his lips, but he was far from smiling. 'The police. They knew I was working on an investigation around Hellyspool. It's a good idea to tip 'em off, or they wonder, especially in country districts. So they got hold of me — I was in Taunton earlier today, hanging round the station on Raeburn's behalf. You know. Waiting. And they had a thought. Something I might have seen. So they took me along to the morgue. Lovely. Just what I like! And it was her, lying there.'

'Her?' I managed to whisper.

'Amanda Tulliver. Reade, rather. Mandy they called her at home. She was the dead woman in Martin's bed.' Then strangely, because I would not have thought him capable of it, he looked genuinely distressed. But he turned his head away, ashamed of it.

Suddenly I felt sick, physically sick. My stomach churned. I'd seen Martin only for a few minutes, at which time he'd been intensely absorbed in Heather. I had no reason to like him. What I'd heard of him, and was still hearing, was in no way calculated to inspire any affection, even minor, even impersonal. What the *hell* was it about him, that I should feel so abruptly and fearsomely distressed on his behalf? But it couldn't be — not that Martin had killed her. By clinging to that thought, I managed to control my physical nausea.

Oliver said, 'Get in the car.' He was speaking to Peel. Then, to me, 'Coming, Phil? Are you all right?'

'Yes, thank you.'

'It wasn't me,' said Peel. 'I swear it wasn't me.'

'What wasn't?' I managed to ask.

'Wasn't me who told her where he'd got to.'

I didn't say anything, but got in behind the wheel. Oliver now sat beside me. I thought he'd detected something in my attitude, but he didn't comment. I started the engine, slipped the box into 'drive', and it wouldn't move.

'The handbrake, Phil.'

The warning light was showing. I hadn't seen it. I slipped off the handbrake and we moved.

'That's better,' said Oliver. 'D'you want me to take over?'

'I'm all right.' And to prove it I speeded up,

and took a corner only a little too fast.

In this way, fast because I was in a hurry to get rid of Peel and talk confidentially to Oliver, I got us to Hellyspool. We dropped Peel outside The Rolling Stone.

He waved nonchalantly as he walked away.

I turned the car in order to return to Heather's place. Now I was driving slowly.

After half a mile Oliver said quietly, 'We could just keep going, you know. Home. And then phone Heather from there.'

I didn't reply.

'She wouldn't notice we'd gone,' he said suggestively. He clearly wanted to see an end to it.

'I don't know what to say. We just can't leave it like this. I don't *know*, Oliver.'

'It couldn't have been him, Phil.'

I had to guess which 'him' he meant, and which 'it'. 'You mean Tulliver's death? Amanda's father's.'

'It just doesn't fit, my love.' He patted my knee. I hate that. 'Even if he did it a month after he'd left her, because it would've looked bad if he'd done it when he was living there, he'd have returned to her. Sometime. And it's been ten years. He obviously didn't know she'd inherited all the money.'

I'd had much the same thought. Oliver put

it in more basic words, that was the difference. 'You're assuming he's always had his mind on money?' I asked.

'That's how it's beginning to look. And surely . . . you've seen what she's like . . . he certainly wouldn't have married that June McBride for affection.'

'No. I can't imagine that.' I was now drifting along at about five mph. The car did it with my foot off the throttle. 'But — if Amanda came to him, and he hadn't known her father was dead — surely, if you *will* insist it was always money . . . ' I stopped, having talked myself into a verbal trap.

'Yes?' he asked politely.

'Well — damn it — if it was money on his mind, and Amanda turned up, just in time, tipped off about Heather's marriage, surely, then, he'd have gone back with her. With Amanda. She *was* his wife. Then at least he'd have been deserting one of his women before marriage . . . Heather. He'd have gone back with Amanda. Surely.'

He was silent . . . then, 'Stop at that farm entrance, Phil, turn around, and go back to Martin's garage.'

'Why? The fuel gauge is all right.'

'You said it yourself. Twice. You said: gone back with her. With Amanda. In what, though? How did she get here — if she did come to him? Walk? No . . . so, where the hell's her car?'

'Oh,' I said. 'Yes,' I said.

I backed up, and we returned to Reade's Rapid Repairs, parking on the forecourt and well back from the pumps.

The obvious place to leave a car was with the others, his second-hand wrecks so optimistically offered. There were six of them. We walked over to have a look. Not one of them in any way resembled a car Amanda Tulliver would have driven. They each had a uniform coating of dust. One even had a flat front tyre.

'That's how he spent the night,' Oliver declared. 'He took her car and he dumped it somewhere. There must be hundreds of places around here where nobody ever goes.'

'Nonsense. Rubbish.'

'And walked back,' he persisted.

'So why would he leave her dead body in his own bed?' I asked with scorn.

He shrugged. 'Just a thought.'

'You're slipping, Oliver. Shall we get on to Heather's?'

Then he was grinning at me, mockingly. 'Just tossing rocks under your feet, Phillie.'

'Rocks?'

'To stop you running headlong into trouble.'

'Let's get in the car.'

I was starting the engine when he slammed his door.

'Let's drive home,' he said.

'No. It's not finished.'

He fastened his seat belt. 'I'm not sure I want to see the end.'

7

They were having a coming-out party, or rather, Heather was attempting to promote one, with Martin's assistance, but Rupert and Kathie were not noticeably in the mood. Drinks were being handed round. Rupert eyed his with distaste, and Kathie put hers on a side table.

'Oh . . . here you are!' Heather cried. 'Where have you *been*?' She, at least, had already drunk more than her share, and alcohol had never suited her. Martin waved his glass in our direction. 'Join the party,' he invited loudly, but there was no joy in it.

Rupert, in the chair Heather had used earlier, sat stiffly, his document case on his lap. It made his presence official.

Oliver and I accepted glasses of a light golden liquid, a cocktail made by casually mixing whatever came to hand. One sip was enough for me. I followed Kathie's example. There was much musical laughter from Martin, but it was forced, and his eyes were warily on Heather. He was hers. She had bought him. It was a new experience for him. Her contribution to his welfare had already come his way, and had drifted past before he could grasp it.

There was a gap of silence. Into it, Rupert interposed a slap with his palms. A smack. Heather had been naughty.

'Isn't it time we cleared up a few things?' he asked.

'What things?' Heather demanded.

'Certain details, such as the truth. Such as standing still for a moment, Heather, and looking this situation in the face, fair and square.'

She pouted. The flush was still on her cheeks and her hair was untidy. 'I don't know what you mean, Rupert.'

'I think Martin does. It isn't finished, Heather. There's a woman's death . . . ' He shrugged.

She stared at him. It hit her squarely. In some way she had managed to put this completely to the back of her mind.

'Martin!' Rupert demanded. 'I'm your solicitor now. Your wife's, so yours.'

It didn't follow, but Rupert was searching for something, and was willing to stretch a professional point.

Heather reached back and fumbled for another chair, almost falling into it. Martin went and leaned against one of its wings.

'You're spoiling the party,' he said, but

there was a spark of humour in his eyes, and an alertness in the poise of his head. 'And we're not man and wife, as you very well know. It's all come out, now. Heather doesn't care, married or not.'

She lifted her glass and grimaced at him, patting his hand with the other one. 'Of course I don't, you silly.'

'Well . . . ' said Rupert. 'I ought to mention that Martin, having been separated from his first and real wife Mandy . . . Amanda . . . could have applied for a divorce himself. It's been ten years, and though it was he who deserted her . . . ' He shrugged, looked down at his document case, then up again and directly into Martin's eyes. 'Though I can see you wouldn't want to reveal your whereabouts by taking out a petition yourself.'

Martin nodded. 'Something like that.'

'Not reveal it to either of them, June or Amanda, I gather. Miss McBride had to have you traced.'

'Vicious, that woman,' said Martin, though without malice.

'But you wouldn't describe Amanda as that?' Rupert was carefully picking his way towards his objective. He saw it as a professional duty, but it gave him no pleasure.

'Oh . . . ' said Martin. 'No. Mandy was a good kid. Sure. I liked her. But, I mean . . . '

He moved away from the chair, away from Heather, who reached after him with her eyes. He stood in a clear space on the floor, as though dissociating himself from us, from his own former self, even. But he was now more relaxed, suddenly, his gangling awkwardness more apparent. This was the naïve Martin — which must have been a large part of him — who was ready and willing to confide, even to glory in confiding.

'I mean . . . ' he said. 'It wasn't going anywhere with Mandy. Oh, we had some grand times, but it didn't turn out like she'd said. Promises, promises. It was her doing. Not me. I didn't ask for anything. When we were courting — hey, there's a nice old-fashioned word for you. That'll suit you, Rupert.' And he grinned at Rupert mockingly.

'When you were courting,' said Rupert, no tone in his voice. 'So?'

'It was she who made the promises. As I said. Oh, I was going to get all I ever wanted — which wasn't all that much. Of course you can, darling, she said. Here . . . ' He made a small prancing movement, the emotion involved in the telling requiring this release. 'Here . . . it wasn't much. Compared. Compared with what her dad had, that is. You should've seen that place! Bigger'n this.

Huge. I reckoned . . . well, she was going to settle it with him. But no — oh no. Come the wedding, and back from the honeymoon — the Bahamas, that was . . . '

Heather drew in her breath and straightened her shoulders. Martin didn't seem to notice.

'When we got back . . . oh, it was all changed,' Martin went on. He flapped his arms, his head bobbing. 'We got our corner of the house. Fine. Privacy. But all the promises came to nowt. He wasn't going to part with his money for anything.'

He stared round for approval, or for our understanding of how badly he'd been treated.

'And what was this 'anything' you'd got in mind?' Rupert asked coldly.

'Is this some sort of test I've got to pass?' Martin flipped a hand and waggled his head towards Heather. 'Never mind. I don't care. Heather's got to know the lot, sometime. Might as well be now. Nothing to be ashamed of, you know.'

Heather flashed him a pale smile, then looked down at the interesting vision of her lap.

'So what was it?' asked Rupert, patient, so patient.

'All I wanted was a rally car. Now . . . is

that much? A rally car and a garage to work on it in.' He frowned at that. 'Where I could work on it. And there were lots of spare garages, there.'

'That was refused, I assume?'

'Yeah. Said he wasn't having any son-in-law of his up to his elbows in grease. Have you ever heard anything so daft!'

'But you gave it time?'

Martin shrugged. His angular shoulders shrugged well, right up to his ears. 'Well, you've got to. Not push things, you know.'

'And after two years, you gave up and walked out on her?'

Another shrug. 'Put it like that if you want to. What else was there?'

That earned him a silence. He looked round with raised eyebrows. Rupert patted his lips with his handkerchief. This was perhaps worse for him than for Martin, as Rupert knew how much it would be hurting Heather. It was a duty, though, which he clearly felt was necessary. How else was he going to be able to rescue Martin from his legal difficulties? He had to have the background details. To Martin, it was a release from suppressed frustrations. There was no pain involved. He didn't even seem to realize Heather might care.

'All right, so I left,' he said, conceding that

146

the silence was not one of approval. 'I can't see how it matters to you.'

Rupert sighed. 'You're in trouble, Martin. It's true that you're now free of the bigamy charge that June McBride levelled at you. And the wrongful conversion claim . . . ' His raised eyebrows made it a question.

Martin smiled. It cut his face apart, a delightful smile, a smile that drew you to him, that embraced you. 'My clever little girl, here.' He reached sideways, as though about to pat her head.

'But now there's a murder hanging over you,' Rupert reminded him solemnly,

'Well, that's just bloody well stupid. Excuse the language, ladies.'

Rupert frowned. 'Very well. Let's hear about the wrongful conversion thing, first. That sounded very unethical to me. If not downright illegal. But I don't know the details.'

Martin came alive. I'd thought he was fully activated already, with his bubbling enthusiasm. Now it was like a spring unwinding. It set him to pacing, long and ponderous paces; it set him to gesticulating, with all his body, hands, arms, head, shoulders; it set him to pausing and bending forward like an entertainer talking to the first row of the stalls. And his voice rose and plunged, exploring octaves of verbal expression.

'You'd never believe . . . but it was great! So simple. There she was, that June, cock-of-the-hoop, if a female can be that.' He cackled; laughter, not impersonation. 'Oh, she had her fist tight on the reins, you can bet. Hey-up, if I tried to get a bit more spending money out of her. Clothes, shoes, all that . . . oh, she piled them on me. To show me off. Elegant, that was what I was supposed to be.'

He wriggled his delight at this, an undulation slithering down his body, then he parodied an erect, correct and practised walk, prancing across the floor. He flung glances at me, for approval. I tried not to respond. But he was enjoying it. He could be fun to be with.

'But no real cash I could get my hands on. Penny-pinching, she was. Mandy hadn't got any, and June had got it all — and none for me.'

Somehow, he graciously omitted to mention that Heather had it too, and it would be all for him, if he asked. Two for the price of one.

'The fraud,' whispered Rupert into a sudden, brief silence.

'Yeah. Well.' For a moment he was still. 'She'd got this Merc on order, see. A 500E, the big saloon with the five-litre V-eight engine. Lovely job. But what good was it for *motoring*! No life in it. Fancy taking that rallying!' He laughed then, a bright and clear bell of a laugh. 'She'd ordered it from Birmingham Motors, their Erdington branch. Nigh on £25,000 it was, with a few extras. They had to order it. It'd be six weeks. So I went to their branch along the Wolverhampton road, and I ordered a Dolomite Sprint. Special. Prepared. The eighteen hundred overhead job, with sixteen valves. And with all the gubbins: fireproof bulkhead behind the seats, interior rollcage, uprated alternator and control box. I kept tagging stuff on, getting it up to the £25,000 mark. Got 'em to change the shockers and fit a competition clutch, and in the end they had to throw in two more wheels and tyres. It wasn't yellow then. I had to respray it. Pale blue, it was . . . '

He took a breath. During this his head had been darting around, confirming our realization of how glorious this was. Nobody spoke. Only Heather was viewing him with anything approaching admiration. When he came close enough in his prancing, she patted his arm. He kissed her forehead on the way past.

I could share his enthusiasm in one way. My father had owned a Dolomite Sprint, one of the first out of the factory gates. I'd been fourteen when he taught me to drive in it, cushion on the seat, blocks on the pedals. I'd even helped him with the tuning — those two Stromberg carbs, they were the very devil to keep balanced. It was a period of my life I dared not mention to Oliver. He would use it as evidence against me, that my father had tried to make a tomboy out of me. He'd already hinted at this.

Martin was continuing with his story. 'So she gave me the cheque to pick up her Merc. I said I'd go there on the bus and drive back. Wasn't far — we were living in Edgbaston. She still is, as far as I know.'

'She still is,' said Rupert. 'Carry on.'

If he'd intended Martin to strip his conscience clean, he was succeeding. If Martin could be said to have a conscience. But Rupert's eyes were on Heather, who was now very still and silent, her face expressionless. She had always needed assistance with her decisions. Facing her was a big one. Was Martin's behaviour admirable or contemptible? Who would help her with that? Martin?

'Obvious, isn't it?' Martin asked. 'I took the certified cheque to my branch of Birmingham Motors, collected the Dolomite, and drove away. It was payable to them, anyway.'

'Out of her life?' asked Rupert.

Martin nodded. 'Nearly. Caught up with

me though, hasn't she?' He straightened his shoulders. 'But by heaven, I've had some grand rallying in that Dolomite. Came third, one year, in the Lombard RAC. Grand!'

And now it was a clapped-out and yellow wreck, as his women had become. At least, Amanda had never recovered. Perhaps June was hiding a deep hurt inside; she wouldn't show it. And Heather?

She raised her face to his, smiling. 'What a clever darling he is!' And he bent and kissed her on the lips.

Then at once his eyes met mine, a wealth of meaning in them, and I knew it was my approval he sought. I wanted to look away. I hadn't decided. Damn it, I hadn't decided, when I knew I ought to be intensely disliking his casual self-approval. Hating it. But he had a way of drawing you into his enthusiasms. He shared his life. That was it. If you wanted to share, he would offer you the lot. This is me — take me as I am, it's all there is.

Rupert was silent. Oliver said, turning to me as though we were alone, but intending it for the whole group, 'So isn't it a pity there's a murder hanging around? Don't you think, Phil? You can't do a murder with the best intentions. Not and mean no harm.'

'Yes,' said Rupert mournfully. 'The murder. Don't get too euphoric about your situation,

Martin.' Martin blinked at that. 'You're in difficulties. You probably know, better than any of us, what you're up against. Shall I list them?'

'Oh — list them,' Martin permitted, flipping a hand, his whole arm. 'Let's have your little list.' He looked around. '*The Mikado*,' he explained. 'I always liked that. The best of the lot . . . '

'Will you please be silent.' Rupert's voice now had a cutting edge. 'I have my own little list. First — she was dead in your bed; second, naked; third, dead from a blow behind the ear; fourth, the apparent weapon was on the bench in your workshop. And fifth . . . ' He sighed at the fifth. 'Fifth, an alibi that can't stand up to official examination.'

'Now *that* just isn't true!' Martin poked a finger angrily in Rupert's direction, advancing so that it was almost in his face. It was the first time I'd realized he could be angry, anything other than complacent. He and Heather were twin souls. They craved approval, and a wrongful accusation would upset them desperately. 'I can't help it if I was where I was,' he said. 'In that lay-by. And as an alibi it isn't all that weak. They've already found a patch of oil where I told 'em I was parked. Exactly where. I'll have to check Jeff's

Fiesta again. It's the washer on the drain plug.'

'Keep to the point,' said Rupert.

Oliver glanced at me. I knew that Jeff Carter, his best man, would now be minus his car. The police would have it in. They would check oil samples, the dripping drain plug, any evidence of the car having been slept in. And all for nothing, because none of these needed to have happened on the night in question, even if they *had* happened.

'The point is I've got an alibi. It's up to the police to prove it.'

'Not exactly. It's for the defence. That's me, ultimately.'

'You'll be lucky.'

'However you'd like me to be, Martin, I'm checking your alibi now. Can there be any chance your mates played a trick on you, by luring a local girl into your bed?' This, I realized was a catch question.

'I'm not going to have anybody in my bed the night before my wedding,' declared Martin nobly. But he was feeling the pressure; it had been in his voice. 'Certainly not a dead one. And she couldn't have been local, or I'd have recognized her. In my bed, I would.' He flicked around a tentative smile.

Rupert looked down at his document case. 'I didn't mean that. But I expect you've had the chance since then. Surely they took you along to the morgue. It would be routine.'

'Yeah. The rotten lot. A nice place to take anybody, that is.'

'Not a local girl, you would say?'

'Never saw her before in my life.'

I watched Rupert's right hand clench. Then he relaxed. 'Never saw her before? Now that's very strange. It may interest you to know that someone else, who *had* seen her before, within the past fortnight, was also taken to see the body. He didn't hesitate. He identified her as Amanda Reade, Martin, your wife. Your first wife, your real one.'

Heather gave a little whimper and rammed her fist against her lips. It was theatrical. It was not Heather. Why wasn't she on her feet screaming — or in a faint on the floor?

'Can you explain that, Martin?' asked Rupert, his voice empty. 'That *you* didn't know her?'

'I kept my eyes shut.'

'Not even a little peep?'

'No.'

'What a pity!' said Rupert, acid in his voice. 'Because then you'd have realized what a fortunate chap you are.'

'Fortunate?' Martin was very still now, his eyes with no sparkle left at all. Beside him, Heather was apparently choking, but he

154

didn't glance at her.

'Though of course you might well have known that,' said Rupert.

'Talk sense.'

'Oh, I am. Believe me. I meant: if you'd known it was Amanda, your first wife, from the moment she came to you the night before last — '

'That's just a cheap sneer.'

'Allow me one sneer, Martin, please. But if you didn't know it before, and if you'd looked at her dead body in the morgue with wide open eyes, you'd have known at that moment. This was your wife, dead, and dead on the night before your marriage to Heather. Yes . . . marriage. Because, you see, if Amanda died that night — no, I'll amend that. She *did* die on the day before the wedding. The pathologist has confirmed that. And that has to mean that when you married Heather you were a widower — which makes the marriage legal and positive. What a pity you didn't realize that! You could have greeted your new bride with that information — a kind of wedding present.'

Then he sat back, apparently exhausted. It might have been the light, as another storm was brewing, but he looked grey.

Heather was lost, her emotions all tossed around. She now had all that her heart had desired, but she didn't know whether to laugh out loud with delight or whimper herself into a sloppy mess.

But Martin knew exactly where he was. 'Ain't that bloody great!' he said, but the twist to his so-flexible lips was sardonic.

'Well, yes, it is.' Rupert got to his feet. He had to assist himself with one hand on the chair arm. 'Particularly as it will also mean you'll be Amanda's legal beneficiary. When she died, you were still her legal husband. So all her wealth will be yours, Martin. At last. It's all yours. Don't let it go to your head.'

There was no indication that this was marvellous news that was now flooding over him. Martin spoke coolly, sarcastically. 'Are you leaving, Rupert? Have you said your piece?'

'Not quite.' But Rupert was watching Heather. 'I'm just wondering how long it will be before you leave Heather. You have your own money now, and a splendid home — where is it? Shropshire? And Heather's already contributed her portion, in order to get you free. So there's really no need for you to stay. Make it soon, Martin, make it soon.'

It was a splendid exit line. He closed the door very gently behind him.

But it was open again ten seconds later, Kathie making a distressed exit. I couldn't

156

decide whether she wanted further words with Rupert, or was heading for her kitchen for a damn good weeping bout.

What they left behind was chaos. Heather flung herself into Martin's arms, crying, 'You're not going to leave me! Tell me you're not, darling.'

'Of course I'm not, sweetness. Of course not. When I love you? Leave you? Nonsense.'

He might have added that he would not need to desert her on the grounds that she kept him short of funds. He would have his own. He could afford to buy a whole fleet of rally cars, and run them as a team.

He might also have added that, now with his own money, he would not need to cling to her, and he would be held to her by only one tie, his love for her. She would have to work at it. Martin's affection was reserved for himself.

'Let's get out of here,' I whispered. I meant out of Martin's presence.

'A second, please, Phil. There's one more thing to say.' Oliver spoke quietly.

'There's more?' I felt hollow.

It was then that Martin noticed us, over Heather's shoulder. 'You're not leaving?' It could have been sarcastic.

'One little word,' said Oliver. Heather had gone very stiff in Martin's arms, but she didn't turn to face us. 'Something I ought to point out.'

'Say it then.'

'You heard Rupert. He forgot to mention that Mandy's death, at just that time, adds the one little detail the police need for their case against you. Think what a wonderful motive it gives you, Martin. Your freedom to marry *and* all that wealth, and in one second, the second when she died. Add that to your rotten alibi. And add it to the fact that she was naked in your bed, which would look like a wife who's just found her husband and is welcoming him back to the fold. And add that to the weapon found in your repair shed . . . '

'What weapon?' Martin demanded, as quick and as sharp as you please.

'An adjustable spanner.'

He laughed shortly. 'Not mine, then. I don't own one. No self-respecting motor engineer would be seen dead with an adjustable in his hand. Get your sums right, feller.'

Heather clung to him, shivering. Martin smiled placidly at us, and as we turned away he winked at me. If I'd been close enough to him I could have punched him in the eye for that. And then kissed it better?

As Oliver closed the door behind us, I was aware that I was now thinking of Martin as a

158

spoiled child. Two for a pair, they were, he and Heather. So . . . who would comfort whom, and do all the encouraging when things went wrong?

'There's the man for you,' said Oliver. 'You'd know he wouldn't be marrying you for your money.' He laughed, so I kicked him on the ankle, and I certainly wasn't going to kiss that better.

He yelped, then he limped around the hall, making a performance of it, a mockery of Martin making a performance of it. Then he stopped in front of me.

'Vicious,' he said. 'That's what you are. I feel like getting a bit of fresh air. Coming?'

We went out to the front entrance steps, which were almost like a terrace, leaving the front door slightly ajar. It never seemed to be locked, except at night. To our left, light swam from the drawing-room window, as nobody had closed the curtains. Oliver led the way down to the drive. We stood there a moment. He jerked his head towards the window.

'The loving couple,' he said.

'I don't want to look.'

Again the storm clouds were swarming in the sky, but it was cooler than the previous night. There was a faint stirring in the air, but not enough to rustle the trees. My car stood on the drive, Heather not having had time to direct me to a garage. There was a complete and utter silence.

'Shall we look round the back?' he suggested.

'Why not?'

It was all quite amicable, but I could feel a coolness that wasn't from the night air. Our feet crunched on the gravel until we reached the vast and extensive lawn at the sides and the rear, which seemed to go on for ever. Here, in this district, it was all wide, flowing pasture land. I missed the hills, crouching against the sky of my own Shropshire.

He paused. 'A well-matched couple,' he observed, no tone in his voice.

'Oh . . . very. Perhaps too well-matched.'

'You think so?'

'Well, yes,' I said thoughtfully. 'Look at it . . . Heather with her absolute necessity for care, attention, cosseting and encouragement. And Martin with his insistent demands for the same encouragement and attention . . . and admiration, applause, involvement.'

He stopped, facing me, his face no more than a lighter patch against the sky. 'You think he might supply what she wants?' He was very close to laughing at me, I felt.

'If he can find time to forget about himself . . . yes.'

'Ah. Cynical. And she — can she supply what *he* wants?'

I laughed lightly. 'Isn't it obvious? She dotes on him. She'll soothe his ego — stroke it till it purrs.'

'But not the involvement?'

'In what?'

'His obsession, my love. In his cars and his rallying.'

'She'll stand and watch.'

'Not get involved? No, I suppose not.' He was amused at the thought. 'But he'll expect that.'

'How could she . . . '

'They have navigators,' he explained, 'these rally drivers. Maps on their knees, and all the details at the snap of a finger. Tight right-hander in a quarter of a mile. Steep hill, poor surface. Road narrows past the trees. It takes concentration, I'd expect, and lightning-fast reactions. No — I can't see that from her. Heather in a zip-up suit and a crash-hat? Oh . . . never!'

'Idiot.' I punched him lightly on his good shoulder. 'Now who's being cynical?'

'A mental image,' he claimed. 'I can imagine *you* doing it, Phil.'

'Doing what?'

'Navigating for him. Now, that's what he needs — a partner who'll navigate for him.'

'Don't you dare start that again!'

'No . . . sorry. My mistake. I can imagine you, much more clearly, doing the driving.'

'I'm warning you . . . '

'Do you think he'd let you do the driving, Phil?'

I decided to play his game, and pretend to take it seriously. 'I'd insist. He could do his share of the navigating.'

'He wouldn't stand for that. In *his* car? Never.'

'I'd insist,' I insisted.

'He'd break your arm first.'

Then I realized he wasn't pretending; he really meant it.

'What . . . Martin?'

'Yes. He's single-minded. Completely. And people like that allow nothing to get in their way. Both his previous marriages — he was determined to satisfy his own wishes. He would stop at nothing. Nothing.'

We walked on again, silently now because there seemed no more to say, and because the grass was soft beneath our feet. We circled the house slowly. At last I spoke, softly because the night was so hushed. 'Are you warning me, Oliver?'

'If you like to take it that way.'

'Not to oppose him?'

'No. Something different. I'm telling you

he realizes we're on Heather's side, and that makes him uncomfortable. He can't do anything about me. He knows damn well I find him revolting. But you . . . he thinks he might gain your sympathy.'

'Oh. Well, thank you for the little lecture, Oliver. I'll bear it in mind, if we're ever alone together.' I halted him with a touch to his arm, the better to look up into his face. 'You're certain he killed that woman, Mandy, aren't you?'

'Not quite certain.'

'You said he would stop at nothing. Isn't that what you meant?'

'We won't quarrel about it.'

'Of course not. Certainly not.'

But the silence of the night seemed even deeper as we completed our circuit of the house.

Then, when we were just about to place our feet on the gravel again, Oliver put a hand to my arm. It was a restraining hand. He moved it to cover my lips.

'A shadow,' he whispered, his head close. 'Moving into the trees.'

I lifted his hand. 'A night animal?' I breathed lightly, interested.

He shook his head, then he relaxed. 'It's gone.'

'A person?'

'I thought so.'

My obvious thought was for my car, but out here, in this vast stretch of emptiness, who would come to steal from my car? I moved towards it, and as I did so a high, piercing scream cut the silence apart.

'Heather!' I gasped. The hysteria was typically hers.

We began to run to the front door, two at a time up the steps. The door was a little wider open than when we had left it. We burst in, just as Martin ran out from the drawing-room.

Heather was standing beside the phone table in the hall. She had obviously seen the partly open door, and had been heading towards it. Now she stood, staring at her left palm and screaming fit to burst, as she didn't seem to pause for breath. Her other fist was against her mouth.

'Heather!' I caught her shoulders and shook her. 'Stop it! D'you hear? Stop it!'

Martin was hopeless in a situation such as this. He was dancing from foot to foot, not sure whether to scowl or grin. I slapped her face. Slapped it again. Then she subsided to a shaking sob, and she held out her left palm, not speaking.

Lying in her palm was a brooch that I recognized. Her father had given it to her on her sixteenth birthday. Heather. It was a sprig of heather he'd had specially crafted in silver and gold, with tiny chips of ruby and turquoise, which blended into the bloom of heather.

When I took it from her she collapsed, and Martin managed to make himself useful. There had seemed to be no strength in his gangly and uncoordinated frame, but it was there. He took her from me, and half carried her back to the drawing-room, and she was no mean weight.

Oliver watched them go. He shook his head. 'What is it?'

I showed him the brooch. 'She was coming to the front door, to close it, perhaps. This must have been on the table.'

'Yes. Left on the table.'

We closed and locked the door and went into the drawing-room, Kathie bustling in from her quarters, all anxiety and concern.

Martin had Heather on the settee. He held a glass containing a tiny quantity of brandy to her lips. She was now nearly over the shock, and managed a weak smile when he kissed her on the lips, then licked his own appreciatively.

'Kiss it better,' he said. Then he straightened and faced me, and for the first time since I'd met him, he was serious. Nothing now masked his emotions.

'Thank you,' he said quietly. 'I could never have brought myself to slapping her.'

I half smiled and quickly turned away. Damn it, there had been frank admiration in his eyes.

8

We were in our room, and nothing was the same. There was a distance between us that wasn't physical.

'Perhaps we can get some rest now,' said Oliver, not looking at me.

We'd heard them come past in the corridor, laughing and joking to their marital bed, perhaps with all its four posts.

Our bed seemed wider than it had been. I wanted Oliver's arms around me.

'I don't think we're going to get the storm after all,' I decided.

'No. Perhaps not. Can we go home tomorrow, Phil?'

I turned away from him. 'You know it isn't finished.'

'I know it's barely started.'

'You don't have to be clever, Oliver. I'm tired.'

'But *shall* we go? Finished or not — just go.'

'Could you really bear to leave it now?'

'Easily. With alacrity. We have the car there, outside. We came only for the wedding, and there's been a wedding.'

'For heaven's sake, Oliver, she's my friend. You know as well as I do they'll be coming to arrest him any time now. Tomorrow, probably. Then where'll she be?'

He looked at me from beneath his eyebrows. 'Your loyalty is admirable, Phillie. Nobody's questioning that. But is she really worth it?'

I shrugged, reaching for the zip on my slacks. 'I don't know. I don't know anything any more. I'm just confused. But if we were to leave I'd be worried stiff. My conscience, Oliver . . . You know what a conscience is?'

'I do indeed. Here, I'll help you with that.' The zip had stuck.

As he did, I was assailed by a thought. It had been in the back of my mind for quite a while, since I'd seen my BMW sitting by itself on the drive. As I peeled off my blouse, I said, 'There's the question of transport, you see, Oliver.'

'Oh yes? Such as?' He didn't meet my eye — he'd realized the problem himself.

'Her car — you saw her Mercedes at the church — well, that happens to be in a long-stay park at Heathrow. How are they going to manage without it? How are they going to pick it up?'

'Ah! The ubiquitous motor vehicle! How? Martin can walk to that garage of his and take

168

his pick from what's on offer, that's how. He can buy one from himself.'

'Those wrecks? He'd be ashamed to drive . . . especially with Heather beside him.'

'Or he can put his Dolomite back together.'

'Talk sense, please, Oliver. Are you all right with that jacket?' I watched him shrug out of it. 'The trousers, then . . . '

These were difficult for him. He couldn't reach forward with his right arm.

'I can do it by stepping out of them.'

I hadn't watched what he'd done the previous evening. Now I realized his difficulties. He couldn't do it as he said. The trousers fell to the floor and tangled themselves round his ankles. He was close to stumbling, to falling on that arm. I stepped forward and grabbed his good one.

'Sit down on the bed,' I told him. 'Now. There. That was simple enough, wasn't it?'

'How'll I manage without you, Phil?'

'You won't need to.'

'I trust not.'

I changed the subject. 'We'll have to fetch her car for her.'

'We? You and I?'

'Yes. Well . . . I don't know.'

Then we had the struggle with his shirt. With his face concealed he mumbled, 'What don't you know?'

'I don't know whether her Merc's got an automatic box, and I bet it hasn't got the power-assisted steering . . . and really, you need those.'

'The Merc's sure to have both. But it doesn't matter, anyway. I'll drive yours back, Phil. Easy. You with the Merc.'

But on the way here he'd become tired inside seventy miles. This was a longer trip, and involved a lot of motorway driving. It was too big a risk. I didn't say that.

'I don't want to drive her car,' was what I did say. 'I might scratch it, dent it, or crash it.' I tried to frown worriedly.

'Nonsense. You could drive anything, Phil. His rally car, even.'

A dig, that was. He was steering us where he knew I was heading.

'I'd prefer not to take the responsibility, that's all.'

'Very well. Take Heather.'

'In that state she's in!'

'That leaves . . . him.'

We were now down to briefs and bra for me, boxer shorts for him. As before. But it didn't feel the same. There was no wish, this time, to admire myself — in the mirror or in my mind.

'I'll take the same side,' he said, seeing that I was lost for a moment.

'Yes. You do that.' I watched as he swung himself sideways on to the bed, and as he did his little wriggle. And it *was* a little one, not leaving enough room for me to lie facing him that side.

'You know very well,' I told him, walking round behind him and finding it easier to say it to his back, 'that you're just dying to spend some time in the village, nosing around and picking up scraps of information.' A pause. 'Am I right?'

No response.

'And on the way down to Heathrow, who better than me to pump Martin for anything he might let slip? You think he murdered Mandy, don't you?'

Still no response.

'Well, don't you?' I insisted. 'Or are you concerned that he might have a go at me?'

That got him. 'He wouldn't stand a chance with you, Phil.'

'Hah!' I said. 'But that's no answer.'

'Yes, I think he killed Mandy. And Luke Tulliver, too, if you must know.'

'So maybe he'll let something slip. It's a long run to Heathrow. D'you think I'll get nothing from him?'

'Oh no. You'll strip him clean.'

'I'm not sure I like your choice of words, Oliver. And it's you I have to strip. I enjoy that. Oh yes. And I intend to return for some more of the same.'

'Huh!' he said.

'Or d'you think we'll run away together . . . Martin and I?'

'Not a perfect match,' he grunted.

'And leave you with Heather. You could marry *her* for her money.'

'That's all she has to offer, as far as I can see.'

Then he shuffled over to the centre, and I ran round to the other side.

But it was not the same. There was no storm that night.

Sadly, miserably, I realized that we had to find some truth in the situation, if only to release us from it, and quickly.

As I was dozing off, he whispered, 'Where have you got to? I can't feel you touching me.'

I smiled. It was his abdication.

But in the morning everything had changed, and decisions were taken without any consultation. Kathie had had the chance to get herself organized, so that we ate in the dining-room. Heather had recovered completely from the previous evening's upset. In fact, I thought her to be quite domineering. Perhaps, in the night, she had sorted out her relationship with Martin. In any event, everything was arranged for me.

'I suddenly thought, Phillie,' she said, wading into bacon, egg, sausage and kidneys, 'about my car, stuck there at Heathrow. I don't suppose you would lend me yours, to go and collect it?'

'You suppose quite correctly,' I told her.

'Yes. I thought you'd say that. You'll want to drive it yourself.'

'Quite so.'

'And I can't let your dear Oliver go away . . . I mean, if any police came . . . your Oliver will know the ropes. Martin's useless. Aren't you, my pet?'

He nodded, mumbling with his mouth full, and Oliver lifted his head. Her logic baffled him.

'The police would more likely want to see him here than me.' He raised his eyebrows.

Heather smiled at him sweetly. 'That's what I mean. Martin's better out of the way.'

'Oh,' said Oliver, defeated.

'And he does so much want to try my Mercedes,' Heather went on, waving her fork. 'He keeps arguing about the gearbox, so now's his chance to drive it.'

'Yes,' agreed Oliver, and Martin winked at him.

Martin had probably done all the driving to get them to Heathrow.

'Good. So that's settled.' Heather smiled

173

happily around the table. Martin opened his mouth, then closed it.

This mode of reasoning was typical of Heather. Try to argue with her and she'd have you stammering and lost in two minutes.

She was wearing the brooch, and there was no mention of her hysterics on recovering it. After breakfast she came out to watch Martin and me leave, and leaned half-way into his open window to kiss him goodbye.

'Have a nice trip, darling,' she said, suddenly clasping at her bosom. 'Oh . . . *that's* how I lost it.' She looked past him. 'The brooch, Phillie. Leaning over the car, it got knocked off, and some kind person must've picked it up and left it on the table in the hall. Oh, I do hate mysteries. I'd have been worrying all day.'

That she would conceive such an idea was acceptable. Her mind took her where she wanted to be. That she'd expect us to believe it was ridiculous.

'As you say, sweetheart,' Martin agreed dutifully. 'Be a good girl.'

Then I drove away because I'd had enough of Heather for a while.

There were three cars out on the road. Two men and a woman tried to get us to stop by standing directly in the way. Without slowing

174

I continued onwards, nearly nipping a couple of toes.

'The press,' I explained, trying to sound nonchalant.

He turned in his seat, looking back. 'The dregs.'

'It's to be expected,' I said.

But he was silent.

I chose the same route as before, heading for the motorway, but Martin knew a better way, and directed me into minor roads, which he claimed would knock a few minutes off it.

'No hurry, is there?' I asked.

'None at all. I'm enjoying this. Fast right-hander coming up. Take it wide, and clip it when you see you're clear.'

'Allow me to do the driving, Martin,' I said. 'And let me do my own bit of enjoying.'

He sat back, and didn't speak for a while, except for the necessary directions. It seemed that he carried a map in his head.

'How d'you like navigating for a change?' I asked, just to break an extended coolness.

'It's not really navigating. Not rally stuff, if that's what you meant.'

'It was.'

'You have to work together for years on that, to get it right. The navigator's got to be top-rate, and the driver's got to know he can rely on him. Up to the hilt.'

'And vice versa?'

'Oh sure. Rely on me not to roll it, for instance.'

'Which I suppose you'll have done?'

He laughed lightly. 'From time to time. Hey! I liked that.'

'What did you like?'

'The way you got the nose out on that left-hander, then powered it round.'

'Thank you. But it's not a rally car.'

'No. Pity about the gearbox.'

'Why?'

'Too soft, these auto boxes. No bite in them. The connection between your foot and the back wheels, I mean. You've gotta be able to chop right down through the box. Top to second and get the engine spinning . . . '

'I can do that, with this.'

I did it on a hill, slapping the gear lever down from drive to second and banging my foot down. The car flew up it.

'So you can,' he said. 'But it's still soft. You ought to have got a bit of tail wiggle there.'

It was a different Martin. Gone was the hyperactive behaviour, the performance, the craving for admiration. In a motor vehicle he was a technician. It was his very existence. He had devoted his life to it, ploughing through all obstacles.

'Jeff's been with me for years,' he said, a few corners later.

'Jeff? You mean Jeff Carter — your best man?'

'That's our Jeff. Yes. A genius, he is. Lets me know everything that's coming up, in detail.'

'Lets? You mean he still is? You'll be going on with it then?'

'Of course. Now I've got my own money — oh Lordy-me, yes. Just let me get my hands on that cash!'

Which he wouldn't do, if they found him guilty of the murder of Mandy. I didn't mention that.

'No more clapped-out Dolomites? One or two new specials instead, with all the gubbins, as you called them?'

'That you can believe. And a proper workshop. Oh brother!'

'You'll dump your Dolomite Sprint, then?'

'No. No, no. I'm working on it now. Changing the shockers and doing over the engine. I'll do her up to top pitch, respray her, and she'll be good for a dozen more rallies.'

'But you said . . . new cars.'

'Don't *look* at me. Never look at your passenger. Concentration on the road, that's what it's all about. Concentration.'

I was learning more than he guessed. 'Yes sir,' I said. 'The Dolomite . . . '

'Oh, I'm gonna give that to Jeff. He's a dandy driver, you know. He's always wanted his own rally car, and we've spent hours together in that one, weeks. We've about lived in it.'

I was silent. He could now afford to buy Jeff a car, but he wanted to give him one he'd brought to perfection himself, one that Jeff had lived in too. I had a good idea that Jeff would appreciate that.

I drove along, pensive now, trying to understand this strange and startling man beside me, one minute completely thoughtless about other people's feelings and their distresses, the next minute so enthusiastically considerate for their pleasures. He was sitting there, actually gloating at the thought of Jeff's coming joy.

'If you breathe a word to him, I'll kill you,' he said at last.

I darted a forbidden glance at him. He nodded to himself. Nothing was ever allowed to deprive him of a delight he'd promised himself, of watching the smile spread on Jeff's face.

Good navigator or not, he'd not noticed the Saab that had been behind us for the past ten miles.

'You'll be short of a navigator,' I observed casually.

'True. Want to try the job?'

'What! Me!' As though I'd never given it a thought. 'You've got Heather.'

'Can you imagine it! No. Not Heather. She's scared of everything.'

'Then it's a good job she's got you.' And he could take that any way he liked.

'You'd better believe that.' For a moment the flippancy had gone from his voice. Then it was back. 'Why not try driving, then?'

'You mean rally driving? Oh no. Not that, either. I'd be dreadful.'

'You wouldn't. You've got this.' He reached over and slapped the dash. 'So you can afford a rally car. And the way you've been handling it, you'd lap it up. Just try it some day. A genuine rally car. You'll know you've never done any real motoring before.'

I didn't know whether or not to laugh at him. 'Thank you.' I tried to look demure, in case he was looking.

'And you've already got your own tame navigator. I reckon that's a police car that's been tagging us for the last few miles. Want to drop him?'

'Do *you* want to?' I asked. 'That's the point. You've probably been told not to leave the district, and the first thing you do is just that. And you head towards Heathrow! Of course it's a police car.'

He seemed unconcerned. 'Let him sit it out. Why would I want to run? Tell me that.'

'Because you're in trouble, you damned fool,' I said angrily. He seemed blissfully ignorant of his situation. 'Why can't you get that into your thick head?'

'I didn't do it. They don't send innocent people to prison.'

'It's happened. It can happen again. They wouldn't let you go rallying, you know, in Gartree Prison.'

'But I didn't do it.'

I was silent down the slipway while I concentrated on easing into the traffic stream on the motorway. Then I went on:

'Try proving it. Try proving that damned silly alibi of yours — and make no mistake, it's for the defence lawyers to prove an alibi. Look at all of it. Your first wife must have heard where you'd got to, and that you were getting married again. Amanda, I'm talking about, assuming there's been no more. There's been a private detective on it who could well have been paid for telling her where to find you. If so, he'd have to admit to that in court. *Then* look at the picture you get. Wouldn't she come rushing to you, to claim you and to stop you committing bigamy? And she'd bring with her the fact that she had her father's money now. So . . . wouldn't you allow her into your bed, your real and genuine wife? You did say you liked her?' I paused. 'So why you left her . . . '

I risked a glance at him. He was staring ahead, his face set. Where had the flamboyant extrovert gone? His lips moved. I could hear nothing, there being a great trailer wagon almost up my exhaust pipe.

'What?' I shouted.

'Pull out. Get into the fast lane. Get past these buggers.' He was angry — at them or at me, I couldn't tell.

I did as he wished. Now, with a police car somewhere behind me, that was taking a risk, because there was a great stream of vehicles in the middle lane, and I intended to build up a fair speed in order to get past them. A black dot followed suit, way back. I allowed it to get closer. It was the Saab.

Then we were clear, and we were back in the central lane.

'What did you say?' I shouted again. 'You said something I missed.'

'I didn't leave her. Let everybody think so, I don't care, if that's what she's put about. But she threw me out. Told me to get lost. And I loved her. Loved her to hell. She was the jealous type, see, and that was the snag.

Oh . . . fun to be with and good for a laugh. But she didn't like to see me laughing with anybody else, and there were women friends of hers . . . you know how it is. I'd have a bit of fun, a bit of a lark. Didn't mean anything. Me — I loved Mandy. There were times . . . Christ, but we had some times! But it all went sour because she was so damned possessive. Yeah. An' it wasn't her dad who didn't want me to have rally cars. It was her. Oh . . . it was too noisy for her, too scary. And there were other women involved. Drivers, navigators, hangers-on. Oh no, no rally car for yours truly. What got up my wick . . . pull out, damn it. Don't let yourself get squeezed.'

He was thoughtful enough to remain silent as I did it. The Saab popped out again. Then, when we'd settled down once more to the beautiful silence of my BMW at sixty-five, I prompted, 'Something got up your wick.'

'Yeah. Well. What really infuriated me . . . oh yes, I was right bloody furious, I can tell you . . . was the reason for it. And I didn't care a tap for all those women ralliers. Only for Mandy. And in the end we had a flaming row, so she told me to sod off, and I did. That's how it was. So why would she come chasing after me? Tell me that.'

I could have wept at his stupidity. 'Oh

Martin, you fool. She was mad 'at you
. . . jealous and possessive, because she was
wildly in love with you. Why else didn't she
divorce you? Ten years! And she still hadn't.
Of *course* she would come rushing to you,
and try to persuade you to come back to her,
by using her splendid body. There that body
was, Martin, dead in your bed — the night
before you married Heather. So how does it
look when she's found there? As though you
didn't want her, because she was messing
things up for you with Heather, that's how.
And they'll say she tried to entice you with
her money, if her body didn't do the trick,
but you would realize that if she was dead
you'd have her money anyway, and you'd also
have a marriage with Heather that was legal.'

'And I'd leave her there, to be found in my
bed? I'd be crazy to do that.' He was scornful,
refusing to see the fix he was in. 'Stupid,' he
amplified.

'It's no defence, stupidity.'

'I could've driven her . . . no, better'n that.
I've got an old inspection pit, not been used
for years, since I had the hydraulic hoist
fitted. It's all planked over. I could've
dumped her in there, and nobody would ever
have found her.'

He was nodding to himself, nodding,
nodding, his chin stuck out aggressively.

'You poor idiot!' I shouted, because here they were again, on my tail. 'It's no defence, what you might've done but didn't. The prosecution would stick to what you *did* do — which was leave her dead in your bed.'

He was thumping his knee. 'Will you pull out! Pull out!'

I complied. It was no good trying to reason with him. When he was more relaxed I said, 'I'll turn in at the next service station. Then you can take over the driving for a while.'

My precious BMW in his hands! But how could I drive safely with my mind all jumbled up with contradictions! And — what had happened to her clothes?

Nine miles beyond Junction 15 I pulled into a service area. I needed to top up the tank, anyway. We had a cup of coffee. Martin seemed morose and preoccupied. Then suddenly he grinned at me, realizing I was watching him closely.

'Who else am I supposed to have knocked off?' He could make anything into a joke.

I decided to quench him a little. 'Her father, Luke Tulliver.'

'What! Hey! What're you talking about?'

'He died. Didn't you know? A short while after you left, his car ran off the road. The suggestion is that another vehicle might have pushed him off. Just a suggestion — I don't know what evidence the police got out of it. But Martin . . . somebody with the driving ability of a rally driver could have done that.'

'What for? What for would I have done that?'

'The suggestion is — '

'Bloody suggestions! Who's doing this suggesting?'

I tried his own technique, grinning at him. 'I am, I'm suggesting you planned that his money should be inherited by Mandy. It was money you wanted for your rallying.'

'But I'd left her. If I'd done *that* — for the reason you say — why didn't I just go back?'

Again I grinned at him. 'But you hadn't left her. You told me that. She'd hoofed you out, you said. But suppose . . . just a supposition . . . suppose all that is untrue. Suppose you did leave her, because her father was holding tight to his own money. Walked out on her for *that* reason. Then you might kill him so that she'd inherit, and crawl back to her, all abject, and saying you'd never leave her again.'

I hadn't realized before that his eyes were a clear, piercing grey. They were now fastened on me, cold and angry.

'I didn't leave her. I told you. And I didn't go back to her. She'd chucked me out for good and all.'

'None of which could be true — or all of it. Don't you see, you idiot, if you breathe a word of this to the police, they'll say it gives you an even better motive than they had before. They'll say, yes, you had left her. But then you killed her father, and you went back to her at that time.'

'She threw me out.' His voice was very low, contained forcibly. 'I did not kill her father. I didn't go back to her.'

I shook my head solemnly. 'Perhaps you did leave her, as she claimed in the first place, then returned after her father died — and it was *then* that she threw you out. Because she guessed you'd killed her father.'

Then slowly his face softened and became mobile. It was as though life flowed back into it. That so-flexible smile returned, and he put out a hand, laying it on mine.

'Hey, you're marvellous. Bloody marvellous! D'you know that? Let's go and collect that damned car of hers.'

Then I knew that I'd gone wrong somewhere. I'd tried to provoke something, but I'd stirred up something else that I hadn't wished to. Even now I couldn't understand whether he was small-minded or brilliant. He seemed to be able to switch. Certainly, whatever it was, he had complete control of himself every second. It was not a matter of what was real and what an act, but rather of which of the many Martins chose to put in an appearance at any one time.

I handed him the keys and allowed him to get on with it. He drove decorously, smoothly, and with absolute confidence. There was none of the flamboyance I'd expected, no attempts to impress me. Without apparent hesitation he chose the correct lanes filtering into the airport, but of course he'd done it once before with Heather's Mercedes. Once was enough for him; then he knew it. He also knew exactly where they'd left her car, and was able to park only two slots away.

This was the first time I'd really taken a look at Heather's car. My only sight of it had been outside St Asaph's, a glance only, though even then it had seemed not really to be the car for Heather. I'd have expected a placid saloon. This one didn't even look placid.

It was the new Mercedes Benz 500SL, crouching low and solid, and fierce. At that time it had its hardtop on, as would be necessary when leaving it in a car-park, but its true purpose was to be driven as an open sports coupé. Heather would have been terrified to sit behind that wheel, though I supposed that it would do what it was made for, to motor smoothly exactly as the driver wished. Which could be a steady fifty, for Heather, but if required up to ... what ... something over 150 mph, I guessed.

'It's yours, really, isn't it?' I asked, finding myself whispering it.

He grinned, running his hands up the back of his hair. 'She hasn't said. But I reckon it's Heather being subtle. Trying to lure me away from rallying. It ain't dignified. You don't wear a tie. So she buys this! Can you imagine! She lays out a fortune on the fastest sports coupé there is around — and the safest. Heavens, imagine all the enquiries she must've had to make in order to find it. It's something she thinks I'd love driving.'

'And I bet you do.'

'Haven't had much chance to try, yet. Coming here, it was mostly motorways. That ain't motoring. You point it, and pray — that's motorway driving. It is not motoring. But ... ' Again that disarming grin. 'But it felt great. Lordy, that's some machine there.'

I walked round it. Then back. My palms were itching for that steering wheel, my foot itching for the throttle pedal.

'And she hasn't driven it?' I asked.

'Must've done. She got it down to the church. There it was, the evening before, up at the house on the drive — and it hadn't been there the day before that. Obvious, it was. Her wedding present to me. So I walked past it and pretended not to notice it was there.'

'That was wicked.'

'Wasn't it!' His hand touched my arm. 'No, it wasn't, it was kind.'

I looked away from him. Up by the entrance the Saab was parked. A large man was standing beside it, but I didn't mention him. Somehow, I knew that Martin had seen him at once, and said nothing. I didn't ask him what he'd bought Heather as a wedding present. Probably a set of spanners.

I just managed not to say it, biting my lip. Spanners — and Mandy had died from a blow with a spanner, one which Martin disowned.

'Care to try it?' he asked casually.

'What! No, no — I couldn't.'

''Course you could. I'll lead in your BMW, till we can get off that damned motorway, and we can head into some country — any old roads — just as long as it's west. And then you can lead, give her a bit of a run-in. See what she's like on corners — then you'll be selling your BMW.'

'Oh no. Never.'

'Go on. Do it.'

'I might scratch it . . . her.'

'I told you. It's probably mine.'

'And what did you buy for Heather?' I couldn't help saying. I felt mischievous, elated.

'A gold Rolex Oyster watch. She hasn't worn it yet.'

I raised my eyebrows at him. 'I thought you were broke.'

He laughed, a beautifully easy and softly intimate laugh. 'I sold the garage. To Jeff. Lock, stock and barrel. He got a bargain. Heather doesn't know yet.'

He was continually surprising me, yet I might have guessed. Money meant nothing to him. It rolled right through him. Either he had it or he hadn't. In either event, he didn't allow it to worry him. A garage for a wrist-watch!

'I shan't tell her,' I assured him.

He dangled the keys in front of my nose. 'So . . . try my car.'

I took them. My cheeks felt hot. 'You lead, then, and I'll follow.' I handed him mine.

As I settled into the seat, and he explained the electrically controlled seating accommodation, I felt myself growing into it, becoming part of it. It would've taken me days to learn all the minor controls, but I soon had enough knowledge to start it and drive it. The gearbox was an auto, the steering was power-assisted, and pretty well every other refinement was built in. It purred me to the exit, where I realized I was paying a vastly higher parking fee on it than Martin was on the BMW.

On the motorway, I simply pointed it, and it went. Martin neatly kept station, two or three vehicles ahead of me, the Saab the same behind me. He didn't push it. There were about 600 miles on the Merc's dashboard clock, and I didn't want to do anything nasty to that engine. Martin was driving meticulously. A touch of the foot, and the Merc would've been past him like a firecracker. But at seventy the engine was turning over at only 2,500 revs. I had to restrain myself.

Once off the motorway, Martin drew into a lay-by. We got out to stretch our legs. So did the Saab driver, way back down the road. I saw him nip behind a hedge.

'All right?' Martin asked.

'Beautiful.'

'You lead now, huh? I can tail you, and watch your line through the corners.'

'And criticize?'

'Afterwards.'

'There may not be anything to criticize.'

'I don't expect anything.'

I laughed. 'You're mad. D'you know that?

And don't just smile. You'd better lead — you know the roads.'

'Doesn't matter, does it? The sun's going down. Keep it ahead of you, and that's the way we go. Just dive down any old side roads you fancy. Head west, and we'll sort it out later.'

I looked at him doubtfully. 'What if I lose you?'

'That's what you try to do. Now, let's start motoring, Phil. Real motoring.'

'Don't you dare roll my BMW.'

'Not a chance. It's solid.'

So we went motoring, which, to Martin, seemed to be an entirely different proposition from driving.

9

I can only assume that some of his madness entered into me. Never before had I driven with such enthusiasm and . . . well . . . joy, I suppose. I went as I wished, how I wished. The car did. All I had to remember was: the sun ahead of us. And always, Martin was behind me, and behind him the Saab. At some time, I cannot recall when, the devil dug a claw into me, and I really tried to drop the BMW. But there he was, always, in the rear-view mirror like a shadow.

And why did that thought make my heart beat faster?

After about thirty miles of this I realized that I had not the slightest idea where we were. It didn't seem to matter, but certainly the terrain was more hilly than we'd been experiencing. At one stage I found myself skirting a valley, on a surface that curved its way around the surrounding slopes, reluctant to descend to the lower level, where I caught glimpses of a narrow river winding far below. Here I had to concentrate. The bends were not acute, but there was no way of being sure, when they were right-handers, how tight they were going to be. The drop, guarded only by a white fence six feet from the road surface, was to my left, and the bank to the right was steep.

I found myself suddenly nervous. Nowhere was the fall very steep, and the Merc was splendidly sure-footed, but the thought of overrunning a bend, of even touching that fence with Heather's paintwork, set my flesh crawling. So I eased back. Six feet of grass were between me and the fence. Martin no doubt wondered why I'd slowed to fifty-five.

I glanced at the mirror. A Range Rover was overtaking him. That a Range Rover could do over fifty-five didn't surprise me. That he would overtake just there, pretty well blind — overtake two cars — was idiotic. But perhaps, with his higher sight-line, he could see much further around the bend, which seemed to be going on and on. I gave him the benefit of the doubt, as I gave him the gender, on the assumption that a woman driver wouldn't be so stupid.

Whatever the sex, there was no doubt now that he was coming on through. I allowed my near-side wheel to hug the grass verge. Still he came on, until he loomed beside me, a battered muddy old wreck of a vehicle, but coming on and overtaking, and, I realized, without any consideration for me at all.

Its tail-end was opposite my elbow when I became aware that he was giving me only a foot of clearance. It became six inches, and then I knew it was being done with deliberation. He was trying to force me off the road.

There were two things I could have done, either put my foot down and take him on the near-side — but I had only six feet of grass on which to do it, and that possibly slippy — or brake hard. Oh yes, he could do the same no doubt, and in the same second, and swing into me. I decided on braking. So I did it. Hard. And I had to pray that Martin's reactions were fast enough.

I might have guessed they would be even faster. He had seen what was going on. He would have seen my braking light, watched my tail-end lift at the fierceness of it, the nose digging in. And he was seconds ahead of my reactions. He knew what to do.

With a howl and a whine — my BMW's engine at full revs in second gear — he was past, then past the Range Rover. Distraction. It worked. The huge vehicle failed to match my decrease in speed, and went ahead. I fell back until I had room, then drew over to the right, intending to do a bit of hard acceleration on my own acount, then we would both be ahead of him and he'd stand no chance of overtaking again. The way was clear; the road was straight for a while.

Even then I'd underestimated Martin's ability and misread his intentions. Two hundred yards ahead of the Range Rover he did a 180 degree skid turn. In my BMW he did it! I know now how it's done — he told me. You yank hard on the handbrake, to lock the rear wheels only, flip into neutral with the same movement to leave the front wheels rolling so that you can still steer. At the same time you spin the steering wheel. I watched it — saw it. My car spun like a top, and miraculously ceased to do so at a moment when the nose was pointing straight back at us.

Then he accelerated hard, head on for the Range Rover. I saw smoke from the rear tyres and he came fast, directly in the centre of the tarmac.

With a turn to the right, the Range Rover would probably have rolled, as the bank that side was so steep. He chose to turn into the fence, then was through it with white timber flying, and in a second the car was fighting to hold a lurching and bumpy line down the steep slope, scattering sheep as it went. Martin skidded to a halt. I did too. The noses of our two vehicles were three feet apart.

I climbed out of the Merc with my legs

shaking. Sweat poured from me, sticking my slacks to my legs, the blouse to my chest. He got out and peered over the edge of the slope.

'He's away and gone,' he said calmly.

'Oh Lord!' I whispered. 'I nearly passed out. Don't ever . . . '

'Your reactions are good,' he commented, and I slapped his face, partly for the condescension. Tried to. His reactions were good, too. He caught my wrist on the way there.

The Saab drew up and parked. The tall young man got out and wiped his forehead with the back of his hand.

'Did you get his number?' we all asked together. Then we shook our heads in unison.

'In *my* car!' I cried.

'It's a matter', said Martin, 'of nerves. If he'd held his line I'd have got him head on, and barely dented him. He didn't have time to work that out, and his nerve went.'

'How fortunate for my car.'

The policeman, though as tall as Martin, nevertheless threw back his head and pushed forward his chest, to gain an inch or two, and said severely, 'You've now added to a possible charge of murder the charge of dangerous driving, sir. May I have your name, please?'

He was not in uniform, but he hadn't forgotten the routine.

197

Martin and I burst out laughing, me somewhat hysterically. The policeman smiled in embarrassment.

'I'd like to see you do that again, sir.'

'Not in my car,' I said. 'You try it with the Saab.'

Then we were all three suddenly sober. Martin wiped a hand across his mouth, and said, 'As I'm in front now, I'll lead from here. I know where we are. Home, I think. Yes . . . home.' So confidently, now, he used that word!

I had a yearning to sit in a seat that was not moving. 'Yes. Let's do that.'

I didn't want to see another of his hair-raising 180 degree turns, and the road was too narrow to allow a backing turn, so he simply drove away in reverse. He seemed to drive backwards as easily as forwards, though more slowly, but half a mile further along there was a lay-by dug out of the bank. He used it in order to turn, and whether the incident had shaken him also I don't know, but from there onwards he drove sedately.

After twenty minutes of this he signalled a left where there wasn't a turn, and drew into another lay-by. We parked behind him and got out. Martin said, 'This was where it was.'

'What was?' I asked.

'Where I spent the night — the night

before the wedding.'

We stared around. It was just another lay-by, as on any other quiet country road.

'How interesting,' I said, weariness prodding me into sarcasm. 'What would you like me to say?'

'They won't accept that I was here.'

'There's nothing positive yet, sir, one way or the other.' The policeman was sounding a little more friendly. He probably wouldn't know, anyway.

'I see the litter-bin hasn't been emptied.' Martin pointed.

'So?' I asked.

'Go and look in it. Should be somewhere near the top — a crushed Coke tin, and a crushed empty packet of Benson and Hedges Gold.'

'Oh — for heaven's sake, Martin!'

'Go and look,' he instructed me. Then he softened. 'Please. For me.'

I met his eyes for perhaps five seconds, then I turned away.

'Not just crushed,' he called after me. 'Screwed.'

'Can or packet?'

'Packet, of course. You're trying to be funny.'

I wasn't. It was just that my heart was sinking. He did, after all, realize how he was situated, he did fear it . . . and he was trying everything.

They were there. A crushed can and a screwed empty cigarette packet. I took them back to him. I showed them to him. I showed them to the policeman.

'There you are, then,' said Martin.

'Why didn't you say this to the police?' I asked.

'Kind of forgot.'

'Oh, Martin . . . oh, you poor idiot . . . it's too late now. There's been time since then for them to have been planted.'

'What time have I had? Tell me that?' He was shaking his head in frustration.

'Not by you. A phone call, and your friend Jeff would do that for you. He'd do anything for you. Deny that. And deny that Jeff smokes Benson and Hedges Gold. And Martin, you fool, you don't smoke. I haven't seen you smoking yet.'

'What do I have to *do*?' Martin shouted. 'What?'

'You're disturbing the peace, sir,' said the constable.

We stared at him, standing there in a vast spread of open countryside, then we looked at each other and spontaneously burst into laughter, in which the policeman joined.

I took can and packet back to where I'd

found them. In spite of what I had said, I knew somebody would be along to collect them. Not looking for fingerprints, not for Martin's anyway, but for Jeff Carter's.

Martin said, 'I'd better lead from now on, in the Merc. It'll look better. We're thirteen miles from Hellyspool. You going to tag along, officer?'

'I'll see you home, sir. Safely,' he added, some doubt in his voice.

He followed us all the way to the gateposts, then got out of the Saab to watch us disappear under the trees. In my rear-view mirror I saw him give a ridiculous little salute.

All three of us completely ignored the seven cars waiting outside the gates. We ignored the photographers, prancing around with their cameras clashing away. Auto film wind, auto everything. You just point, and push the button. Photographers indeed! They got good shots of the constable saluting, though.

Oliver was waiting on the front steps, the door open behind him. He seemed stiff and formal as he wrapped his left arm round my shoulders and kissed me on the cheek.

'You've been a hell of a long while.'

'We didn't waste much time.'

'It seems a long while.'

'Silly.' I put a finger on his lips.

Martin was walking past us, tossing the Merc's keys in his palm. Oliver reached out a hand, just touching him, not restraining. 'Before you go in . . . '

Martin was at once alert. 'Oh? What's up?'

'There's been some more fun and games.'

'Such as?'

'They're in her room. You'd better hear it from Heather, and try to get some sense out of her, if you can. I'm damned if I've been able to. And let me know if you do . . . huh?'

Martin stared at him for a second, then he ran into the hall and I could hear him pounding up the stairs. 'Where are you, lover? It's Martin. I'm here.' We looked at each other, and Oliver shook his head.

'This bloody front door,' he said. 'It's never locked during the daytime, for some damned silly reason. Something about its being too far for Kathie to come to answer the bell. The postman leaves the mail on the hall table. It's *that* casual. Why she can't answer the door herself . . . '

'Get to the point, Oliver, please.'

He took me into the hall and pointed at the table. 'That.'

It was an 8″ × 6″ brown envelope. Its flap had not been sealed. It lay there, plain and unaddressed, slightly plump from its contents. Hand delivered, obviously.

'Found there, like that,' Oliver told me, his voice toneless. 'By Heather, half an hour ago. If I'd only seen it first! It sent her way over the top, hysterics, faints, screaming. Kathie nearly had a fit, too. It's all right, you can pick it up. It's been well handled, you can guess. Thrown on the floor. Stamped on. Pick it up. Smell it first.'

'Smell it?' I reached out tentatively, cautiously opened the flap — and sniffed. Then I recoiled. It had the stench of decay and of dissolution and was quite revolting.

'Fish it out,' he said.

I reached two fingers inside, and slowly drew out a pair of briefs. They were crumpled and stained, originally pink, but now blotted and smeared with green. The texture felt slimy.

'Yuk!' I said. I held them up and stretched them out. 'Too small to be Heather's — '

'Heather's? What the hell're you talking about, Phil? Who said they're Heather's? Think, think. Whose do you imagine they are? Were, rather.'

It was plain that he too had been shaken.

I stared at him above the briefs, my mind not working, free-wheeling, hunting for a gear to engage.

He lifted his shoulders in a gesture of near-despair. 'We've got a naked body, stripped. We wondered where her clothes had got to. Who was it who suggested that Martin had driven out in Jeff Carter's Fiesta, and dumped her clothes in a ditch? Was it me?'

'I think so,' I said quietly, my mind still racing.

'And you said it was nonsense, because stripping her wouldn't hide her identity, she probably being local.'

'You don't have to push it, Oliver.'

'But she wasn't local, was she? She was his first wife. He'd know who she was — and he wouldn't have much time to work in. Whatever he had to do, it would have to be a rush job. Now . . . what sort of a rush job might cover him, if he wasn't to take her somewhere and hide her body away? There was nothing. Don't glare at me like that, Phil. I'm only trying to get some logic into it. He was going to be away for a fortnight. There was just a chance her body wouldn't be found in that time, and he'd be able to go back and finish it off. Perhaps he had his own ideas as to how to dispose of the body . . . '

'Oh . . . h . . . h,' I moaned.

'What is it?'

'The pit. He's got an inspection pit. Oliver, he told me that, with no persuasion. He said

— why would he leave her in that bed of his, if he had that pit? It's boarded over, he told me. She was only a little thing, so it'd be nothing for him to have carried her into that repair shed of his and drop her inside, and then put the boards back. So ... if he'd wanted to cover up, that was the obvious thing for him to have done. But it *wasn't* done. Are you telling me he'd rather leave her lying there in his bed — and the house not even locked up! Don't you *see* what I'm getting at?'

He stared at me morosely. 'I see that you've been with him all day, and you still don't understand him.'

'More than you do, certainly, Oliver.'

'Nonsense. You must have realized that he's a man who plays with danger. He lives for it. It would be dangerous to leave her in the bed for a fortnight, but he'd happily play the chance that she wouldn't be found.'

'Rubbish, Oliver. You're just going out of your way to annoy me. You still don't see ... with that inspection pit there, yet he didn't use it ... Oliver, it simply means that he didn't *know* she was in his bed, naked and dead. Didn't know!'

I had never before encountered the expression he now presented to me, with a stubborn and hard tension around his lips and a sad concern in his eyes.

'You were with him too long, Phil.'

'Oliver, I'm warning you — '

'We haven't all got it, that naughty, lost-boy attitude the women love to comfort, the enthusiasms he involves you with, that mocking — '

'To hell with you then!'

'To hell with Martin, rather,' he suggested softly, his mood abruptly changing. 'Why are we trying to save him from himself? Think! Why?'

'For Heather, Oliver. Not for Martin.'

'Really?' He tried to smile.

'Really and truly.'

Then he succeeded and the smile was genuine. 'So . . . for Heather . . . we proceed. Hah!' It was a laugh, but I couldn't see that it was appropriate. 'Then put those knickers down, love.'

'Briefs, Oliver.' I stuffed them back into the envelope and dropped it on the table, then sniffed my fingers, grimacing. 'Give me time to freshen up, will you?'

'Then we'll take a walk,' he suggested. 'You'll want to stretch your legs a bit, and I could do with some clean air.'

I ran upstairs. We'd both bought fresh underwear in Taunton, and me a new pair of slacks, Oliver his shaving kit. I wished there was time for a bath, but we had to talk. And talk. I ran down again, and found him walking round and round on the gravel.

'D'you think we'll get anything to eat?' I asked, suddenly aware of a pressing hunger.

'You can rely on Kathie, anyway. You first, Phil.'

So I told him about our day together, carefully slanting it to smooth out the corners of my — and I have to admit it — growing liking and admiration for Martin. But Oliver sensed it, I could feel. I didn't omit the fact that we'd switched cars, nor omitted the attempt to drive me over the edge and down that slope.

He barely hesitated in his stride. We were heading straight into the expanse of Heather's grounds, which seemed to consist of a great stretch of grassland on which cattle were grazing. Not her cattle, surely. She probably rented out the grazing.

When he spoke it was in a calm and practical voice, and I'd been expecting all manner of recriminations and protests. But no.

'We have to consider', he said, 'whether the driver knew it was you in that car. Perhaps he was after Heather — it was her car, after all — or Martin.'

'I'd thought of that,' I assured him. 'Yes

. . . Martin, most likely.'

'But who would want — '

'Somebody who believes the same as you do, Oliver. That Martin killed Amanda. Somebody who doesn't like him. Hates him, probably.'

'Not somebody from the village, then.' He was nodding, smiling.

I looked up at him. Walking, he was content. There was no effort involving his arms. The sky was heavy, though the racing clouds were broken, exposing fleeting pockets of blue sky. For June, the wind was cool. Patches of sunlight raced across the grass. I felt a strange desire to detect them coming, so that I could run and get in their path. I longed for clean and bright sunlight on my face.

'Why not somebody from Hellyspool?' I asked. 'It must be obvious to everybody that Martin's suspect number one.'

'Even so, that's no reason for trying to kill him, no reason they'd accept round here, anyway. You see . . . they all love him. It's no good trying to dodge the issue, Phil. It's getting to be too obvious that Martin killed her. You can't argue about that, because there's too much loaded against him. But if he'd run through the village street with blood on his hands . . . '

'Let's talk about the threats,' I said, that terrible smell so close to my memory. 'They're surely aimed at Heather. Wouldn't you say? And try to make sense of that. First . . . her brooch. Now the briefs. The brooch . . . well, she claimed she'd lost it, but when it turned up she *saw* it as a threat. Oh yes, she did. Don't pout like that. If it'd been me, or anybody else, really, then all you'd have got would've been, 'Oh look! My brooch. And I thought I'd lost it.' Anybody else. But Heather went right over the top. It was a threat. To her, it was. The briefs are, too. It follows. She's terrified, Oliver, and you can't get round that.'

'A threat of what? Tell me.'

'You're a man. You wouldn't understand.'

'Try me.' He grinned at me.

'Terrified of losing Martin, you fool. Isn't that obvious? She'd go through fire and water — '

'But I do understand. You mean she knows, in her heart if not in her mind, that he killed Mandy, and she doesn't care, and somebody is warning her that they're in a position to provide final proof of it. And Heather knows it means that . . . or suspects it. No, Phil, don't just shake your head. Heather could be quite convinced he killed his first wife, and she . . . you know her . . . would she

209

care? No — I bet she'd even be proud, that he'd done it for her, so that he could marry her legally. Oh . . . how proud she would be! He's like a knight in shining armour. Don't go on shaking your head, Phil, you'll have it drop off. Consider it, at least.'

I paused in my stride, considering it. A patch of sunlight fluttered across the grass in front of us. I'd just missed it. A cow lowed mournfully.

Oliver said quietly, 'And Phil — have you thought about this? Heather could be certain that he killed Mandy — as I said. But in that event, how long d'you think she'll be able to stand these threats? How long, Phil?'

'Let's go back,' I said, feeling a chill between my shoulder blades.

We turned back to the house, now with the sun bathing it, and I wasn't there. The building shone like a jewel against the darkening grey sky.

'It's going to rain,' he said.

'Let it.' We walked another twenty yards. 'What did you mean, Oliver, that they all love him in Hellyspool? Was that a nasty bit of sarcasm?'

A bit of bounce entered his step. It was as though, in speaking of Martin, he'd absorbed some of Martin's buoyancy. 'Not that, my love. They do. I'll tell you . . . I found Jeff

Carter. He works for a haulage firm, driving. A day off, he said, though I guess it's been several. He'd taken it because he wanted to be around in case Martin needed him. That sounded a little unlikely to me — '

'Not to me,' I assured him.

'In any event, there he was, in the bar of The Rolling Stone. We talked. Phil, he's told the police that spanner was his. *The* spanner. He told them he knew the sump was leaking, so he'd gone along to do it himself, taking his own spanner.'

I stopped, halting him with a hand, turning to face him. 'Is this the truth?'

'It's the truth as I heard it. He was probably lying.'

'When's he supposed to have done this?'

'The evening before . . . well, the evening of the day Mandy died. But Martin had taken the car out, so he couldn't do the job. It was a test run or something. Jeff said Martin's very fussy. He says he left the spanner on the bench.'

'How's that supposed to help Martin?' I asked.

'It throws it wide open for anybody to have used it. That sliding door's always open.'

'But Martin wouldn't lay his hand on an adjustable spanner. Is that it?'

He nodded, a smile hovering, his eyes

shining. 'That's it. But . . . here's the best bit. There're about a dozen other men in the village who'll also say the spanner was theirs. They're lining up behind him, Phil.'

'Friends . . .'

'Yes. All of them. Friends. He'd do anything for anybody. They all knew he didn't mind if they drove up to his repair shed to do their own work on their own cars . . . even if they also borrowed his tools. No wonder he's always broke.'

'Not always, Oliver.'

'Only between wives.'

'And the women?'

We began walking again. The first spots of rain were falling, heavy drops. I could hear them rustling the grass. We stepped out. Oliver was silent for a moment, then:

'I strolled through the village, having a chat here and there. The women adore him. A leaky washer, he'd fix it. A vacuum cleaner not sucking, he'd fix that. And all with a laugh and a joke and a slap on the bottom, and screams from them. His jokes were a bit off, it seems. He doesn't sound real, Phil. He must have lived a life of pretence, always an act.'

The rain suddenly lashed down. We broke into a trot, and reached the porch before getting completely soaked. I'd got a change now, but Oliver had only his fresh underwear.

'Oliver,' I said, still panting a little, 'does Jeff Carter smoke?' I wanted to settle this before we entered the house.

'Like a chimney.'

'What brand? Don't look like that. I'll explain. You just say.'

'It was a gold-coloured packet.'

So I told him about the Coke tin and the screwed cigarette packet. He nodded. It only confirmed what he'd discovered in the village.

'Have you got any idea how much a gold Rolex Oyster wristwatch, ladies' model, would cost?'

'Quite a bit. A dozen of 'em would buy your BMW.'

So I also told him about the Dolomite Sprint that Martin was going to give to Jeff, and about the exchange of the business in order that Martin could buy Heather the watch.

'*Now* what d'you say?' I demanded. 'Is that the sort of man who'd murder his wife, and hide her clothes somewhere in a stagnant ditch?'

'Oh Phil! To say such a thing! Murderers don't look the part. They're just ordinary people, most of the time, who've been pushed past a certain point by something outside their control. Don't let yourself be fooled.'

'In what way?' I asked suspiciously.

'Into liking him too much. He casts a spell. Don't allow yourself to get . . . ' He couldn't find the word, but at least he was now tackling the subject calmly.

'Enchanted?' I asked softly.

'That would fit the case.'

I thrust open the front door, angry now, at myself or at Oliver — I couldn't decide which. And angrier because I couldn't.

The threats were now coming thick and fast. There had been the chance for someone to leave it when Oliver and I were walking away from the house. It was a package this time, not large, and clumsily wrapped in brown paper with a rubber band round it.

I heard footsteps on the stairs. From the top, short flight we would not have been fully visible. On the lower half-landing, which had been constructed exactly for that purpose, it would be possible to lean over the banister and view the complete hall. The hunt ball, the friends arriving, and you standing there in your crinolined dress, and looking down at the throng, with yourself thereby the cynosure of all eyes.

Oliver whipped up the package and thrust it inside his jacket. Both packages. 'In our room,' he said softly. He raised his voice. 'Kathie! Is she all right, now?'

'Quiet. Resting.'

So we didn't want anything else to upset that.

'We've been out for a walk,' I explained.

'I thought so. Dinner will be a little late, I'm afraid.' She was shaking her head in muted distress.

'Never mind. You can't be in two places at once.'

Then we allowed her to pass, before we went up to our room.

We didn't exactly lock the door, but I felt a taint of secrecy, and an atmosphere that caused us to lower our voices.

Oliver took out the new package. He sniffed it, and grimaced at me. Then he slipped off the rubber band and opened it all out on our small table. The same smell assaulted me, the dank stench of decay. He carefully spread out a bra, what looked like a thirty-four, small cup. Once more, too small for me, ridiculously so for Heather. It was in white satin, with a firm shaping. The owner — we were assuming Mandy — hadn't been very well built around there.

'Hers?' he asked.

'The same woman I'd guess. Yes . . . Mandy.'

'The knicks are a small size, too,' he pointed out.

'She was only a little thing. And look — the same green patches. Could anything smell worse?'

He stared at me for a second, was about to say something, and changed his mind. 'I doubt it.'

'You think they were hidden in a ditch, Oliver?'

'It seems obvious. One with stagnant water.'

'Hmm!' I put out a finger tentatively. 'They're both dry now. And with the weather we've been having — wouldn't the ditches all be dry, too?'

'A pool, then.'

'The place *is* called Hellyspool,' I suggested.

'But they haven't got one. There's only a big dent, and that's always dry, they tell me.'

'Perhaps that's why it's called Hellyspool. A corruption of Hell's Pool. There's only dry ones there.'

'Don't be so fanciful, Phil. It doesn't matter where it was, this stagnant water. He found the place.'

'He being Martin?'

'Yes,' he said tersely.

I took up the bra, smell or not. One didn't have to go all fussy. I examined it carefully.

'There's bits of green weed. See — here and here. Dried now, of course.' I took up the briefs. These I hadn't examined carefully before. Now I did. 'There's some weed on these, too, Oliver.'

'As you'd expect.'

'And the green patches. Muddy green.'

'What're you getting at?'

'They're all on the outside, the bits of weed. On the outside. Look at the bra. No sign of weed inside. Not one. And look . . . look . . . The stain's strong on the outside, but less inside.'

'It'd soak through.'

'Yes. I suppose. Oh, Oliver, pay attention. The briefs — the stain's right through, inside and out. But what about weed! There's some here, caught in a seam, and here. All on the outside, but none inside.'

'How d'you know which is inside and which out — with briefs? Now men's . . . because we're mostly right-handed . . . '

'There's reinforcement — see. That's on the inside.'

'Ah yes.'

'But there's not a sign of weed inside.'

'What on earth are you getting at, Phil?'

'Why isn't there? That's what I'm getting at. In a pool — if they were dumped in a pool — it'd get at both sides. Oh, Oliver, what a rotten detective you are. These underclothes — they weren't taken away and dumped in a pool. She was wearing them at the time. When *they* went in, she went in.'

10

It took him a long while to assemble a passably rueful smile.

'It's a pity your name's not Locke,' he said. 'Your father could've named you Sher. That bit of detection's more Holmes than Marlowe.'

'Sarcasm?'

'No, I assure you. I didn't spot that myself. So what does it mean?'

I shook my head. 'That she was drowned?' But I was tentative.

'She wasn't drowned. She died from a blow behind the ear, and that's official. It was her only injury.'

'So it gets us nowhere?' My bit of sleuthing gone up the spout!

'Not at all. It's an advance. She was knocked on the head, she was in a stagnant pool, was later undressed, then she found her way into Martin's bed.'

I eyed him speculatively. 'So now you're prepared to agree that she was not in his bed naked when he was there?'

'Not alive, she wasn't. And would you like to lie with a corpse?'

'Oh, for God's sake! Oliver . . . what're you doing standing in those wet clothes?'

'The same as you.'

'Give me the suit, and I'll take it down and get it dried. I've got spare slacks, you know.'

He grumbled. It wasn't easy for him, climbing in and out of his clothes, but nor would be a nasty chill.

I took his suit down to the kitchen, to see what they had there that could prove useful. It was summer, so there was no big fire. Kathie was clattering madly with her pans.

'There's an electric fire with a fan,' she said. 'Here, let me do it.'

'No, Kathie. You're busy. I'll do it. Where do you hide it — under here?'

It was a powerful heater, and they had an old-fashioned clothes-horse standing in a corner. I fanned it out and spread his suit on it, and my blouse and slacks while I was at it, then stood around while they dried.

'I take it Heather's recovered?' I asked. Kathie wouldn't have been in the kitchen if she hadn't.

'Oh yes. Mr Reade's marvellous with her. A tower of strength.'

'I'm sure he is.'

'Silly joke. A *nasty* joke,' said Kathie with disgust. 'Sending a new bride a pair of briefs! Shocking!'

'Very bad taste,' I agreed.

More clattering. Kathie said, 'It's going to have to be a stew.'

'Put some more spice in it,' I suggested. 'Call it goulash, it sounds better. Paprika, I think.'

'Oh, I couldn't do that. These foreign things . . . oh no.'

I turned his slacks and allowed the other side to steam. My blouse was already about right.

'They'll need some pressing,' said Kathie. 'There's an ironing board in the other corner, and an iron . . . ' She gestured vaguely. She seemed to be uncomfortable, even uneasy.

I found the iron, surprised even that it was an electric one, but it was very old and very heavy. I fumbled with the ironing board in its corner.

'I'm so worried about her,' said Kathie to the window, her voice low.

'Martin can cope.' I found I could say this with complete confidence.

'I'm not sure she would dare to tell him.'

I barely heard that. I was trying to see how the ironing board had to be rigged.

'Tell him what?'

'About the man who came.' Kathie turned to face me as I lifted my head. It all tumbled out of her, she too not being able to cope, but with her it was the responsibility of not being able to speak out. 'Two days before the wedding,' she whispered. 'Such an unpleasant man. If he'd come to my door here, I'd have sent him packing. That man in a nasty shiny grey suit, who was here with that woman and her solicitor.'

I recognized her description of Victor Peel. 'He only wanted to sell something,' I told her soothingly.

'Then he was a long while about it.' Her face was flushed; she felt she was being disloyal. 'He was with her in the drawing-room for nearly an hour.'

The ironing board collapsed with a clatter. I bent to pick it up, glad of the opportunity to hide my face. It was not what Heather had told us, which was that Peel had not got past the front door.

I managed to untangle it, fumbling. My hands wouldn't stop shaking. With the iron hot, I began by pressing my blouse, and made a hell of a mess of the pleats down the front. Kathie found me a clean white cloth to press Oliver's suit. 'If that's wool, the iron'll make it all shiny.' I thanked her absent-mindedly.

So Heather had lied. Peel had lied. He'd been picking up backhanders from every-body.

'She went out with the new car the day

before,' she said to my back.

'The day before . . . '

'The day before the wedding.' Her voice was toneless, but Kathie was crying out for help. 'She was out most of the day.'

I managed to press the trousers only a little off-crease, and half turned.

'You mustn't worry about it, Kathie. She'd naturally want to give a new car a trial run, to get used to it. New engines have to be run in carefully, and they were going to be driving down the motorway the next day.'

I managed to say this with a tone of confidence. But I was recalling that the mileometer on her Merc had read around 600 when we'd picked it up at Heathrow. It hadn't meant anything at that time. It did now. She had driven it, therefore, a matter of 400 miles on that day before the wedding.

Blessedly, Kathie was now silent, and left me to my iron thumping. My mind chased frantically after my thoughts, trying to grasp one and hold it up for inspection.

So Peel had come to Heather only two days before the wedding. Not to question her, certainly. There was nothing she could have told him, if he'd still been conscientiously pursuing his enquiries on June McBride's behalf. No — he wouldn't be asking, he would be telling, hawking his knowledge wherever he could find a market.

And he'd told Heather . . . what? Have a guess at it, Phil, I told myself. So I did. He had probably told her, as a lead-in, that she was about to assist Martin in committing bigamy. I couldn't imagine her paying anything for that piece of exciting information. She would more likely have laughed in his face.

No, perhaps not laugh. More likely, she'd have been hard pressed not to scream, but not daring even to risk a scream, not when Kathie might hear it. Heather had a better control of herself than that, when she needed it. She would have listened with intense concentration.

But now I was understanding a certain strangeness about that scene in the drawing-room, with June McBride and Raeburn and Peel. I had thought at the time that Heather was overreacting. So perhaps she had simply been over-acting. It would have been typical of her. Even she must have realized that what she was doing for Martin was, at the very least, unethical. So there had had to be an act — a scene.

Yet she'd said it herself. She had wanted Martin, and she intended to have him, marriage or no marriage. And who — if Peel's information was correct — was in the way of achieving that? Why . . . June McBride, that was who. And this was because Peel would have been able to tell Heather that his client was taking bigamy proceedings, and had progressed with them so far that there was already a court warrant out with Martin's name on it. This would surely have panicked Heather.

I wondered how much Peel would have demanded for revealing June McBride's address at Edgbaston in Birmingham. So much was becoming clear now. Heather must have gone to see June McBride. They had made a deal. But the lawyer, Raeburn, had not been happy with it when he'd had to lay it out formally. The two conspirators would have been satisfied with the arrangement, June wanting her money, Heather her man. This wouldn't have been enough for Raeburn, who would want to make a big proposition of it.

Perhaps he'd been right in this, I thought. It would otherwise have been degrading to both women, such a cold and bitter disposal of Martin. Raeburn had wanted it to look as though he'd worked hard to bring it about. It was a legally consummated fact only if he wrapped it up in his best legal phraseology. And ultimately he had failed. He had not been able to make it less degrading, and he had failed — or not tried — to prevent the arrest of Martin at Heathrow.

This must have been what had so upset Heather — that she'd thought they had a deal, and that Martin was hers, she having negotiated his freedom.

'You'll have that crease so sharp he'll cut himself on it,' said Kathie, frivolously for her.

'Oh yes. Yes.'

I made a poor job of Oliver's jacket, and I didn't trouble at all with the creases in my own slacks, simply put them on crumpled. As I took it all back to our room, I was miserable at the thought that I would not be able to tell Oliver. What would he do if I did? Why — he would go to Peel and ram his lies down his throat, that was what. And he had only one good fist with which to do it.

Yet I knew I couldn't withhold it from him, because a trip to Edgbaston and back wouldn't account for over 400 miles. So where had the rest gone to? Why . . . on another journey in order to see Mandy in Shropshire, that was the logical assumption. After all, she'd heard of her existence only the day before. She would naturally want to see her. But stupid Heather, had she thought she could make another deal . . . with Mandy? I want to marry your husband! Lovely! She'd have come away with a flea in her ear, but not, I feared, without her own final comment that she was going to marry him anyway . . . so there. It would be typical of stupid Heather, even including the defiance. She would have been incensed by this trick of fate. It wouldn't be fair; it would be infuriatingly beyond all acceptance. And I wouldn't have put it past her to throw behind her, as an exit line, the remark, 'So you can come and watch, if you like. It's St Asaph's, in Somerset.' Something like that.

And was I to assume that Mandy had come to Somerset to watch? Or to prevent Martin from one more bigamy? Oliver would have to be told.

I got my expression together, tried to assemble a smile, and opened our door. Oliver was at the window, and turned.

'You've been a long . . . what's the matter? Something's happened?'

It was just as well that I'd decided, at the last second, not to keep it from him. I gave him his suit, and told him what had happened. In detail, and including my mental probings of it.

'The silly, deceitful creature,' he commented.

'Silly! She's brought all this about, and that's all you can say, silly and deceitful!'

'It's only conjecture. You can't know what

she did. You're building a mountain of theory from a shovelful of information.'

'I'm building it from what I know about Heather. But you can always go and ask her. Want to try that?'

He laughed. 'And drift even further from the truth?'

It was then that the front door bell rang. It must have been somebody who didn't know you could simply walk in — and shout.

We were at the head of the stairs in seconds, Oliver still struggling to zip up his trousers and me fighting my way into my blouse, when Kathie answered it. This was a bustling and obviously annoyed Kathie.

Three men entered the hall, three big men, as I could see as they advanced. They demanded — or rather, their leader demanded — to see Martin Reade, whom they believed to be on the premises.

He was, by this time, beside us on the top balcony, though not even acknowledging our presence. 'That's me,' he said flatly.

'Will you come down please, sir.' It was not a question.

'Who're you?'

'Police, sir. Superintendent Simmons. If you'd come down . . . '

Martin walked down the dozen stairs to the half-landing. From there he had a choice of stairways, either right or left, to the hall. He chose to take neither, but leaned over the banister.

'What's your business?'

'I have a warrant for your arrest, Mr Reade, on a charge of the unlawful killing of your wife, Amanda Reade. You need not say . . . '

And so on.

I heard no more. I was tensed for Heather's screams. But she didn't scream, though she was standing beside me now. She simply whispered, 'Martin . . . ' And passed out.

Yet Martin must have known this was inevitable. Every fact that emerged only implicated him more certainly. The body and its location, the time of the death the day before his third marriage, the murder weapon so easily available. And if the police now had a dozen claims to the ownership of that adjustable spanner, there was no denying that it had been *there*, available to Martin. And I could now add to that — as the police would surely do in the near future — a possible reason for Amanda's presence at Hellyspool.

Martin didn't look back. He walked down the right-hand final staircase, shrugged away a hand that reached for his elbow, at the last second glanced round, then the door closed behind the group.

Kathie stood weeping in the hall. Oliver

was supporting Heather's weight with his good arm.

'D'you think we can get her to her room between us?' he asked. 'She's like a lump of lead.'

'We'll have to.'

By the time we got her there, Kathie was with us. 'On the bed,' she said. 'On the bed. Now leave her to me.' She was still weeping as she ministered to her mistress.

Silently, we went back to our room. The first things that caught my eye were the two packets, the bra and the briefs.

'Shouldn't we let the police have those?' I asked, just for something to say.

Oliver glanced at them. 'No. They're our evidence, not theirs. Evidence for the defence.' He was reaching for the phone directory. 'What was his name? Rupert what?'

'Anderton, I think. No . . . Anderson.' My voice still sounded dull.

He got him straightaway, as though Rupert was always there, waiting for her call. He told him what had happened. 'You'd better get over here . . . He's rung off.'

'Evidence for the defence, you said.' I was still working out what this implied.

'Yes.'

'That means you're on his side, then? At last.'

'I'm on yours. Put it like that. But he said it himself. Why would he be so stupid as to leave her body in his bed? Why so stupid as to take her clothes away? Yes, I know — your clever bit of detection. Ratiocination, Poe called it. But we don't know that he didn't kill her and put her in a pool, then fish her out, then take her home with him. If he *was* stupid, he might even have done that. But he's not . . . is he? Far from it. If he was stupid he'd have insisted on driving the Merc back, then deliberately dropped you — then made a run for it. But no . . . he cheerfully came back, in spite of the fact that he must have known he was going to be arrested.'

'He seemed so confident . . . '

'But wasn't that all for Heather? To reassure her, to protect her. To protect her from the perils of worry and concern. As you've always done, Phil. He came back for her sake. Since then, it's all probably been an act. He's always doing that. Admit it.'

I nodded numbly. But in those two cars it hadn't been an act. That I knew. Nor had my own performance been. I'd met the genuine Martin. We had . . . as he'd have put it himself . . . meshed together like two gears. Mated, the engineers call it. I had to make an effort to shake myself free of the thought.

'We can't leave Kathie with all this . . . to

231

look after her all by herself.' I said it dubiously.

'D'you think she'll be alone? No, there's Rupert. The solicitor. He'll be on it like a terrier, applying for bail and everything else. You know what Rupert's like.'

Yes, I knew Rupert.

'So what do we do,' I asked, 'if we leave in the morning? That was what you had in mind, wasn't it?' To go home was what he'd meant.

He thought for a few moments. 'I think we ought to start at the beginning of it all. Luke Tulliver's death.'

'There's nothing there.'

'No? What else is there for us to get hold of? And you see, from what Martin told you, if she'd thrown him out — and not him walked out on her — then there's no motive for Martin having killed his father-in-law. She wouldn't have had him back anyway, so where'd be the point in him killing Tulliver?'

'And why does that matter now?'

'I don't know. Everything involving Martin matters. It would be nice to be able to add a little confirmation to one thing he's said.'

But I knew there was something else on his mind.

'We don't know where Mandy lived,' I pointed out.

'So we go and ask Victor Peel.' He was very casual about it, but it was what I'd dreaded. 'A diversion to Birmingham — it wouldn't take us far out of our way,' he said lightly. 'His card gives an office address at Dale End.'

I pouted, and left it at that.

I changed into my new slacks, pirouetted for Oliver's approval, and then we set out to see what was happening to Heather, and to our meal. For me, I admit, the meal came first in my mind. One could have enough of Heather's vapours.

We met Kathie coming out of Heather's room. I raised my eyebrows to her. She smiled weakly.

'She's all right. I don't think, between you and me, that she was very surprised. I mean . . . it had to come, sooner or later. She's coming down to dinner, anyway.'

So we ate our stew in the dining-room. There was no wine that might have added stature to the stew, and the pudding was ice cream, because it didn't need cooking.

It was time, I thought, to tell Heather that we must leave the next morning. She looked at me with startled surprise.

'You're leaving me,' she accused, but without force. She knew when fate was hopelessly against her. She would have to sit and lap it up. But sullenly.

'Not exactly,' I assured her. 'There're things to be looked into. Anything we can find in Martin's favour . . . wouldn't that be worth the trouble?'

She looked down at the table. 'I suppose.'

It was our third night at Hellyspool Hall, when we'd not expected to stay one. The sleeping arrangements were now established, but that was all we did . . . sleep. It had all been terribly exhausting.

Heather wasn't down for breakfast. We could say a farewell only to Kathie, who dutifully said they'd been glad to have us. She seemed limp and discouraged.

'Oh, we'll be back,' I said. 'Do try to make that clear to her, Kathie, please. We'll be back . . . whatever happens.'

She waved miserably as I swung the car round on the gravel and pointed it for the tunnel of trees. I felt like a traitor. Oliver said, 'No need to hurry.'

I wasn't, and had no intention to. In practice, I didn't get as far as the road. As we came out from beneath the trees, the sun blinding that morning, Oliver shouted, 'Stop!'

My mind hadn't been on it. By instinct I reacted, skidding on the gravel.

'There's another,' he said, his voice toneless.

He was correct. Something, some item of

clothing, was hooked on the rusted hinge-pin from which iron gates had once swung. In anger, I thumped the steering wheel. Again!

It was fortunate that the press and photographers had not yet put in an appearance, but I was certain that nobody in the village would have offered them accommodation, so possibly they had to come from a distance. But oh . . . what might they have made of this!

I got out of the car and walked over to it. Close to, it was at once apparent that it was a pleated skirt in printed cotton, and that it was fouled with brown and green stains. It was hung by the loop on the waistband. Reluctantly, I reached it down, delicately with forefinger and thumb because I knew already how it would smell. In fact it didn't smell as badly as the bra and briefs had, possibly because it had been hanging in the open air, though we couldn't guess for how long.

Oliver was at my elbow. 'What is it?'

'It's a rather expensive printed cotton skirt, Oliver, as you can see.'

'Let's spread it out on the boot.'

So we went and did that on the closed lid. Inside the boot were the other two items.

'The same stains,' said Oliver. I couldn't understand why he had to sound pleased.

'And the same little bits of green weed. Going brittle now. But inside, too.'

'Yes,' I agreed. 'The skirt would spread out in the water, and the weed could get inside. It got to her briefs, didn't it! But look — there're bits of weed outside the waistband, and not inside.'

'Well of course . . . '

'It's just a little more confirmation that what we worked out must be correct — that she was wearing the clothes when she went in the water.'

'Yes, yes.' He seemed impatient. 'But it's not adding anything. I don't mean to what we know . . . but it doesn't add any reason for doing this. What's the point in producing bits of clothing piecemeal . . . '

'Only the blouse to go, now,' I told him. 'It's all she'd have been wearing, this hot weather.'

'You're missing the point.' His fist made a small thumping noise on the boot.

I understood his frustration. Analyse it, and there seemed no point in it.

'What am I missing?' I asked.

'That there isn't one. First the brooch, then the articles of clothing . . . what're they supposed to mean? What do they achieve?'

I touched his arm. No need to shout — we were of the same mind. 'They achieve the thorough frightening of Heather, that's what they mean, Oliver. Whether they were intended to do that, we don't know. They need not have been a threat. A sort of: 'I know where these clothes have been, but I haven't sent them to the police.' A kind of reassurance.'

'Then it hasn't worked. And: 'This is your brooch.' What about that?'

'If they're linked,' I said doubtfully.

'Of course they're linked.'

'That depends where she lost the brooch.' Then I had a terrible thought. 'Oliver!' I clutched his bad arm in my agitation. 'You're not saying . . . '

'I'm saying — let go of my arm.'

'Oh . . . sorry, Oliver. Really I'm — '

'What were you saying?'

'I was wondering,' I admitted dully, 'whether you were suggesting that Heather hid those clothes — and dropped her brooch when she did it. Oh no! Don't suggest that. It'd mean she helped him . . . whoever. Tell me it can't be.'

'It can't be, Phillie love, because Mandy was in a stagnant pool before she was undressed, and I can't fit that in. Show me a stagnant pool around here.'

'Oh . . . clever you! I had this terrible thought . . . ' And still had. Heather hadn't been 'around here' for the whole day before the wedding.

'But she did scream at the brooch,' he persisted.

'All the same . . . ' I had to try to do something for my friend. 'An item isn't a threat. You don't threaten by producing an item. There would have to be some message involved. A threat has to be verbal or in writing. Not imaginary . . . '

He suddenly grinned at me. 'Perhaps it was.'

And at once I could recall a clear mental image of that moment when I had run into the hall. Heather had been screaming. The brooch lay in her left palm, claiming my immediate attention, and her right fist had been against her mouth. Not her open hand — her fist.

'Let's go back and ask her,' I suggested.

'Yes. Let's.'

I had to drive out into the roadway in order to turn. Just inside the gateway, I stopped again. Oliver was tossing the skirt on to the rear seat.

'Now what?' he asked.

'There's been no messages with the clothes. It was only a thought.'

He nodded. 'Drive on. Let's get it over with. It's obvious. If the clothes were meant for Martin — as they might have been as it's now his home, his address — then there wouldn't need to have been a message. They would shout out: I know where she died. I know you did it and where you left her body. There. Isn't that enough of a threat?'

'Then why weren't they sent to the police? Instead of to Martin.'

'I suppose because he would know what they meant, but they might not. And they might start looking for the person who sent them.'

I said no more on it. We drew up at the house once more, and we climbed the steps. I didn't want to use the door bell, so I pushed open the door.

'We're back, Kathie,' I called.

She came pattering across the hall. 'But I thought . . . '

'There's something we've got to ask Heather,' I said. 'Sorry. It's only just come to mind.'

She stood four-square. 'Oh, I couldn't let you do that. She's resting.'

I'm afraid my patience with Heather was becoming stretched. 'I don't care if she's sitting up and playing the mouth organ, I'm going to see her, Kathie. You can come along. You can be the referee.'

She made a tiny snorting sound, then she

turned around and headed for the stairs.

'Very well. Very *well*.'

Oliver, beside me, whispered, 'Mouth organ?'

'She used to play one, at school.'

'Never!'

'It's perfectly true.'

'Won't you feel a damned fool if she really is?' he asked.

But she wasn't. She was sitting calmly at her dressing-table, tidying her hair. She stared at my image in the mirror.

'Oh hell, Phillie, aren't you *ever* going to give us a bit of peace?'

There's gratitude for you.

11

'Not until we've got this thing all sorted out,' I told her firmly.

'They've arrested him. Isn't that good enough for you?'

I approached her. She watched my reflection all the way to her shoulder. 'Not really,' I said. 'Not by any means good enough.'

'Don't tell me you think you can do anything now.' She swung round on the seat to face me.

'If I ever heard any truth, from anybody, maybe I could.'

On the plate glass surface of her dressing-table lay the brooch. There was also a porcelain tree, on one of the arms of which was hooked the bracelet of a gold Rolex Oyster wrist-watch. She clearly wasn't in the mood to tell me it was Martin's wedding present. She didn't mention the brooch. The old stubborn look was on her face, the lower lip beginning to pout. Pugging, we used to call it.

'The brooch, Heather,' I said. 'That was what I wanted to talk to you about.'

'What about it?'

'You screamed. When you saw it on the hall table — when you picked it up — you screamed.'

'I . . . I was so happy to see it back.' Her gaze wandered past me.

'It was a scream of fear. Terror, even.'

'Nothing of the sort.'

'As though its very presence was a threat.'

Her eyes were going blank. She was shutting her thoughts away, veiling them. She said nothing.

'But how could that be?' I asked. 'A threat. A personal threat, simply because it was *your* brooch. A voiceless threat, if you like. Interrupt me, if you want to say anything, Heather.'

'Yes, I do. Stop pestering me, Phil. Stop it!'

'When you tell me what the threat was, I'll stop. Of course, you could have remembered where you'd lost it, and suddenly there it was, in the hall. *That* might be a shock, if you'd lost it somewhere you weren't supposed to have been.' I ventured this in the hope of jolting her.

'It wasn't a threat,' she said very quietly, no emphasis to it. She seemed not to have heard my last few words.

'So possibly the brooch wasn't the actual threat. Maybe that was written on a bit of paper, which you had screwed up in your other hand, Heather.'

It was perhaps the fact that I was questioning her, and severely, that unnerved her, her friend Phillie, whose job it had always been to protect her from the evils of life, not lay them out under her nose.

'No . . . I can't . . . oh, go away, please.'

'Have you still got the note?'

'No, I . . . '

There'd been hesitation, and even then she'd got it wrong. 'Threw it away?' I offered this to her as a way out. Her eyes opened wide. Her fingers fluttered.

'Or did you keep it?' I persisted. 'Yes, you did, Heather. You'd have to keep the threat, to look at it from time to time, to try to read something else into it. Where is it, Heather? Please.'

The moving hand settled. It gestured. 'In the . . . the box,' she whispered.

She meant the pine box with the brass corners, which I saw she had on her dressing-table. This was her jewel box, though Heather had never worn much jewellery. I reached over and lifted the lid. A pearl necklace, discreet, a small diamond pin, a bracelet, gold and amethyst. And beneath them a piece of paper, flattened out but showing creases.

I lifted it out. It was a page torn from a pocket diary. The week shown was this week, and in the space allocated to the day that had been the fatal one, the day prior to the wedding, was printed: *Keep your mouth shut.* I put it down on the table again.

'And this frightened you?' I asked gently. At that moment, she was very fragile.

She was silent, looking down at the fingers on her lap, where they were twining and untwining. She murmured something I didn't catch. I put a finger beneath her chin and lifted it. There was no resistance; she was now praying for my help, pleading for it.

'It was on *that* day that you lost the brooch?' I asked, removing the finger in order to indicate I meant the day on which the message appeared. She nodded.

'So somebody found it and returned it with this message: keep your mouth shut,' I said, softly, gently. 'About what, Heather? About where you lost it? About where it was found?'

She gave a tiny, choked sob. No more.

'Is *that* what matters?' I persisted. 'Where it was found?'

Her head was lowering again. She couldn't meet my eyes.

'You went out in the car that day, didn't you, Heather?' I asked. 'The day before the wedding. You were out a long while. A very long while. That day you drove over 400 miles. The mileometer told me that. You must have been away for at least ten hours.' I put it this way in order to imply that I'd reasoned it out myself, and thus to spare Kathie. But Heather guessed. Sometimes she could be quite astute.

'Oh . . . Kathie!' she sobbed.

And Kathie sat down suddenly on the side of the bed. I glanced at Oliver. I'd been hoping he wouldn't interrupt. He inclined his head marginally, a tiny smile on his lips. It was all mine, heaven help me.

'Isn't that when you lost the brooch, Heather?' There was no response. 'Shall I tell you where you went? Shall I tell you *why* you went?' It would save her the shame of admitting it. 'You can interrupt me wherever I go wrong. Shall we do that?'

There was no sound from her, but she covered her face with her hands. It was all I could do to continue.

'Very well. A man came to see you, the detective, Victor Peel. He didn't try to sell you anything, except information. No encyclo-paedias. Perhaps you paid him, Heather. I don't know. But the information he must have let you have was that the man you were going to marry — it was two days ahead at that time — that man, Martin, was already married. He'd been married for twelve years. Not only that, but he'd married a second time, and that second wife, as we'll call her, had employed Peel to trace him, and had taken him to court for bigamy. I'm sure he would've given you all that absolutely free, Heather. As a gift. What he still had to offer was what he *would* charge you for. And wasn't that the names and addresses of the two women involved? Did you say something? No? Never mind, I'm sure I'm correct. And didn't you, on the day you went out with the car, your new Mercedes . . . on that day didn't you visit both these women?'

There was silence.

I sighed. 'Didn't you, Heather? A trip to Edgbaston in Birmingham, and then on to Shropshire to see Amanda Tulliver — I'm sure you'd rather think of her under that name. Wasn't that what you did?'

She nodded slowly, twice, her hands still over her face.

'No, Heather, don't hide your face. You'll have to take the story from here. How can I guess what happened when you met them? Or what you did when you met them? Or what was said. Heather . . . please. Try to help yourself. This is for you, you stupid creature.'

That got her. Her head came up, her angry eyes matching the amethysts in her bracelet.

246

'I am *not* stupid, Philipa. I knew what I wanted — I wanted Martin. I wanted him then, and if it hadn't been for you I'd have him now.'

'What?' Her logic confounded me.

'You and your interfering. All you do is irritate them, and then they turn nasty.'

'Who?' I asked, lost.

'The police, silly.'

'Ridiculous. Don't talk such nonsense. They're naturally like that. If you're not nasty, they don't let you join, in the first place.' I didn't dare glance at Oliver.

'All the same . . . ' she said stubbornly. 'Surely you can see, Phil. I had to do *something*. Two days from the wedding, and *that* had to happen! Of course I went to see them. I had to.'

'It didn't occur to you to take the easy way out — and talk to Martin about it?'

She lifted her chin. There was no sign of distress now, she was bright and sharp, and even aggressive. She had learned to fight back. 'Now how could I have done that?' she demanded. 'It would only have upset him. Heavens, he might've taken it into his head not to come to our wedding. Perhaps three would've been too many for him, especially if I knew . . . You know what he's like. Anything like that, and he'd be hurt. It'd show him I

247

didn't trust him, and that's what marriage is all about, isn't it, Phil — trust? Of course I couldn't go to him.'

I managed not to smile. 'So you went first to June McBride?'

'Yes. She was the major snag. I mean, *she* was the one who'd been talking about bigamy. Oh Phil, have you ever driven there? To Birmingham. It was awful! All that traffic, and those no-entry signs and one-way traffic. Oh, I could've wept. And when I *did* find the place . . . who on earth would want to live *there*! All those houses and always the traffic, not so far away, and streets lined with parked cars. I hated it, hated it! And hated her. It only took one glance, and I could see right through her. D'you think she cared one jot for Martin? Not a bit of it. I soon got *her* measure. It was her money she wanted. Hard, she is. But I wasn't going to let her have it all her way. Oh no. I said — how much? That got her. How much did she want to call it all off — this bigamy thing? I tied her down to it. Got her wriggling.'

I found it difficult to accept the domineering and imperious June McBride wriggling beneath Heather's blue and guileless eyes. Or flinching at her scorn. I said, 'And you got her to agree?'

'Oh yes. Of course I did. She said she'd

have to see her solicitor and get it all laid out legally. I told her she wasn't getting her money until she did — and that was that.'

'Not quite, it wasn't.'

'The stupid woman wasted time. That . . . that horrible arrest at Heathrow! I could've sunk into the ground.' Then she flicked a wry smile at me. 'But it all came out right in the end.'

'It did.' I had difficulty not making that a question.

The two women had arranged it, but June McBride had had to make a scene out of it. Perhaps there had been something evil behind her attitude. In any event, she had succeeded in terrifying Heather, suggesting she had changed her mind — or why come to the house? Even, perhaps, she had been suggesting that her demands had grown beyond Heather's financial reach. And Raeburn had connived in it.

But I couldn't just stand there, facing her. It was like an inquisition. I went to the window and looked out. She was well launched now. I asked casually, 'And did it work out, too, with Amanda?'

There was a slight pause, then she said, 'Not so good.'

'In what way?'

She avoided a direct answer. 'Now there's a

beautiful place to live, Phil. Out in rolling country with a bit of a stream running through the grounds. Shropshire. It's called Fillingley Towers. That's because the house — oh, it's huge! — it's got towers, four of them.'

'I wouldn't have guessed.'

'And you'll never believe it — an actual gatehouse, with somebody living there, too, though there wasn't anybody there at the time. And a housekeeper, I'd guess, it's so big, and probably maids. What d'you think of that?'

'It sounds wonderful,' I conceded.

'And Phil, d'you realize . . . ' Her voice became animated. 'I've just thought . . . it all belongs to Martin now. Perhaps we'll go to live there. Oh yes. That's what we'll do. I'd love that.'

'I hope you will.' That covered a lot of the aspects. 'And you succeeded in getting to see Amanda?'

'Oh yes.'

'You talked it over with her?' I managed not to glance at Oliver.

'Of course. It was what I'd gone for, after all. I told her I was going to marry her Martin, and we discussed that. We walked out into the park, as she called it, and talked about it. She wouldn't have me in the house, and she seemed to be edging me towards my car. I'd left it half-way down the drive. I'd got out, see, to have a better look at the place, and between you and me, Phil, it wasn't all that grand, when you *really* looked. Sort of scruffy . . . oh, I can't describe it.'

'Then don't try, Heather.' Though she was doing fairly well. 'It's not relevant, really.'

'I thought you'd want to know,' she answered petulantly. 'But please yourself. Anyway, she must've seen me there, and came out to see what I wanted. And we had ourselves a grand bit of a chat.'

'Are you telling me that you two discussed your forthcoming marriage with her husband — and calmly?'

'Not calmly, Phillie. You know that. Why say such a thing? No. She was annoyed. Really angry. The way she shouted . . . you'd have thought I was stupid or something, the way she went on. But really, it was she who was stupid. She said Martin was *her* husband, and she wanted him back. As though I'd just hand him over! I told her he loved me, and we were going to get married, whatever she said. And I told her she could come and watch, if she didn't believe me, and told her where it was going to be. I thought I was *very* reasonable. I went out of my way to be kind to her, but some people will never be told.

Never. That was when she started shouting.
So undignified . . . shouting!'

'And you shouted back?'

'Of course not. This was business. After all,
it'd worked out all right with that June
McBride. Offer them money. So I did. I said
it was all her fault, because she ought to have
divorced him long before this. Ten years ago,
he'd left her. She told me that. So why hadn't
she divorced him? And I suggested — I mean,
I wasn't *telling* her, just suggesting — I said,
if she would start it off — the divorce — now
she knew where he was, I'd make it worth her
while. As I pointed out, she could do with
some new curtains, and — '

'But a divorce would take months!' I
interrupted, somewhat exasperated. 'Your
wedding was the next day.'

Heather reached out a hand soothingly.
'Well, of course it was. But as I pointed out
— words of one syllable and in a calming
voice — it didn't matter to me if we weren't
properly married, as she called it. I would get
the Church's blessing, and that was good
enough for me. And we could do it all again
later, after the divorce came through.'

Surely even Heather couldn't be so blandly
naïve! But in some ways she was correct.
These days, the ritual of marriage is not of
paramount importance — but people don't

usually get married again while there's still a first spouse hanging around.

'I didn't care,' said Heather, with a blissful mangling of logic, 'if we *would* be living in sin, as long as we had the Church's blessing.'

'Did you say that to her?'

'Something much like it, but different words.'

No wonder Amanda had got to the point of shouting. 'And then what?'

'Then she went at me like a wildcat.' Her eyes were huge. Even now it was unbelievable to her. 'All flying nails . . . and such vile language! Silly little thing — she was only tiny, you know. I just held her off until she was quiet. She tore my blouse.'

'And then?'

'She burst into tears and ran back to the house. I think. Or round the side, anyway. And me with a torn blouse! I didn't dare be seen . . . but with a bit of luck . . . you know, you have to trust to luck sometimes. So I just got inside the car, all shaky, you know, and had to sit a minute. Then I did a big, skiddy turn on her grass. Serve her right.'

'I'm sure it would annoy her,' I agreed.

'I think that's where I must have lost the brooch,' she said quietly, as though it was an admission of guilt.

'Where you fought, you mean?'

'Yes. Perhaps then. Or when I got into the car. Then somebody must have picked it up.'

'Hmm!'

I glanced again at Oliver. Now I was lost, and couldn't think how to pursue it. He read my thoughts.

'And that's why you screamed?' he asked, his voice full of understanding, as though he too might have screamed on finding the same brooch on the same table.

'Yes,' she whispered.

'Because it proved you were there?'

A slight hesitation. 'Yes.'

'That and the message. What did it say, Phil? I didn't quite catch it.'

'Oh, sorry, Oliver. It reads: keep your mouth shut.'

'I see. And *that* made you scream, Heather?' he asked her. 'It was a threat. But what about, that's the point? It hadn't been too shocking, if it was known you'd visited Mandy. It was nothing you'd need to be terrified about.'

'Oh no. But somebody else might've thought it was bad. Such as Martin. I was worried.'

'I'm sure you were.' He smiled. 'But what did it mean? You must have realized at once. Keep your mouth shut — about what? You can't have needed to be told to keep your mouth shut about your own visit. So it was something else. It made you scream. What was so terrible?'

She said nothing. Her eyes had glazed.

'Wasn't it,' asked Oliver gently, so gently that I knew this was the crucial question, 'that you realized it was really saying: keep your mouth shut, and I will too. Something both of you knew. You and somebody else. So . . . what could that have been?'

She shook her head stubbornly.

'What did you think it might have meant?' Oliver was persistent. 'You can say it here, you know. We're all friends. Keep your mouth shut . . . about what?'

Her hand reached out for mine. She gripped it so hard I nearly cried out, but I managed to smile encouragingly and nod. She whispered something.

'I'm sorry,' said Oliver. 'I didn't hear that.'

'Martin was there,' she said, on a sob.

Inwardly, I groaned. She made it worse and worse for Martin, the more she opened her mouth.

'You saw Martin there?' I asked.

'Yes.' So quietly, this was, that I had to lip read.

'So he would notice *you* were there,' I pointed out. 'But how could it be such a frightening threat . . . '

'Oh, I'm sure he didn't . . . didn't know it was me. I was in the new car. He'd never seen it before. It was supposed to be a secret.'

'What time was this?' With Heather it was hard work, but I wasn't going to let it go, now we were getting somewhere.

'Oh really, Phillie! You're the limit. As though I'd been watching the time. I was back here just after seven in the evening. I remember that. Kathie was worrying about the evening meal.'

So she'd probably left Fillingley Towers at around three.

'And where did you see Martin, Heather?'

'He was in a lay-by, a hundred yards from the gatehouse.'

'You mean he was parked there?'

'His car was.' She was now speaking in a numb tone. The emotion had drained from her. Now it was simply a flat statement of fact. She didn't know what Martin's presence there might have meant, having forced herself not to think about it. Dreading to.

'*His* car? Not the yellow Dolomite Sprint, surely? But that was on the hoist, being gone over . . . '

'No, no. That Fiesta of his friend's. What's his name — Jeff Carter. Our best man, he was. That car was there, parked.'

'But surely, Fiestas are quite common. You

wouldn't recognize one from another, parked in a lay-by. Why would you even glance at it?'

'You *are* slow, Phil. Really you are. He was standing there by it.'

'Doing what?'

'Nothing really. Just standing, and looking over the hedge towards the house.'

'So he didn't see you in the Mercedes? Didn't recognize you?'

She shook her head violently. 'He wasn't looking my way. He glanced at the Mercedes. Well, he would. He's a car fanatic, and it's the latest model. But he didn't see me in it. It's got tinted glass. I mean . . . he wouldn't have expected to see me there, would he? So he didn't.'

That was a neat bit of logic, to come from Heather.

'No, he wouldn't even glance at the driver, Heather. That's true.'

But he would certainly examine the car with keen professional approval. And remember it. He'd said he'd seen the Merc in the drive the day before the wedding. The evening, that would be, after they were both back in Hellyspool. *Then* he would remember it, and where he'd seen it. There wouldn't be many of that specific model on the roads yet.

Didn't she *see*, the stupid woman? She was making everything worse for Martin. He had been *there*. He might even . . .

'Would it have been possible, Heather,' I asked, tentative because everything she said was disastrous, 'that from where he was standing Martin might have seen you two fighting?'

'Oh no!' She shook her head again violently, hair flying. 'There're some trees, where he was standing. I'm sure he couldn't have seen.' She stared from face to face. 'And is that all? Can't you think of anything else you can frighten me with, Phillie?'

'No, Heather. Nothing else for the moment. We'll get off now, Oliver and I. It's not finished yet, you realize, so we'll surely be back.'

She raised her chin. 'You're always welcome, you know that.' But it would be a cool welcome. 'And do bring some clothes the next time you come.' She clearly had not understood.

'We'll do that.'

I went to Oliver at the door, giving Kathie a rueful smile as I passed her. 'Look after her,' I mouthed. She nodded. She, at least, could understand that we were on their side.

We closed the door quietly after us, and I hurried Oliver down the stairs.

'No need to rush, Phil, is there?'

'Yes, there is. I want to get to the phone

258

before she rings him.'

'You *are* mysterious,' he grumbled. 'I'm lost. Rings who?'

'Rupert Anderson, of course.'

We reached the hall and I grabbed up the phone. Heather wasn't speaking, so I had the line. Let her listen, if she wanted to. My other hand was flicking the pages of her notebook on the table.

'Here it is. His office.'

I dialled, and got a woman's voice. 'Mr Anderson is very busy.'

'I know, I know. I'm speaking for Heather Payne. Reade now, I suppose. It's very important.'

He came on at once. He sounded tense, his voice dead. 'What is it, Heather?'

'It's Philipa Lowe. Heather's been telling me things I don't like the sound of. If you see her, ask her where she was on the day before the wedding — but that wasn't why I called you.'

'What was?' He was short with me, impatient.

'Have you been able to see Martin?'

'Of course. I was there all last evening. Please don't ask me to reveal — '

'I wouldn't dream of it. No. What I wanted to ask you . . . could I see him? Would they let me?'

'I'm quite certain they wouldn't.'

'Then — next time you see him — could you ask him two questions for me? Or maybe three.'

'If it would help.'

'I'm afraid, if my guess is correct, it'll land him right in it.'

He sighed. 'Very well. Ask your questions. I can write shorthand.'

So I rattled them off briskly. 'Did he take the Fiesta — that's his friend Jeff Carter's Fiesta — out for a run early in the day before the wedding? If so — why did he need to take it out for a test run later that night? You can see . . . '

'I see. Any more?'

'Yes. Why, when he took it out earlier, did he drive to his wife's place in Shropshire? That's the first one, the real one, Amanda. Was it because he'd heard from her? And *did* he see her?'

'Shropshire! Shropshire? What the devil's this about Shropshire?'

'Amanda's place,' I said. 'It's called Fillingley Towers. Did he go there that day? Was it because he'd heard from her? Did he actually meet her and speak to her?'

'Do you expect answers to these questions? If he *did*, he wouldn't dare to admit it.'

'I'd expect him to tell the truth to his solicitor.'

'Hmm!' he said sceptically. 'To a lot of people, a solicitor's a person you visit to lie to. Like the opposite to a priest.'

I didn't reply. It hadn't demanded a reply.

'Can I expect you to tell me the significance?' he asked.

'I'd have thought — '

'It was obvious, yes. I'd like to know, though, what it might explain, and how it could help me.'

'When I know, I'll call you again. Later. All right?'

'If it helps my client — yes.'

He hung up. As I replaced the handset, Oliver said, 'Can we get away from here, Phil? I'm beginning not to like it.'

'Yes. Let's get going.'

'Where to?'

'To Shropshire, of course. To Fillingley Towers.'

We were travelling light. All we had to do was walk out of the front door, step into my BMW, and drive away. Oliver made no attempt to appropriate the steering wheel. I felt he needed time to think. In any event, he wasn't saying anything, but hunched himself down. It was only when we drove out from beneath the trees that he sat up abruptly.

'Bloody press!' he said tersely.

But it wasn't, though they were now clearly on the job. I'd seen them lurking amongst the trees, cameras at the ready. Their cars were scattered along the lane, a TV mobile van amongst them. But no member of the media would climb into his vehicle at the sight of us, and drive away. Not away. And what this man had climbed into was a Range Rover.

I put my foot down. The BMW did a skid turn on to the tarmac, and we set off after him.

Oliver was silent for a few moments, then he said, 'I hope you haven't got the idea of retaliating. I mean, you couldn't push that thing off the road with your lovely BMW.'

'I merely wanted words with him.'

'Then that's all right. Me too. Once we're not moving I'll toss you for who goes first.'

But the Range Rover didn't seem to be making a run for it. It proceeded with sedate dignity. I gave him a blast with the horn, but all he did was draw over for me to pass. This was no good. If I stopped ahead of him, he would simply drive on past. I blew the horn again. I flashed the lights. He flicked his taillights. I flashed again.

It could have gone on for miles, but in the end he drew into a lay-by and stopped. I drew in behind, as he jumped out. We slid out. Together, Oliver and I advanced on him.

He did not flinch. He did not seem the sort of man who would flinch from anything. Fair, curly hair, slightly thinning, crowned a square and dominant face. Grey eyes, which were now cool, stared out uncompromisingly from beneath a broad brow. His face was rugged and wind-blown, his mouth wide and flexible. At the moment there was a sternness in its firm line. He stood with legs slightly apart, clad in cavalry twill, above this a tweed hacking jacket with leather elbow reinforcements. He might have been returning from a cattle auction.

'You wanted to speak with me?' he asked, voice low-pitched and cool. But polite.

By this time I wasn't certain that I did. This Range Rover didn't look the same one. It was clean; it was unblemished. It's true that a hose can do wonders with a coat of mud, but somehow this man didn't seem, either, to be the same driver. I hadn't actually seen the other driver, but all the same this was not the type of man to deliberately run people off the road. If there is such a type. I hesitated, and Oliver rescued me.

'We only wondered why you were hanging around outside the gates,' he said genially.

There was a faint twitch at the corners of that wide mouth. Then he said, 'I wouldn't call it that.' His voice was deep, ponderous, measured. 'I didn't see you stop and question that gang with the cameras and mikes. So why me?'

'You were the only one who drove away. Nothing would shift that lot.'

He shrugged. 'I got bored. Nothing was happening.'

He seemed to be confidently in control of the situation, so I tried another tack. 'The last time, I was driving a Mercedes coupé.'

'Indeed?' He looked past me at the BMW. 'You collect cars, do you?' This was not put in a sarcastic manner. One eyebrow was raised. He seemed vaguely amused. I shook my head with impatience, at myself really. I'd made a mistake.

But Oliver took it on. 'One might describe it as suspicious behaviour. Or at least . . . '

While they continued with this, I walked round to the front of the Range Rover. They're built like a tank, so I didn't see any damage, such as might have been inflicted by a paltry wooden fence. Absolutely nothing. Pristine. Not a touch of white paint on the solid black of the huge bumper, not a sign that a headlight might have been smashed and replaced.

I walked back, pursed my lips at Oliver, and shook my head. Oliver smiled, but not at me.

'Perhaps we owe you an apology,' I said. 'All the same . . . '

To some men, victory, even such a small one, exerts a softening touch. Especially men who have found life a continual struggle, with defeat more often the end result. Now he did smile.

'I was merely wondering,' he said, 'if Martin might be home?' The raised eyebrows made it a question. 'I believe that place to be his new home.'

'It is, and he's not,' Oliver told him.

'A pity. Mind you, there was always the chance he'd be too deeply involved . . . but it was a matter of urgent importance to me. I had to know, you understand. To know how it's going to be, I mean.'

'How what is?' Oliver asked.

'The tenancy,' explained the man simply. 'My landlord, my cousin in fact, has recently died — and that's what's brought me to this district. It's not a time to intrude, I know. But I need to get the facts, and in writing, if possible. Quite simply, I wish to know if the tenancy will be allowed to continue on the same terms. As a matter of fact, it's really urgent. I have forty-five acres of barley and two hundred of wheat, all coming along quite nicely. I need to know. I'll be going into the red, anyway, hiring the reaper and operator. Do I make myself clear?'

Then I knew what had been nudging at my subconscious. I had, in the middle of Somerset, been listening to a Shropshire accent. And somebody had said — was it Peel? — that Fillingley Towers had a home farm, which was farmed by a relative of Mandy, whose name . . .

'You're Clive Garner, aren't you?' I asked him. 'The tenancy, you said. You're the one who works the home farm at Fillingley Towers.'

He turned to me. The recognition seemed to please him, though he was clearly surprised. 'I am indeed. And who are you, may I ask?'

'I'm Philipa Lowe, and this is Oliver Simpson. Friends of Heather . . . er, Reade, I suppose.'

He inclined his head.

'And I'm afraid Martin isn't available,' I went on. 'If I'm correct, weren't you speaking about your cousin, Mandy? Yes? Well, I'm afraid Martin's under arrest for her murder.' There was no point in attempting to soften the impact. In fact, he seemed satisfied with the information.

All the same, he said, 'I'm sorry to hear that.' He paused, then added, 'I'll have to leave the question of the lease until later, then.' That, apparently, was his main concern.

12

Clearly, this encounter might save us a trip to Shropshire if we handled it correctly, but I had the idea we might miss something by not going there to see for ourselves. All the same, the opportunity was not to be tossed aside. He, too, seemed prepared to talk.

So we strolled up and down that lay-by, talking. After a long drive, Garner was pleased to stretch his legs, which were probably more used to striding on grass. A Welsh collie put its head out of the car window and watched with interest.

It appeared that the lease in question had first been brought into effect a long while ago. Somebody's great grandfather and somebody's great-great grandfather. One of them owned Fillingley Towers, the parkland, and the home farm. The lease on the farm was nominal, Garner explained, and had continued so, at a peppercorn rent.

'Peppercorn?' I asked. I had heard of it, but didn't realize it still existed.

He explained. 'There has to be *some* payment to make it legal. So . . . it was a peppercorn per annum in the old days. And so it's gone on. My cousin Mandy was, until recently, my landlord. I paid that, though in practice it's now money. One penny per annum.'

'Not a peppercorn?' I was disappointed. A peppercorn was romantic.

He laughed. A fine, free laugh, this was. He paused to let the dog have a bit of a run, opening the door. The collie came to me for a fuss.

'If I cared to grow *Piper nigrum* I'd have enough peppercorns to last a hundred years in one crop from a single shrub,' he told us. 'You get red berries, and they dry off black. That's a peppercorn. Maybe I'll do that, if Martin takes over the lease. One peppercorn per annum, and I'll stick it right up . . . ' He drew in his lower lip, and gave a sharp whistle. The collie, who'd been investigating a farm gate, ran back to heel.

I smiled sympathetically. 'It doesn't sound as though you like him.'

'Hate his guts,' he said flatly, smiling a thin, cool smile at me. 'No depth in the man. And what he did to Mandy . . . When he could see there was no money coming his way, he was off and gone. The silly creature — this is Mandy I'm talking about — the silly creature, she wouldn't cut him right off. Wouldn't divorce him. I was . . . well, I thought it was all arranged. When she got to be eighteen, she was going to marry me. I'm quite a bit older — eighteen years — but it was kind of settled . . . between us. Her father — Luke Tulliver, this was — he seemed to be happy enough with the arrangement. It kept it in the family, you see, as it's always been. I'm not exactly family — or of course we couldn't have married — but we were cousins on her mother's side. Then she had to go and marry that . . . that . . . ' He moved his hand angrily, and the collie gave a little whine. He glanced down and pulled her ear. 'Worth her weight in gold, this one is. You can trust a dog. Know where you are with a dog, you do.'

'And you don't know where you are with Martin?' Oliver asked. 'I can understand that, believe me.'

'Whoever did know? What if he refuses me the lease? What if he asks a fortune? He might. He's got no reason to like me. Tcha! I can pride myself on that, anyway. But I'll have to crawl.' His lips twisted sourly. 'I'm just about hanging on now, but with farm subsidies being messed about, and the like, you're almost running at a loss anyway. I *need* that damned lease, and more than a penny a year will just about finish me.'

I glanced at Oliver. He pouted. There seemed to be nothing to say. Garner fished out a pipe from his pocket and stared at it.

'You say he's not available?' he asked, stubbornly hoping.

'I'm afraid not,' I told him. 'And it looks as though he might spend a long long time away. It's murder, you know, and there's nothing anybody could say in mitigating circumstances. In his favour,' I said, as he'd frowned.

'And he can rot there, as far as I'm concerned,' he said.

'*Then* what about your lease?'

He looked startled. 'Perhaps it'll still be legal, signed in prison. Even more legal, most likely.'

'I think,' said Oliver gravely, 'that you ought to get a solicitor's advice on this. You really should.'

'What? Yes. Yes, I suppose so.'

But his mind was miles away.

'You were heading back home?' I asked, because we needed to know.

'Oh yes. Nowhere else to go, is there? Oh goddamn it, now I've got to get all fouled up with the law. Give me a field, let me walk on it, and I'll tell you what it'll grow. The law . . . it just confuses me.'

'All the same . . . ' I was sympathetic.

He blew down the stem of his pipe. 'Nothing goes right. Now my pipe's stopped up.' He lifted his shoulders in resignation. 'Oh well, better be off, I suppose.' He clicked his fingers. 'Meg.' The collie jumped inside the Range Rover. 'Nice to have met you.'

We watched him drive away. Oliver was motionless until the car disappeared into the distance.

'Oliver?'

'Hmm?'

'What're you thinking?'

'If I was Clive Garner I'd drive like hell, straight to my solicitor. Oh, he's sure to have one. All farmers have to, these days. And there . . . ' He paused, shaking his head and half smiling.

'What is it you're thinking?' I asked again.

He grinned at me. 'Don't tell me you haven't thought of this, too. The inheritance, Phil. Not just the farm but also the whole property. Martin's, he said. It'll all be his. But will it? If Martin's found guilty of murder and is sentenced, he won't be able to claim any inheritance from the person he's killed. You know this, Phil. You must.'

'Shall we get back in the car? It's a long run.' I knew what he was getting at, but I was thinking back. Garner hadn't shown any sign that he knew about this, otherwise he'd have been less concerned. 'I know all about it,' I said, as I pulled out of the lay-by. 'But I don't think Clive Garner did.'

'But he will. If he's Mandy's closest relative, now . . . probably the only one, from the way he was speaking . . . then *he'll* inherit the lot, Towers, parkland, the home farm, the lot.'

'It would save him planting his *Piper nigrum*,' I commented.

'You're not taking it seriously.'

'Is it serious?'

'If he discovers this on his way home, what'll be the point in our going there? It'll suit him to have Martin convicted. So he'll throw every obstacle he can find in our way, just to stop us from discovering anything in Martin's favour. We'd simply be wasting our time.'

'Would we?'

'You know damned well . . . '

Then he was silent for a long while, until at last he spoke quietly. I'd been building up the speed, anxious to get there, to see it.

'No need to hurry, you know,' he said, noticing. 'I thought it might be a good idea to go back to our district, seeing we're heading for Shropshire. You could drop me at Penley, and you carry on to Hawthorne Cottage in Lower Streetly. We need a break. Change of clothes, a bath each, and . . . ' He allowed it to fade away.

'And what?' I knew what he was thinking,

that, away from this district and back in our own, we might take stock, and see this affair with a fresh perspective. From a distance it might all seem paltry and none of our affair, anyway. Our affair *was* ours, between Oliver and myself, our personal affair, which had progressed further than I had anticipated when we came to Hellyspool, and in a direction I hadn't expected.

I glanced at him. He was pensive, and hadn't replied. 'And what?' I repeated.

He turned to me. I caught just a glimpse of his smile, the smile he'd had for me the first time we'd met, when his raised tweed hat had introduced us, and that damned smile of his had been my undoing. Undoing? What am I saying? The wakening of my whole life, that was what it'd been.

'And pick up our life where we'd left it,' he suggested.

'It seems to me it's picked up more than a little, since we left Penley.'

'There're plans I want to discuss, Phil.'

'Not now,' I said, too quickly, because the way I was feeling I would agree to anything he produced. Anything, to be with him. Never to be parted again.

And — creeping into my mind and influenced by this wretched business of Martin — was the realization, which I was trying to reject, that marriage would not be the bond I had assumed. It didn't seem to have bound Martin very much; he'd flung aside the restraints when it suited him. There was also the point that I was now aware that nothing was going to bind Oliver and me closer than we were at that very moment.

That was ironic, when you come to think about it. I'd taken Oliver to this wedding, having had to use every persuasion I could unearth — and the hint of a few mild threats — under the impression that he would find the occasion emotionally persuasive and become enthusiastic about marriage. Damn him that I'd come to this: my actual pleading, if silent and only psychological, for him to marry me. How fatuously unfeminine! How degrading! And the outcome had been nothing but a damper on my aspirations, and a near-surrender to his point of view.

Oh, the temptation to drive away from the situation we found ourselves in for good, to remove both of us from the influence of greed and acquisitiveness!

'You're driving too fast,' he said. 'There's no hurry.'

'Of course there is.' I could hear that I was being short with him, as though I might have been speaking my thoughts aloud. 'We need to get there before him.'

'Do we? I thought we'd decided — '

'He'll go straight to his solicitor. It'll take time. We might be able to use that time to good purpose, before he puts a stop to us. You said that yourself.'

He grunted. 'You mean, before he puts a stop to our efforts to prove Martin innocent? But I don't like the man, Phillie. Martin, I mean. I don't see why we have to put ourselves out for his sake.'

'It's for Heather. She's my friend, Oliver. Silly, ineffectual and childish, but she's still my friend.'

Again he was silent. Questioning somebody, he can come out with queries and demands like a rapid-fire machine gun. Emotional problems take a little longer. Then at last:

'Why don't you marry me, Phillie?' he asked.

I nearly had us in a ditch. 'What! You were digging your heels in . . . '

'Stop the car.'

'No. You say your piece, damn you.'

'You need somebody to keep a short rein on you, Phillie. Somebody to watch over you and tell you where you go wrong. Watch the road, blast it. And I need somebody who'll take not a blind bit of notice, so that life stays as damned interesting as it is now. So watch

276

the road . . . and drive, woman, drive.'

Naturally, I skidded to a halt. 'If you think I'm going to marry you on those terms — '

'State your terms.'

'Oh damn you, Oliver.'

A BMW is not a car in which to embrace — it's too wide. It was not satisfactory. The kiss wasn't. The contract was all right as far as I was concerned, but I was not going to tell him that. Terms! I wasn't going to commit myself to any terms. All or nothing is my motto.

'So now,' he said a little later, 'can we do some motoring? If you feel up to it.'

The word motoring was Martin's. It was different from driving. More purposeful. Oliver didn't seem to realize he'd jolted my thoughts in a direction I didn't want to explore. So I motored — as Martin had taught me. But with more than a little perturbation I realized that, after all, I wasn't doing this for Heather, I was doing it for Martin.

It's all right talking about motoring to Fillingley, but getting there was a different thing. We hadn't many clues, only that it was in Shropshire, and the mileage Heather had done that day. But Shropshire is a sizeable county, and though our own district was also in Shropshire, neither of us had ever heard of

Fillingley. Having regard for Heather's native ability to lose her way, we had to reckon on a trip from Hellyspool as being about 200 miles.

Oliver had to work this out, and make a few guesses, and his eventual decision was that Fillingley had to be to the north of Shropshire, near Whitchurch or Ellesmere, an area that neither of us knew very well. So it was Taunton to the motorway first, then head up the M5 to Worcester, we decided, and take ordinary roads after that, heading a little west of north through Kidderminster to Shrewsbury, then north to Whitchurch. Then we would start asking.

Oliver was very good with the map, tipping me off very neatly as to how many miles it was to the next bypass, the next major junction. He would make a fine navigator, I decided, but had to put a rein on that thought. I really hadn't any intention of going in for rally driving. Or had I?

At Whitchurch we stopped for a break, coffee and a sandwich. Oliver wanted to do some of the driving, but I said we daren't lose his skill as a navigator. He smiled. I didn't dare to guess why. But we had one bit of luck, the purchase of a guidebook to the county. And there it was: Fillingley Towers. Formerly (they were writing about the seventeenth century) the residence of Lord Wilton Crewe, but now much reduced by the spread of the township of Fillingley. *Some of the fine park still remains, in the care of the Tulliver family, whose purchase dates from the Industrial Revolution.*

How very pleasant for one's name to appear in the guidebooks, I thought. But now, with the death of Amanda Reade, née Tulliver, that name would disappear. That family would. The entry would require amendment. *Is now in the care of the Reade family, and comprises an extensive fun park and motor racing track, constructed by Martin Reade.*

'Let's get going,' I said. 'It can't be far now.'

But we had been feeling our way, had several times explored territory that turned out to be of no assistance. Clive Garner would've known the best route. He might at that very moment be sitting in his solicitor's office. Time was running out fast, perhaps had already disappeared.

We found the Towers, though not until after a slight error at the last moment. We had been looking for a lay-by, the one Heather had mentioned. One was there, on our right, and I slowed as Oliver said he'd just spotted a tower through the trees on that side of the road. I had even turned into the entrance of a lane just beyond the lay-by, before I noticed a sign: *Home Farm*. It was nailed to a tree. I backed out. Wrong lay-by, wrong entrance.

About a quarter of a mile further along, there it was, the lay-by where Heather had seen the Fiesta parked. It was just a hundred yards short of what was clearly the imposing entrance to Fillingley Towers, complete with gatehouse.

I drew into the lay-by, and we got out to have a look. There, below us, because the Towers was in a shallow valley, was spread the property. It was completely open, the drive being a bare and straight run of rather decrepit tarmac, perhaps two hundred yards long. And here were the trees Heather had mentioned, but they were by no means a solid barrier. Trees never are, unless dense. There was no more than a thin line, and from the lay-by, Martin — assuming it had really been him — could have seen anything and everything that might have been happening down there, merely by moving sideways, this way and that.

And — come to think about it — I had been stupidly slow in my reasoning, when I'd not questioned Heather more deeply on this. Of *course* he would have been able to see Heather and Mandy in violent conflict.

Heather had clearly assumed that Martin had sent the brooch, however she might have skated around it, therefore she had assumed he'd actually seen it fall. Perhaps the sun had caught a wink of reflection as it fell. But certainly, if it had been Martin — or Jeff as his courier — who had returned the brooch to her, the two women must have been closely observed if the brooch had been recovered from the drive, where Heather had said they'd had their little dispute.

We continued to the gatehouse, drove just inside the gates — still in perfect condition — then stopped, got out, and went back to speak to the occupants.

As Heather had indicated, they were merely tenants, and had no connection with the owners of the Towers. The woman I spoke to recalled nothing unusual about the day I specified. It was her day for shopping in the town, she said, and Mrs Thomas, who was apparently the housekeeper at the Big House, had taken her there in her little car. No — the house was not open to the public. As far as she knew, a lot of the old furniture and fittings had been sold. 'The death duties were something terrible,' she said. She must have meant on the death of Luke Tulliver. 'And now there's another, so I hear. Amanda. That poor woman . . . and so pleasant, so brave.'

'Brave?'

'Her husband left her.'

'Ah yes,' I said, nodding.

'You're not news people?' she asked anxiously and belatedly. 'We've had enough of them around here.'

'No, no,' I assured her. 'Friends.'

She smiled. It was just as well she didn't ask: friends of whom? I'd have been hard pressed to answer.

It did seem, now, that Martin wouldn't be in line for any grand inheritance. Bricks and mortar and a huge responsibility, that was what it would be. Martin wasn't the type to take that on. Oh no. He would be negotiating in no time at all with the National Trust for assistance. And Clive Garner could say goodbye to his peppercorn rent. Martin would ask the earth, now, for the annual rent on the home farm.

I wondered whether Garner realized the full implications. Would he see the possible dissolution of what he'd spent his whole life fighting to preserve?

'You're very thoughtful,' said Oliver, as we drove slowly down the drive.

'Sorry. Yes.'

'Isn't it what you expected?'

'Oh yes. Just as grand, just as imposing.'

As indeed it was, but I had no eyes for it at

the moment. I was looking to right and left, and then I spotted it, a circular sweep, churned into the grass, soft from the recent storms. This was where Heather had said she'd turned the Mercedes. It indicated anger, and it also confirmed part of her story.

Then I had time, drifting the car onwards, to pay more attention ahead. The Towers lay in the valley below us, beyond it a belt of trees, and just visible, to one side of them, the gleam of water, no doubt a stream. We had plenty of time to appreciate the frontage, the pillared, wide porch, the curved sweep of steps up to it, and, as we came closer, the deteriorating paintwork, the crumbling brick-work, the general impression of dilapidation. The front indicated no signs of occupation. Weed clumps were scattered on the approach steps and along the front terrace.

At the bottom of the drive we were offered a choice, swing left across the frontage, or slightly right and then along the side. I chose the right. From what we'd heard, we could hardly expect a frock-coated butler to answer the door bell — if it still worked.

This secondary drive soon terminated. On our right, now, I could see a run-down vegetable garden. Amanda hadn't been dead a week; she must earlier have allowed the gardeners to find other employment. What had been a rose garden, further to the rear, was now a jungle.

I drew to a halt. There was a simple paved yard, and a door set in the wall to our left. The tradesmen's entrance, no doubt.

'What now?' said Oliver.

'We take it as it comes,' I told him, not feeling as optimistic as I sounded.

There was a bell-push. It brought us, after a minute or two, a plump and indignant woman, dressed in black. Mourning. Amanda was missed. This woman blinked at us, bewildered. She'd been having a nap.

'Yes?'

'We're friends of Amanda,' I said, reaching for a lead-in.

'Oh no, you're not. Reporters! You get away. This is private property.'

What I had said had been partly true. We were trying to discover who had killed Mandy. That made us friends, anyway, if posthumously. They had clearly heard, here, that her body had been identified.

She stared at me blankly.

'Friends of Martin Reade,' I tried suggestively.

The door began to close.

'Friends of Mr Garner,' I ventured.

Hesitation. 'He's not here.'

'I know. We were speaking to him earlier

today. He said he would be delayed, but we could have a look round.' I watched her frown. 'Until he gets here.'

'He doesn't live here. He's at the home farm.' She nodded vaguely towards the rear of the house, where I could see no more than the belt of trees. 'There's only me here now.'

I smiled. 'It's a big house for one.'

'I don't pretend I can look after it. Why . . . Miss Amanda, when she was . . . when she was here . . . ' She bit her lip. 'She lived in just two of the rooms.'

'I see,' I said.

'It's nothing but a mausoleum. That's what I say . . . a mausoleum.' She nodded. So there! 'When Mr Luke died . . . Mandy's father . . . that did it. Death duties. Tcha! Robbers. Thieves. Take the bread out of a child's mouth, they would. Poor, dear Amanda. I don't know how she could manage to live through . . . live through . . . Oh dear!'

Then she clamped her hand to her mouth and closed the door on us.

When I'd imagined that revised entry in the guidebooks I'd been fantasizing. But now . . . now, if Martin inherited, that was what it would surely become. A fun park or a safari park. Oh yes, one could imagine Martin making a success of it. And then the home farm . . . he'd have that out of Garner's hands in no time at all, and make it into a racetrack, Formula 3 to start with. And Clive Garner would be offered the job of senior track steward . . . There I went again, my imagination leaping about.

But Garner — if he inherited it — what would *he* do? Plough it all up, including the house? Leave perhaps one tower standing, and call it a folly?

Oliver said, 'That seems to leave us a free hand,' and I took a second or two to understand what he meant.

'Yes,' I agreed. 'Let's have a look around.' But somehow the heart had gone out of it.

There seemed to be nothing to stop us wandering about. What was there to steal? We strolled to the end of the building, stood there, and admired the view.

There was a long terrace across the rear, with pots and urns that ought to have had something growing in them and didn't, apart from straggly weeds. The row of windows, some of them opening on to the terrace, could have done with a cleaning. Faced with that task, I'd have walked away. Steps ran down to an extensive lawn. Perhaps it had been possible, at one time, to play croquet on it. Now, you could do little of interest there, apart from going on a safari, machete in hand. Beyond this, beyond the sagging tool shed in one corner, was the row of trees we had seen from the gatehouse. Stout oaks, were these trees. These alone had stood the test of time.

We took the narrow path beside the lawn and headed for the trees. They were further away than they'd seemed, and thicker. It was not a row, but a small wood. But beaten paths guided us, slightly upwards, to the peak of a low hill. There the trees ended, and we came across a fence with a stile in it. On this we sat, side by side, resting. There was a deep silence, which seemed to have width and depth, a huge black hole of silence that stretched out in all directions, a thick silence that demanded concentration to confirm that your hearing hadn't failed. But then, almost as though the landscape had been waiting for us to settle tranquilly, the air came alive with sound, birdsong, the caws of crows, the soft rustle of a breeze in the trees behind us. And, projecting the hearing forward, it seemed that the rustling came from ahead, from the shimmering of an apparently limitless expanse of mature barley, still green, but waiting impatiently for the gold of the sun. I realized I could watch pockets of breeze playing with the barley, see them gather themselves to chase across the expanse, like sea waves, dark and then flickering bright.

Between us and this delight, which almost demanded that I should rush hysterically into that elusive sway and rustle of barley, was, fortunately for my dignity and common sense, the brook we had seen from the distance. Almost opposite us and to our left there was an old water mill.

It was built this side of the brook, but the water wheel was sited on our side. Clearly, a long time ago, a channel must have been cut to divert the fall of the water around the mill, using sluice gates. The building itself was built almost into a hillside on the far side, as a wooden chute projected, high from this hillside, to channel the water to the top of the wheel. It was an overshot mill, which I would have thought to be rare in this country.

But now no water fell from this channel. Perhaps a trickle when there'd been a storm in the hills, but now the diverting channel would be blocked off, as would be the channel that had directed the water back to the stream, lower down. The wheel was disintegrating, few of its paddles left. The mill itself stood firm, but had been built of overlap pine, and a lot of this had rotted away. The roof was an unusual design for this country, having two slopes, like a Dutch roof. It had been slated. How close they had been to the Welsh slate quarries! But a lot of these had fallen free, exposing naked black slats and beams.

Due possibly to the slope against which it rested, it seemed that the building was leaning. I got down from the stile and walked closer, along the line of the stream, to confirm this. The path was beaten out of the earth by foot traffic, but, there having been little of this lately, was rapidly becoming overgrown with nettles and giant docks. I had to place my feet carefully, keeping my exposed ankles clear of the nettles.

Behind me, Oliver said, 'That must be the farmhouse, over there.'

I stopped, and looked where he was pointing. It was a red and fawn toy house, sitting above the barley, way up on the far slope.

'Watch your step,' he warned, as a slip would have sent me down the slope towards the stream, where the weeds were a wild and tight tangle.

But I was already clear of the worst, as the surface now opened out as a flat and smoother expanse, from which an insecure set of wooden steps, with only one sagging handrail, led up beyond the wheel to an open doorway on the upper floor. It seemed there had never been a door. The opening was complete in itself.

'However did they get the stuff here?' he asked. 'The wheat or whatever in, and the grain out?'

From where I was standing I could see further past the mill than he could. 'There's a sort of track, heading away towards the farmhouse.'

From behind me, he suggested, 'Shall we go and look inside? While we're here. If those steps are safe, that is. Come on, Phil, don't just stand there.'

But I didn't dare to move. That was what I felt. There was something elusive, nudging at my senses. It seemed that if I moved I would lose it and never retrieve it.

'Oliver . . . ' I whispered.

His voice was abruptly tense. 'What is it?'

'Come along a bit closer.'

He did that. Right behind me.

'Stand still, and what . . . '

But he had it. 'That smell! Oh good Lord, *that* smell.'

Slowly now we moved on, cautiously so that we wouldn't lose track of it. The smell of decay and of putrefaction — it was there. We moved on until the source became visible almost at our feet.

Below the wheel — in fact, a small section of it lived in the water — there had formed a pool, fed by the stream from a tiny leak of water that filtered past the barriers. The pool was some ten feet by eight. We knew that smell. Perhaps other stagnant pools smelt as revolting, but logic indicated there ought to be a difference, depending on the origin of the rotting leaves and seeds that fed it. This one had its own specific smell, yet with a sweetness behind the basic tang, which seemed only to sicken the stomach rather than alleviate the impact of the basic background pungency.

Oliver bent and picked up a stone. The surface, still and placid like a green carpet, was three feet below us. He tossed his stone into the middle. It made a round black hole in the centre, as the algae oozed away from the disturbance. In the murky darkness below it we could detect a lazy waving of weed, awakened, resenting it. And slowly the hole closed up again. The oily ripples died. The surface was still.

And it had flung its smell at us in defiance, a sudden blast that almost had me recoiling.

'This was where she died,' said Oliver hollowly. 'Or rather, this was where she went into the water, clothes and all.'

I couldn't answer. I was fighting a nausea that had me retching. Then his hand was on my elbow.

'Let's get out of here,' he said.

I wanted to cry out, 'Don't let go of me, Oliver!' But it would have come out as a cry of horror and fear. For a moment I stood, swaying I think, then I managed to take a deep breath, turning my head away, not wanting any tiniest part of that pool inside my lungs, and forced myself to say, 'No. We've got to see inside. Got to. Now we're here.'

He said, 'Damn you for a stubborn female.'

13

From this side of the building there was no way in except the uncertain outside staircase. The alternative would have been to leap the stream, but it was too wide, swollen by the recent storms. I eyed the staircase with uncertainty. It was too close to the pool for my liking.

'I'll go first,' said Oliver, although the rail was on the side of his bad arm. 'If it'll take my weight, it'll take yours.' He smiled at my expression. 'And if it collapses, you can fish me out of the pool.'

'I wouldn't be able to force myself into taking your hand.'

He twisted his mouth at me and began to climb the stairs, taking each step with care. I watched critically. They seemed firm enough; they didn't rock and they didn't creak. He reached the top, turned, and waved.

'It's all right. Come on up. The handrail's not too good, though.'

I went up with hesitant legs, yet Oliver had been quite correct. He had gone inside, so confident he'd been.

The light was poor, from two small

windows, one overlooking the pool, one in the wall opposite. Neither showed any indication of ever having possessed a frame. Perhaps any windows had been fastened to the surrounding woodwork. Now they were blankly open to the air, and unfortunately part of that air rose from the pool. But the smell was now different. A dank odour of rotting wood had joined it.

There were half a dozen stairs down to the floor surface, here. The rafters were close to our heads. Once again, Oliver led. These stairs were firmer, having had some degree of protection from the weather, though I could see clouds sliding past lazily in a weak blue sky, where slates were missing.

It was here that the shafting from the great wheel entered horizontally, low down towards the floor, one straight shaft of oak six inches square, where it was slotted into a small wheel, and pegged. The small wheel meshed into the protruding pegs of an eight-foot horizontal wheel, wood again, but made up of shaped pieces, in the centre of which another squared oak shaft, even heftier, led down through the floor.

It was all in wood. How many centuries ago had men fashioned this mechanism, tenderly and painstakingly, to handle the chilling power of the overshot wheel? What secrets of seasoning had preserved the wood until now?

I found it awesome and at the same time frightening. Powerful mechanisms have always held an hypnotic power over me. Their immensity overcame me, until it became an effort not to go too near, not to reach or lean over, in a psychological urge to become part of that massive force, to become involved in menace. Even now, with the wheel still and silent for so long, I dared not go too close.

Against a side wall there was a bench, which must have held the rudimentary tools that were necessary to keep this machinery operating. Now, on its surface, there were scattered several more-modern tools, wood-working equipment in the form of a handsaw and a cross-cut saw, a plane (but a wooden one, not the modern metal ones), chisels, a mallet, and a couple of heavyweight spanners. Spanners? But surely, spanners were for metal fastenings, for nuts. Nothing but the bearings were metal here, and they appeared to have been shrunk on to the shafts, probably red-hot, like a steel tyre on a cart-wheel. They were all rusted solid, now.

Oliver was leaning out of one of the windows. He had seen all that I had, but in one sweeping glance. But he would not have been awed by the wheels, as I was. Sometimes

I envied him this lack of imagination.

I say leaning, but the opening was barely wide enough for his shoulders. He said, almost pensively, 'Come and look at this, Phil.'

I had not the slightest desire to do so. The mill was beginning to exert its influence on my mind. I felt uneasy and insecure. But I went to see what he meant.

Taking his place, I risked a quick look. The sill, if there had been a sill, came barely above my knees, the top of the opening just above my head.

The pool was directly below me. As I watched, something stirred, down inside it, perhaps a pocket of gas. The surface moved like treacle, parting to emit a bubble, which collapsed rather than burst. The ripples sluggishly rolled away.

Then, from somewhere deep down, disturbed by the bubble or perhaps the cause of it, there floated to the surface — or just below the surface, because there was no definite outline detectable — a shape that I recognized. It held a glow of colour. Red perhaps. It had the shape of a shoe, a woman's shoe, with a heel strap. It turned lazily and sluggishly, kicked the wedge heel at me, and then, as though called from below by a higher power, sank down into the oily darkness, and silently the algae collected together and closed in, sealing it off for ever.

I drew back. Perhaps I made a sound, because Oliver said, 'It's all right, you know.'

But it wasn't. I wanted to scream out at him, but no sound came. My throat seemed to be closed, obstructed. I felt sick. I wanted to get out of there.

'It was here that Mandy died,' he said quietly, in his official voice. So damned practical, he was! I had difficulty restraining myself from kicking his ankle. 'It's obvious. Did you notice the tools, Phil? Two adjustable spanners amongst them. Perhaps there were originally three.'

He crossed to the bench, just when I needed him to be leant against.

'What the devil would anybody want with spanners, in here?' he wondered. 'There's nothing metal around.'

'Only the bearings, so far,' put in a new voice. 'I haven't made up my mind yet.'

My nerves were in no condition to stand this form of treatment. I felt my cheeks tighten as the blood ran from them.

Clive Garner stood there. I glanced at Oliver, who was peering through the window opening opposite. He nodded to me slightly — yes. The Range Rover was there, outside.

Garner had brought it down from his farm. He would have coasted down, in order to surprise us. He had succeeded. I had just shed a year of my life, and was desperately clinging to my stomach contents.

But he seemed quite relaxed and amiable. 'I saw your BMW round at the front,' he explained. 'I knew you'd want to have a look at my mill. Everybody does. Isn't it wonderful . . . beautiful?'

I wouldn't have used exactly that description. He saw that in my expression.

'Ah!' he said. 'But wait until I've got it all done. All my life I've wanted to restore it to its original condition. When I was a lad I used to come down here and sit and look at it, and stand in here — or go down to the lower floor and stare at the millstones. Eight feet across! Would you believe! Massive. It's the great power involved that fascinated me. But it's all wood, you see, and I'm a metal worker. You have to be, on a farm, or lay out a fortune to the pros. I can weld and I can grind, and turn a shaft on a lathe, and forge. But with wood I'm hopeless. Isn't that a terrible admission? It isn't hard enough, you see. You've gone too far before you know where you are. Have you been down below? The millstones are well worth seeing.'

'We haven't been down, no.' I said this

hollowly. I didn't want to see his damned millstones.

He came and walked past me, and peered out of the window space. 'I want to clear that pool, but I can't till the paddle wheel's operative. That's the first task. Get the small gear off here, so that the main shaft will revolve, and then get the paddle wheel turning. Think of that! There's a waterfall the other side. All it needs is the old diverting channels clearing out. But I daren't. The paddle wheel's got to be done first. And how the hell am I going to get *that* off? It'd take a dozen of us. Fifty, perhaps.'

'You've surely got enough friends.' I managed to say this with confidence.

'Certainly. They'd pour in from the village — everybody. They'd want to see it being done. It's the local treasure, this mill.'

'Then do it,' I said. 'Don't think about it . . . but I'd drain that pool to start with.'

He glanced at Oliver. 'Is she always like this?' he asked. It was a polite question; perhaps he really wanted to know.

'Very determined,' Oliver told him gravely.

'If there's a problem,' I said, trying to justify my determination, 'it doesn't go away if you stand and look at it.'

'There's philosophy for you,' said Garner, smiling that slow and easy smile of his, but with something cold about the look in his eyes.

In some ways he was very like Martin. They both cherished an obsession. But Martin had not spoken to me with an underlying mocking tone to his voice. He hadn't at any time condescended, as Garner was now doing. Because I was a woman? To Martin, a woman was a special type of person, possibly to be seduced. To Clive Garner, a woman was an inferior being.

He came to stand beside me, to look out of the window opening, as though checking the feasibility of my suggestion to drain the pool first. Now I had an explanation of the impression I'd received when he first entered the mill. I'd seen no cedar in this building, and yet he seemed to have brought it with him. Closer now, I realized it was his aftershave, or even a body spray.

It was the same smell I had felt wafted at me when Oliver had lifted the sheet from Mandy's dead body.

I knew, then — knew as opposed to suspected — that Garner was the one who had taken Mandy's body from that pool, had stripped her and cleansed her . . . heavens, how had he done that? Had he laid her in the yard at his farm and hosed her down, with the casual lack of emotion he would use when

300

hosing down his Range Rover? Had he then sprayed her with his own body spray — a sentimental gesture? Internally, I shuddered. Now I knew it was he who had taken that stripped body to Hellyspool and left it in Martin's bed, and had taken along with him the spanner that had killed her. I knew that. I could accuse him of it right there and then, and he would treat the accusation with the same smiling condescension he'd been aiming at me all the while. He would say: so what? I could tell him so what — that it was a legal offence to remove a body from its place of demise. That's what.

Yet he would do no more than laugh at me. It was also a legal offence, and a personal one, to leave a dead body in his pool.

And none of it had any backing of proof. It was a feeling, because it fitted the background facts. It was as elusive as the scent.

Oliver must have realized what I was thinking. I glanced at him, and slowly he shook his head. It would get us . . . where . . . if I made this accusation? It would assist Martin . . . how? It was possible to explain how the body came to be in his bed; it wouldn't in any way cover the question of who had killed her. Martin had had the opportunity to do that, because he had been in this area at the right time. And so, come to think of it, had Garner himself. And the motive, too, Garner had had that, if he'd known earlier than he'd implied what the result could mean to himself.

In order to think this out I'd turned away, so that Garner might not guess my thoughts. I had even peered out over the pool. It took only seconds. It seemed that Garner continued speaking without a break.

'Mandy was very like you,' he was saying. 'Not to look at, oh no. But she was philosophical, too. And full of determination. A little firecracker, she was.'

'Philosophical?' I asked, picking it up. Something to say, something casual.

He shrugged. 'She was always saying it would work out. Something would come along. Nobody could've guessed it would be her death.'

'But it worked it out, didn't it?'

He frowned, not understanding, or pretending not to, and slid away from it. 'We used to meet here, Mandy and me, when she was a kid and me in my twenties. She loved the mill too. She used to say, 'You'll have to get it working, Clive. Have to.' That's why it's even more important now. In her memory.'

He didn't seem so emotionally vulnerable, that he should carry his mourning to the extent of erecting a monument to her — this mill. And yet . . . the cedar body spray!

I said, 'It'll cost money. A lot of it. You must realize that.'

He shrugged. 'Money . . .'

'You've seen your solicitor,' I stated. There could be no question of it.

'Oh yes. Thank you for your advice,' he said to Oliver, turning. 'I'm very clear on the situation now. If Martin goes to prison, I'll inherit it all. As simple as that. Am I supposed to cheer, when it arises from Mandy's death? No!' Then he spoilt the noble sentiment by saying, 'I'd inherit a headache, anyway. The Towers is a millstone already, and Mandy couldn't keep it up. Perhaps we can rent it to some grand international corporation, as their headquarters. Very impressive to the visiting executives, that'd be. Or so my solicitor says.'

'You're anticipating things a little,' I pointed out.

'Seems pretty certain to me. Martin was seen here, you know, on the day before that farce of a wedding. Hanging around with that car of his. What's the odds he'd heard that Mandy had found out about the wedding? It's possible. There was another suspicious character — sounded like a private eye to me — who came to see Mandy, weeks back, now. Mrs Thomas at the Big House told me. What say Martin heard something from him? Then he came to see Mandy, to try to stop her interfering with his plans. That sounds likely to me. And Mandy — what a thing to ask her! She'd be there at the wedding like a shot. So what could he do about that? He'd have to keep her silent, somehow, if she went there.'

It was just what he would say if he hadn't known she'd died here, and fallen in the pool outside. It was just what he would say . . . if he *had*. It was also the sort of thing I'd have expected him to say in a voice full of sorrow, and a catch in his throat. He had delivered it in a flat voice, and only the clenching of one fist betrayed any emotion.

'They used to do their courting here,' he said blandly. 'Mandy and Martin.' He made no emotional issue of this, either, when it must have been disturbing to him. He was a man who hid his emotions deeply, and he didn't seem to realize that he was implying they had met in the mill — here — on that day before the wedding. Their meeting place, it'd been.

'Not the atmosphere, I'd have said, for courting.' I was looking around, trying to imagine it.

'For Mandy it was,' he assured me. 'It was a romantic place to her. She said the years were in the wood, and the stream of life was in the millstones. Strange thing to say. I never could understand half she said.'

Well, of course he wouldn't. But it helped me to understand Mandy. Nobody but a wild and dedicated romantic would cherish the memory of a strayed husband as long as she had. Nobody but an emotional and perceptive woman would have recognized any worth in Martin, and treasure it like a gold nugget found in an apparently barren mine. And if that made me the same, damn it I'd be proud to admit it.

'Yes,' I agreed absent-mindedly. I was now trying to maintain a conversation whilst my mind was elsewhere. It had been a romantic place to Mandy. It was to this mill she would no doubt have retreated if she was disturbed and upset. It would calm her. It was to this mill she would have come after the encounter with Heather.

And here she had died? To her had come Martin? Or . . . Clive Garner? Or somebody . . .

Suddenly I felt cold. It seemed that the sun shunned this tiny, historical spot, and that the shadows lingered in order to cast it in the cool of their shade . . . until the next cloud could take over. It was a cold and miserable place. A place of evil.

'Would you like to come up to the farm?'

Garner asked. 'A cup of tea and a slice of cake.' Then abruptly the smile was shy and self-mocking. 'I do my own cooking and baking.'

'Thank you, but no,' said Oliver. 'I really think we ought to be leaving, Phil.'

'Oh yes.' I glanced at my watch. 'We really must.'

'What a pity.' Garner seemed amused. 'Some other time, perhaps.'

'We'll look forward to it,' I assured him.

He stood aside politely. 'It's much better to go out from the milling floor,' he told us. 'Safer. Here . . . may I lead?'

We followed him down a fixed ladder, through a hole in the floor, down to where it was so heavily shaded that I could barely detect the millstones. But I had my glimpse of them. They would rumble and shudder as the top one rotated. I didn't want to be there when it did.

He took us out into the sunlight, through a wide doorway opening. There, his Rover was waiting. 'There's a safer path this side,' he explained. 'You'll come to a foot-bridge over the stream — only two planks but they're very firm. There's a stile right opposite. Then back the way you came, through the trees.'

We thanked him. He stood and watched us walk away, feet apart, firmly planted on his land. I didn't turn to look back until we came to the bridge. He was just getting into his Range Rover. I didn't wave.

Because we were returning through the trees on a different path from the one we'd used before, our first sight of the Big House was from a different angle, so that I became aware that we were facing, adjoining the house, the rear of a line of stables. They would surely now be garages. I had not noticed them when we'd gone to Mrs Thomas's door. I could see her kitchen window. I could just detect a pale face behind the glass. She would be worried as to our activities. I decided to give her something more to occupy her mind.

'We'd better look at the stables,' I suggested.

'Oh . . . why?' Oliver seemed eager to get away.

'When he spotted us, on our way to the mill, probably sitting on that stile, he needn't have used his Range Rover to get to the mill from his farmhouse. What's your mental image of a farmer, Oliver? I'll tell you mine. It's of a man walking, with one thumb hooked in his belt, the other gripping a knobbly stick, and with a collie at his side. But no — he'd driven down to the mill. He's been pushing that clean and innocent Range

307

Rover under our noses, Oliver. I believe we ought to look for a non-clean and guilty one. Don't you think?'

'Phil — you're the limit! You suspect everything and everybody.'

But I was leading him towards the garages. 'Somebody tried to force me off the road.'

'Or Heather, or Martin.'

'Force somebody off the road, then. It wasn't imagination, Oliver.'

'I'm sure it wasn't. And you're remembering that Mandy's father possibly died in the same way.'

'You're a mind-reader. Shall we start at this end?' It was the end closest to the drive; it was logical.

There had been stabling for fourteen horses. The stables had been converted into seven garages, giving plenty of available space. Each had double wooden doors with hasp fastenings, and not one had a padlock for its hasp. That would have been superfluous, out here in the placid country and far from the mayhem of the cities. But murder spreads to remote places, in the same way as its motivations hide in remote corners of minds.

In the first garage there was a Ford Sierra. Mandy's, most likely. It seemed to confirm that she had not driven herself to Hellyspool, but had been taken. In the second, seeming lonely and lost in all that space, there was a battered Citroën 2CV. Probably the house-keeper's. In the next, nothing. In the fourth, fifth and sixth . . . nothing. In the seventh, a Range Rover.

I had been aware that Mrs Thomas had come out of her lair to watch us. Slowly she was following our progress, seeming to be nervous of us, this perhaps generated by our confident behaviour. I *had* been confident.

'Is this it?' asked Oliver.

I didn't reply. It had the same muddy appearance of the one I had encountered. I ought to know; I'd been six inches from it. But mud is part of a Range Rover's uniform. They ought to send them out from the factory pre-muddied. So it meant nothing.

As it was parked nose-in, I had to walk round it. The front bumper was a mere foot from the rear wall, and it was dark back there. It was necessary to lean over and look carefully. And yes, there were marks of white paint. Tiny bits of wood were caught in indentations. It was *the* vehicle. It was the car that'd nearly killed me. But I'd not been the target. Martin must surely have been the intended victim. Logically, it should have been Martin at the wheel of the Merc.

That had to mean that Clive Garner had

been behind the wheel of this Range Rover. If he hadn't been driving such a vehicle, he might well have died himself, and I couldn't help but wonder whether, in the last split second, he had recognized Martin behind the wheel of the BMW heading directly at him. But it had to mean that Garner had realized that Martin's death would have left him, Garner, as the owner of . . . everything. And all this without the benefit of a solicitor.

I stood back from it, viewing its rear. The image of this was imprinted on my mind, the Merc's nose having been nearly under that blank and uncompromising back end. Range Rovers acquire their individual stickers and decorations. This vehicle it was.

And during this inspection my mind was carrying it along. It was a natural progression. From the thought that Garner must have known the legal effect of Martin's death, it was possible to believe — if not be certain — that Garner would equally understand the effect if Martin were to be tried for murder and found guilty. To ensure this, he had taken Mandy's body, possibly in the vehicle I was staring at, to the place where her death would implicate Martin. That he'd found the perfect place, Martin's empty bed, had been sheer luck.

But why had he thought it necessary to go

to such lengths? If Martin had been seen in this district, and wished to see Mandy, it would be assumed that the mill was the place for such a meeting between these two, especially if Martin had seen Heather disputing with Mandy. So . . . if Mandy was dead and in that terrible pool, there would have been no point in Garner doing anything other than phone the police.

'Phil . . .' Oliver was wondering why I was standing there, staring. But the express train of my thoughts wouldn't stop and let me alight. I didn't dare to do anything but travel with it.

So why hadn't Garner left Mandy in the pool? The case would still have been solid against Martin. But perhaps Garner hadn't wanted her to be found there. It could allow suspicion to ooze sideways and involve others, maybe even himself . . . even an anonymous woman who'd been seen arguing on the drive with Mandy. He would know Heather now; he wouldn't have known her then. She was just a woman who might have become involved, and perhaps some element of chivalry had entered into it. Garner was the old-fashioned type, rooted as he was in the tradition of his land. He would want to keep her out of it. And keep Martin well in it. So Mandy's body had to be where it belonged — with Martin.

'Phil . . . Mrs Thomas . . . '

I turned. Had I been standing there for ages, or had it been only a few seconds? I turned, smiling. It was an effort to produce that smile.

'If you're thinking of buying it,' said Mrs Thomas, 'I don't think it's for sale. It's all very complicated . . . ' She stopped, lost and confused. Her own life was in a turmoil.

'No,' I said. 'We're not really thinking of that. It's just that I thought I recognized it. Seen it somewhere.'

'Oh no, you couldn't have. It won't go. I'm sure it won't, not after all this time.'

It had been going very well when it'd overtaken a Saab, a BMW and a Mercedes.

Oliver said, 'The engine ought to be turned over every now and then, if they're left standing. How long has it been here — like this?'

He was merely seeking confirmation that it was *the* Range Rover. But Mrs Thomas wouldn't be able to say much. The grounds were so extensive that there had to be other ways out that were beyond her observation.

'Oh . . . years,' she said, blinking at the effort of remembering. 'Must be ten.'

I glanced at the registration. Yes, the letter

indicated it was twelve or thirteen years old.

'Since Mr Luke died,' said Mrs Thomas sadly.

'He was driving this when he had his accident?' I asked.

'Oh no. No, no.' She was shaking her head violently. 'That was a . . . a . . . I can't remember what they called it. Not worth saving.'

'A write-off?' Oliver suggested, taking it gently, smiling at her as though this was of only vague interest.

'Yes,' she said. 'That was it. A Vauxhall, it was. I don't know what sort . . . ' She stared at her feet miserably. It wasn't the exact model she didn't know. There was something she didn't want to remember.

'Then how did the Range Rover . . . ' I knew I had to do no more than prompt her.

'It was Miss Amanda,' said the woman miserably. The memory had been trapped in her mind for nearly ten years. It struggled to get free. 'She took this one out. Mr Luke had gone off to see an agent or somebody at Llanrhaeadr, or somewhere like that. He'd forgotten his cheque book, Mandy said. She went after him in this one. But they'd been having a row. Oh . . . it was always rows, rows, rows. Over that Martin, I'd bet. He'd been gone two months then. But I knew Mr Luke. He hated upsets. If you ask me, all he was doing was getting away from Mandy. But she went after him. She told me later he tried to . . . to lose her. Is that right?'

I nodded. 'Lose. Yes, that's right.'

'And he went too fast. I was told when I was young never to drive when you're angry. I've always held by that. It's so true. He . . . he did a turn too fast and went down a hillside full of trees, and it was all mangled up and him dead in it. She came back hours later, still as white as a sheet. She put that car where it is now, and she never went near it again.'

I had been engaging her attention, nodding, smiling, while Oliver slid quietly down the near side of the Range Rover.

'How terrible for her,' I said sympathetically. 'I can't imagine *anybody* would want to drive it again.'

'But if you did want to . . . ' Mrs Thomas had realized that this would be part of the estate, and that her own future might depend on the financial outcome. 'If you *were* interested, I'm sure it *would* go. Mr Clive comes down from the farm now and then and turns it over, as your friend said. Charges the battery — that sort of thing.'

'Oh,' I assured her, 'I'm quite certain it will go.'

We said our goodbyes. We omitted to explain why we had come here. Let her assume we were considering buying the whole caboodle. We strolled round to the front, when I ached to hurry. I allowed Oliver to slide behind the steering wheel. You shouldn't drive when you're angry, Mrs Thomas had said. I was angry, I was miserable. I wanted to cry.

'There were abrasion marks along the near side,' Oliver observed quietly. 'Towards the rear. There hadn't been any attempt to retouch them.'

'For God's sake!' I cried out. 'I didn't need that.'

He started the car. We drove sedately from the drive and headed back the way we had come. We'd covered two miles before I was able to touch his arm and murmur, 'Sorry, Oliver.'

'It's all right. I felt the same myself. Home? Do we head home? It's not far from here.' He said this hopefully.

'Find a café, Oliver,' I said, sighing. 'I need a cup of tea. I need to think.'

'Yes.'

'And I need to find a phone.'

'What for?'

'To get Rupert Anderson, if I can. He might have the answers to my questions by now.'

There was a long pause. 'Let's do that,' he agreed at last. But he was far from happy about it.

14

It was nearly five o'clock when we found a café. Oliver stopped the car outside on the road and eyed it dubiously.

It was a log cabin affair, up on a rise from the road, with lead-in and lead-out drives each end, both quite steep. There was an extensive parking area, seeming too large for such a small café, and it was packed with motor vehicles. Where were all the passengers? They certainly couldn't all have been inside, not without the walls collapsing outwards.

The answer came when Oliver drove up to it and found a parking slot. As we walked back to the café steps, I saw the National Trust sign. There were signposts pointing up three separate paths through the trees, which clothed the hillside beyond. It was a walkers' paradise. The signs indicated that the Ramblers' Association had erected them.

Consequently, we were the only customers. The facilities were geared to the certainty that the hikers would descend on them, ravenous, at about sunset. At this time the fare was slim. We could have baked beans on toast or poached eggs on toast. We ordered, each, baked beans and poached eggs on two pieces of toast, ice cream to follow.

'There was a phone in the lobby,' I said, as we waited.

'Eat first, phone afterwards,' said Oliver practically.

It was sensible. I contained my impatience, and we ate. Then, having paid, I asked, 'How much change have we got?'

We put it together. It would suffice, I hoped. I dialled Rupert's office from memory. But he could well have left for home. I realized we ought to have done this before eating.

I was lucky. He'd been just about to leave. His secretary had already done so, it seemed, because it was he who answered.

'It's Philipa Lowe,' I told him.

I thought he sighed. His voice conveyed a deep weariness. 'Ah!' he said. it was close to a groan.

'Have you seen him?'

'I have. I've been there most of the day.'

'And did you ask him my questions?'

'Where are you?' he asked.

'We've been to Fillingley Towers, and we're on our way back. Asking around . . . you know.'

'Then I wish you'd waited. There're

questions you might have asked while you were there.'

I pounced on that. It implied that there was uncertainty, that the case against Martin was not yet solidly based.

'Ask them later then, Rupert,' I said, feeling I might use his Christian name. 'It's possible we might be able to supply the answers.'

'Very well. We'll see. I asked him about having taken his friend's Fiesta out earlier in the day. He didn't hesitate. Oh yes, he said. He went out about ten in the morning. This is the day before the wedding.'

'Understood. And he went where?'

'To Fillingley Towers. He made no attempts to hide that fact.'

'Did he say why he went?'

'Oh yes. He wanted to see his wife — Amanda. Or rather, she'd phoned him. No . . . don't trouble to ask me. A man had been to see her, and told her about the forthcoming wedding. He'd given her Martin's number, the phone in his pre-fab.'

I hadn't noticed a phone there. 'He was quite open about this?'

'He's a beaten man, Miss Lowe. Very down and very low. Weary. He didn't make any effort to work round the point, evade, or try self-justification. He just told me what I'm certain was the truth.'

Martin bowed and beaten I found difficult to imagine. I had trouble in speaking for a moment.

'Did he tell you what he did there?'

Rupert hesitated. I heard him take a deep breath. 'He stood in a lay-by and looked out at the house. I can understand that, but I don't want it to get to Heather. I believe he still felt something for that woman — Amanda. I believe he still wanted her. Deep down . . . underneath. But he was uncertain of what to do. If their feelings had been mutual, perhaps, that day, he would not have returned to Heather. But if not . . . if Amanda simply wanted to see him in order to tell him how much she hated him, and to tell him she intended to stop this ceremony going through . . . he just didn't know what he would do.'

'And what *did* he do?'

'He got back in the car and drove away. He didn't even speak to her.'

'He explained all this — why he didn't go to the house?'

He cleared his throat. 'Not in so many words. I've had to put it all together and fill in a few gaps.'

'So he never actually spoke to her?'

'Haven't I already said that?' he asked wearily.

'Sorry. But do you realize that this only

makes it worse for him?'

'I'm not a fool, Miss Lowe.'

'Sorry.'

'We're all tired. Yes, it makes it worse. Even if he didn't see her, she would still, probably, have made an attempt to see him at Hellyspool. Later in the day.'

'But she didn't,' I told him with confidence.

'Are you sure of that?' His voice held slightly more interest.

'Her car's in the garage here.'

'Ah. Yes. Umm!' He brightened. 'That, perhaps, helps him a little.'

'It doesn't, I assure you. No . . . please listen, Rupert. I'm not arguing. There's something we've found out. Amanda didn't die at Hellyspool. We've found where she died. We have evidence that links up, and almost makes it certain. She died at an old water-mill in the grounds of the Towers. She then fell — or was pushed — into a stagnant pool there. That's why she was stripped of her clothes and washed — '

'Washed!'

'Yes. It was a very smelly pool. It would've been necessary to hide the location of the place where she met her death. And it was necessary that her death should be linked with Martin. So her body was brought to

Hellyspool, and dumped on him. Maliciously.' Wrong word, Philipa, I told myself. For gain. For gain.

'Good Lord! But he's said nothing to me . . . not mentioned any such possibility.'

I sighed. Oliver had been listening at the lifted ear-piece and feeding in money. We were running short. 'I'm nearly out of change, Rupert.'

'Wait! Your number?'

I told him, just as we lost the connection. I hung up, and we waited.

Oliver said, 'I'd have expected Martin to deny he'd been anywhere near the Towers.'

'And he doesn't seem to have mentioned having seen the Merc.'

'Perhaps he didn't know whose it was.'

'He didn't at that time. Later, he would've recognized it in Heather's drive. It's a brand new model. He knows cars.'

The phone rang, and I snatched for it. 'Tell me more,' said Rupert, who'd had a minute or two to ponder on it.

So I told him the lot, how Martin had been seen in the district, and why I was convinced that Clive Garner had found her body in the pool, and how he must have taken her clean and washed body to Hellyspool. No, I told him, I hadn't questioned Garner on this — I was just certain. In the same way, I was certain that Martin had seen Amanda's struggle with Heather, had seen the brooch fall — it would glitter in the sunlight — and had, whatever he said, entered the grounds in order to retrieve it.

'What!' said Rupert.

'What!' said Oliver.

I groaned. 'Do let me say it. He would naturally go and pick it up for her. And later, when he knew it might be difficult for Heather if she ever had to admit she'd even been there, he would get it back to her.'

'He had no opportunity,' put in Oliver.

'Who's that with you?' demanded Rupert.

'It's only my friend, Oliver.' Oliver put a finger in my ribs. 'It's all right, Rupert. Listen. Isn't this all useful to Martin, at the very least? Have you managed to arrange bail for him?'

'No, I haven't. I'm going back there now. I may be able to use some of this. The brooch — it matters. How could Martin have got it back to her? I understand it turned up on the table in the hall.'

'Yes,' I agreed. 'But just ask around. The village is full of his friends. I'll bet Jeff Carter would do anything for him.'

'I have no intention of asking around, I assure you.'

'Then I will.'

'You do so, then. In the meantime . . . they wouldn't allow bail because they thought they had a good case. I'll take these facts — bare as they are — to Martin, and if his answers are satisfactory . . . why, it would open up the case splendidly. There'd have to be an investigation at the Fillingley end, so keep your fingers crossed.'

'I will,' I assured him. 'But Rupert — why are you so keen to see him free?' This was a personal question. I tried to slip an impersonal note into my voice, not too successfully, it seemed.

'He's my client,' he said sharply.

'But I felt your heart wasn't in it.'

There was a moment of silence, then, quietly, 'I'm thinking of Heather.'

'Well, of course,' I said heartily. 'Oh . . . one more thing.'

'Not more!'

'One little point. If Martin got back in time for his stag party, having driven the Fiesta all day . . . why would he take the Fiesta out again later, after the party, half drunk and dead beat? *That's* a snag, Rupert. It affects his alibi. He'd have to justify it.'

'Strangely enough,' he said acidly, 'I've worked that out myself. He told me that he'd flogged it, by which I assume he meant driven it hard.'

'Motored,' I murmured. 'Martin calls it motoring.'

'If you so wish.' He was cool. He was tired of my persistence. 'I asked him that exact question. He told me he'd pushed it hard, and it'd run off-tune. Engine rough, was the way he put it. He took the tappet cover off — I am using his words — and adjusted the gaps. *Then* he took it out again, to make sure.'

'He must have been near-exhausted, by that time.'

'He was. That was why he drew into that lay-by. To rest. He simply fell asleep. Frankly, that didn't really convince me.'

'Thank you.'

He hung up abruptly, before I thought up any more questions. But I wasn't going to question that last little detail. I could believe it unreservedly. It sounded just what Martin would do. He'd promised his friend to tune his car, so that was what he would produce, a perfectly tuned one. If he dropped.

'And what d'you make of that?' I asked Oliver.

We were walking back to the car.

'Want to drive?' he asked, realizing we were now in a hurry.

'Yes.' I slid in behind the wheel. 'Well . . . what *do* you make of it?'

'If I was in charge of the investigation,' he said, fastening his seat belt, 'I'd see that my case against Martin could now find itself sewn up tight. Let Rupert be optimistic. But I'd get permission to come along here and have a look for myself. I'd ask around — and I'd finish up with an absolutely unblemished case, every little hole in the original theory neatly tied together and invisibly darned. That's what.'

'Yes,' I said. 'It's bad — just the matter of him being there at all. But don't forget, we know a lot more than the police do, at this stage. To them, it might look different.'

'If we don't reveal it all.'

'Yes, we'll have to be careful not to.'

'Concealing evidence . . . ' he began. Then he decided not to go on with it. I was aware that he'd glanced at me sharply, but I applied myself to my driving. It was going to be a long and tiring haul, and I realized I was already feeling exhausted, physically and emotionally.

For quite a while Oliver said little, nothing but instructions on our route. We hit the motorway somewhere around Stafford and headed south. It was the M6, and it was commuting time, and it was hell. But it eased a little once we got on to the M5. I thought Oliver had dozed off, but no. He suddenly said, 'It didn't have to be deliberate, Phil.'

'No.' I knew at once what he meant — the death of Luke Tulliver. 'That Range Rover's covered a vast number of miles. The scratches could've come from anywhere. But Mandy was pushing him, Oliver. For Mandy, one gathers, an unfinished argument with her father remained unfinished until she got her way. Can you imagine that, against Martin's quiet stubbornness?'

'Yes,' he said.

'Good. There's a service area ahead. Let's have a break.'

'But in any event, Mandy would've witnessed her father's death. I like to think she didn't cause it,' he said morosely. 'Especially if it was to get Martin back.'

'Me too. But Martin had been gone for two months. The word is that he left her, walked out on her because he couldn't get his own way. But *he* said she told him to sod off — his words, Oliver — because of a row they had arising from her jealousy.'

'Did you tell me this, Phil?'

'I thought I had. He told me on the trip, when we went to get the Mercedes. Why d'you think I wanted it like that, if not to get information out of him?'

I turned off on to the slipway to the service area. We parked, and I walked around a little.

Oliver asked if I'd like him to take over, so I said yes. It wasn't until we were seated with a couple of coffees that Oliver took it up again.

'What was she jealous about?' His smile told me he was assuming it was women.

'He said — because he was always fooling around with the young girls.' I grimaced at him. 'Of course, it wasn't that. She was jealous of his obsession with rallying, when he ought to have been obsessed with her.'

'It's a sad fact of life.'

'What is?'

'Women not understanding men.'

'Hmm,' I commented. I intended to take him up on that later. In depth. 'But you can see, Oliver, that if she *had* lost him because of his obsession with rallying, would she deliberately bring about her father's death so that she'd be able to have Martin traced, and persuade him back by offering him unlimited rallying facilities? Would she?'

'If her mind was as devious as yours, Phil — probably yes.'

'Oh, you're an unimaginative idiot.'

'True. But I'd imagine — she being a woman who was still yearning for him after all these years of loss — she might have done anything. Literally anything.'

I stared at him. He smiled at me blandly. 'But she *didn't* have him traced,' I said. 'She

328

didn't try to get him back.'

'You don't know that, Phil. And anyway, she'd have discovered the financial situation wasn't what she'd expected, and there wasn't going to be any spare money around. She'd got nothing left to offer.'

'And cynical,' I decided. 'Would you like to do a bit of the driving?'

'With pleasure. I thought we'd decided that.'

I think I fell asleep. There is no memory of the rest of the journey, and Oliver must have navigated it without my help. I awoke as we were approaching Hellyspool. It was dark, with the headlights on. We were moving more slowly, which was probably what had awoken me. I was fuzzy. It took a full minute to search out my brain and assemble its scattered pieces.

'Where are we? Oh, I see. Not up to the house, Oliver. Not for a moment. What's the time?'

'Getting on for ten.'

'The village first, then. There's something we've got to ask Jeff Carter.'

'Is there?'

'We'll try the pub. Eh?'

'Oh, sure.'

We didn't reach the pub. As we were drifting along I was idly casting my eyes around, and when we were opposite Reade's Rapid Repairs, which was in darkness, I thought I caught a glimpse of light from the direction of the repair shed.

'Oliver!' I said. 'Stop for a second.'

He did. 'What is it?'

'I think somebody's trespassing on Martin's property. In the repair place.' It wasn't Martin's now, I reminded myself. It was Jeff Carter's.

'Then we'd better have a look,' Oliver agreed.

He backed up, and turned on to the forecourt. We got out and walked up the rutted driveway. After the rain, it was considerably softer underfoot, half-way between ankle-twisting and ankle-sinking-into. The light definitely came from the permanently open sliding door. We turned in through the gap.

The lights were on, the ones up in the roof. Above the bench and the surrounding other working areas there were adjustable bench-lamps and spotlights. These were not switched on. The illumination was therefore dim. I was not particularly concerned about intruders, as I recalled that this repair shed was open house to the men in the village. Trust, more often than not, generates honesty. The man standing there with his back to us was doing nothing suspicious, just standing and quietly smoking a cigarette. A Benson and Hedges would've been my guess.

We must have made some minor sound, because he turned. Jeff Carter. For one moment he looked startled, then he managed to speak quietly and confidently.

'Do I know you? Yes . . . I do. Hello.'

We strolled in, and I left it to Oliver. It suited me, anyway, as my interest was to the workbench, and the half-stripped engine on it. How many years was it since I'd last held a spanner? Fifteen to twenty? Back to the age before I decided it wasn't ladylike to go around with cracked finger nails and black grease ingrained into my palms, that was what it was. In other words, since I'd noticed there were boys around. But the interest was still there.

The rocker-box cover was off, the cam-shaft and rockers exposed. *Triumph*, it announced proudly on the cast aluminium cover.

Oliver was saying, 'We're friends of Heather, Martin's wife. Friends of Martin, too, but you'll have to take our word for it. Do you mind answering a few questions?'

He was suspicious, darting his head up to look into Oliver's face, and across to me when I glanced that way. 'Depends, don't it?'

he said cautiously.

'Depends on what?' I asked. 'On how much you can trust us, or on what the questions are?'

He thought about that. 'Both,' he decided.

'All right.' I nodded to Oliver. 'We'll try the questions first. Shall we do that?'

'You ask 'em, if you want to. I ain't promising anything.'

'That's fine then.' Oliver picked it up. 'I understand you're Martin's best friend.'

'You could say that. Who told you?'

'Martin did, himself. He thinks you're the best rally navigator in the world — from what I heard.'

Jeff shook his head, glancing at his feet. 'Not quite. Not that good. But he's definitely the best driver. You ought to see what he can do with a car.'

'I've seen,' I told him over my shoulder. 'I was impressed. I'm still alive, and I might not have been if Martin hadn't done a few things with my car.'

'That so?' He was only vaguely interested.

'This is your place now, isn't it?' Oliver asked, probing for a little enthusiasm.

'It sure is.' It was there, Jeff gradually unwinding. 'A bargain, this is.'

I wouldn't really have said that myself. Martin hadn't managed to make a go of it, he'd been too obliging to friends. A bit in here and there from the odd repair, the few gallons of petrol, there'd be next to nothing coming in. And a few sagging cars for sale on the forecourt . . . they'd been there for ages. Oh, and yes . . . I was forgetting, and with a clapped-out Dolomite Sprint all to himself — and there it was, still up on that hydraulic hoist. It was to be hoped that Jeff was as good a mechanic as Martin.

But Martin had said the Dolomite was going to be a gift to Jeff, and not to breathe a word about it until he'd tuned it to perfection. I decided not to mention it.

Jeff felt the pressure of the few seconds of silence. He was prodded to say, 'Work it up a bit, and I reckon the place'll pay its way.'

'I guess, from what I hear,' said Oliver, 'that you'd do anything for him.'

'Pretty well.' But there'd been just a hint of hesitation.

'Such as rig a Coke tin and a screwed-up cigarette packet?' I put in, still hovering by the bench.

'How d'you know that?'

'He showed me. He took me to that lay-by.'

'Did he?'

I could almost feel his brain racing. How far dared he go?

'He did,' I assured him. 'He said you were

his mate, so I guessed it was you who put them there. For him. It *was* you, wasn't it?'

He shrugged. 'The coppers reckon it was, so I suppose it must've been.'

There was some splendid logic in that, Heather's brand. I pursed my lips at Oliver, and he nearly laughed aloud.

'So,' Oliver said, 'if he wanted to do a quick trip to Shropshire, say, and the Dolomite was sort of stripped down ... ' He gestured towards the yellow car on its hoist. 'Then he'd probably have borrowed your Fiesta. He'd be welcome to it, I suppose.'

'Any time.' Jeff was beginning to relax. 'He knew that.'

The Fiesta! I thought. Where was it? Was it that dark shape towards the rear? I strolled in that direction. No, it wasn't. This was a larger saloon. I recognized its lines. A Triumph 2000. That was another car my father had owned, before he'd switched to the Dolomite Sprint. I'd helped him strip the 2000's engine. A six-cylinder in-line engine, it was. All the correct words were coming back to me now. How much clearer is the memory for the distant past! I'd have been — what? — oh, eleven. Eleven! And I'd fitted brake pads before I'd fitted a bra; knew more about engine oils than I did about bath oils. So I knew a Triumph 2000 when I saw one.

'And if he wanted to do a very fast trip of it,' Oliver went on, 'he'd need a navigator. An expert. He'd ask you. It was your car after all. Where is it, by the way?'

'The police've got it. Won't let go of it.'

Of course — I should've known. I could have kicked myself. I continued my wandering.

'*Did* he take you?' Oliver asked.

'When was this?' Jeff was trying to make time. He strolled over to the bench, now that I'd moved from it. He weighed a spanner in his hand. 'When . . . exactly?'

'The day before the wedding. Martin's wedding. Remember it?' Jeff still had his back to him, but Oliver persisted. 'The stag party was that night — after the Shropshire trip.'

'Yeah, I remember.' Jeff turned, leaning back against the bench nonchalantly. But he was as tense as a coiled spring.

'You'd be only too willing to oblige him, if he'd wanted a travelling companion,' Oliver suggested.

Jeff screwed the cigarette end into the layer of black grease with his heel. 'I didn't mind.'

'So you were with him when the Fiesta was parked in a lay-by on a road in Shropshire, overlooking a huge private park with a great big house in the middle of it?'

Jeff was now definitely on the defensive.

'Yeah,' he said at last. 'He told me he used to live there. Crazy. Martin never had any spare spending money in his life. Live there! I just couldn't see it. But he got out of the car. I thought he was going for a slash, but he just stood there.'

'You beside him?'

'Not me. Who wants to look at a lot of country? I see nothin' else around here. Bloody boring. Me — I stayed in the car.'

That explained why Heather hadn't seen him. She'd seen only Martin. Well, she would — in the same way as Martin had seen only a Mercedes sports coupé. Or had he? If he'd been gazing down at that great, open park, he'd have seen Heather having her little dispute with Mandy. Couldn't have helped but see them. So he would have known it was Heather in that Mercedes.

'Did he say anything when he got back into your car?' I asked, giving Oliver a break.

'No. He didn't.'

'Didn't say anything?'

'Didn't get back in the car,' he said casually, as though it meant nothing.

'Didn't he?' I tried to sound uninterested.

'He just stuck his head in the window and said he'd be a minute or two, an' he walked off.'

It had possibly not been a good idea to

question Jeff, if we'd wanted something that helped Martin. I wondered whether he'd told the police all this. No — they hadn't known of any trip to Shropshire. But they would when Rupert proudly took the information to them!

'He just walked off?' asked Oliver. 'Where to?'

'In the entrance. I could see that.'

'The entrance to the drive?'

'Yeah.' But Jeff seemed uncertain. I suspected he was having to reorganize the facts in his mind. 'I said that.'

Blast the poor lighting! I couldn't see his face clearly, so had no way, except the tone in his voice, to guide me to a judgement.

I was now standing beneath the car on the hydraulic hoist, which was the type that had four legs, one at each corner. There was room to move about, and I was short enough that my hair didn't get tangled in the messy transmission underneath. My father hadn't got any of this fancy sort of equipment. If he'd wanted to lift the engine out, he'd had a tripod with a handle for winding it up, and a chain to go under the sump. I could see him now. 'Watch the clutch cover, Phil. Forward a bit. That's it.' And I'd been eleven! I'd been fourteen when he bought the Dolomite Sprint. Sixteen valves and sixteen tappets.

No . . . thank you! And Dad had laughed. I'd become concerned about eight fingers and two thumbs.

Hell! My attention was wandering. Jeff was speaking. 'Then I didn't see him again for a bit. Couldn't see anything 'cause of the hedge.'

'So you didn't see where he went?' Oliver asked blandly. 'Not exactly?'

'Couldn't.'

'But you *did* see the house and the grounds? You knew what it looked like.'

Jeff answered as though Oliver was stupid. 'I got out at first. When we got there. Had a quick look, then I got back in again. Didn't interest me, that sort of thing.'

Now every word was being chosen with caution. Oliver had been pressing the point, so that Jeff must have realized that it mattered.

'Away long?' I put in casually. 'Was he away long?'

He stared towards my voice. It was dark under that car.

'Couldn't be sure of that. Yeah . . . I suppose so. Me . . . I was sitting there thinking. I mean, you gotta think of yourself, an' the missus wasn't keen on me taking time off. So when you get the chance . . . I'd had this offer of a new job. A factory they've built

338

at Hellston. They make jam or somethin'. So I had to have me a good think. I mean, I'd got *this*. Hadn't I! The business. Maybe I dozed off. I dunno. Anyway, next thing I know he's opening the door an' getting in.'

He'd over-elaborated, a sign of nerves. And coming out with that . . . he'd dozed off! A veteran of a hundred rallies, involving hour after hour of night driving . . . and he'd dozed off after a little jaunt of 200 miles in the daylight! I just didn't believe it. He'd resorted to a pack of lies.

'Then what happened?' I asked.

'Eh?' Jeff had lost his direction of thought. 'Yeah. I remember. He'd got a brooch in his hand. Fancy, it was. Said he'd seen the lady drop it. Took some finding.'

'It would, I suppose. All that drive to look at.' Oliver turned, as though explaining it to me.

'It would,' Jeff agreed. 'Then later on he said, would I slip it to her? Heather. Mrs Reade. Would I slip it to her? And he handed it to me. 'Cause he wasn't going to have the chance, I suppose. So I did. Popped it on the hall table. They always leave the door open.'

'That's all very clear,' I assured him. 'You've been very helpful, Jeff.'

But Oliver wasn't satisfied. 'Just the brooch?' he asked. 'No note?'

'Well now . . . ' Jeff had to stall for time on that one. 'Well . . . it wouldn't do, would it, without some sort of message? It'd look like we'd been spyin' on her, sort of.'

'You didn't say you'd seen a lady. You said you'd seen nobody. Nothing. So how could it have been spying?'

Oliver was pushing now, trying to shake Jeff by repeating his questions. I didn't know what he was after. I looked down at my feet. The surface felt different from the greased concrete. I realized I was standing on the old inspection pit Martin had mentioned. The boards felt like old railway sleepers.

Jeff had hesitated long enough. He now hurried on. 'Martin said: the lady. Well . . . ' His voice gained confidence. 'Stood to reason, didn't it. And he told me who to slip it to. His Heather. Sometime or other.' He smiled round for approval, a strangely shy smile.

'And whose diary lost a week?' I asked casually. I moved forward into the light. 'The message was on a page from somebody's diary.'

'What?' He darted suspicious glances from face to face. Oliver nodded.

'Well . . . mine,' he admitted. 'It was my idea, see, the message.'

'Kind of short, wasn't it?' I asked, to let him know I'd seen it.

'Well . . . ' He dragged his hand through his hair and tried a weak grin. 'It wasn't somethin' she'd want known, was it! A bride the next day, and visiting Martin's first wife. Well . . . was it?'

'I'm sure you're correct, Jeff,' I assured him.

'Did my best.'

'Well . . . that seems all clear.' Oliver glanced at me. I nodded.

'Can I lock up now?' Jeff asked.

'Lock? This place?' Oliver laughed.

Jeff grinned. I think it was the first time I'd seen a genuine grin from him. Relief, I suppose.

'Put the lights off, then,' he amended.

He headed for the open door, Oliver at his heels. I diverted to the bench, but didn't reach it. The lights went off.

'Been nice talking to you,' said Oliver, when we were outside.

'Sure, sure. Anythin' I can do to help Martin . . . you know where to come.'

We walked with him down to the forecourt. 'We do,' I assured him.

Then we got back into my car, me behind the wheel. Jeff stood there, watching us go.

'To help Martin?' Oliver asked. 'That

wasn't helping him much.'

'That's what he thought he was doing,' I said, but not very pleased with the result. 'Just look what he's given us. It could've taken Martin three minutes to find that brooch on the drive. It was where the two women argued, and Martin had the tyre tracks to give him a starting point. But how long was he missing? And why did Jeff try to cover up for that? How long would it have taken Martin to reach the mill — he'd have known Mandy would head there. Oh hell, Oliver, let's get it over with. Let's go and tell Heather the brooch was no threat.'

'But . . . ' Oliver was plucking at his lower lip when I glanced at him. 'The note with it — the wording wouldn't have been Jeff's. Of course not. It exactly fits what Martin would *have* to say. Keep your mouth shut. Yes, then nobody need ever know he'd seen her there, that they'd both been there. Not a threat, Phil. Good advice.'

I said nothing, simply driving steadily and thinking.

'The briefs were, though. The bra was, the skirt was, we know that now.' Oliver was quietly persistent.

'But Oliver, love,' I said, trying to contain my patience, 'the clothes must have been

Garner's threat — to Martin. Not to Heather.'

'Then it all went wrong. Martin hasn't seen any of them. Let's go and get it over.'

I drove on slowly, a hundred yards before his meaning came through. Then, 'Get it over? Get what over, for heaven's sake, Oliver?'

'Phil, Phil, think about it. We now know what information the police are going to dig out at Fillingley Towers. We know more. But I could put a case together now, motive, means, opportunity, the lot, because we're ahead of them. The best we can do is warn Heather that Martin's going to be formally charged with the murder of his wife, Mandy — even if he hasn't already. The whole story's clear — in detail. We can't do anything but warn her. Phil? Are you listening?'

'I'm trying not to scream,' I told him angrily. 'Martin didn't do it. I know he didn't. We need one little detail . . . I know he didn't . . . one last detail.'

I'd allowed the car to drift to a halt.

'Isn't there a personal interest drifting into this, Phil?' That was Oliver, trying to be delicate.

'Damn you, no!'

'Ah!'

'And if you ah me again I'll thump your

bad arm. I *know!* Do you understand?'

He smiled that smile of his. I nearly collapsed against his bad arm. He said, 'You know. Right. Fine. Then let's go and tell her that.'

The house was dark and silent. The Mercedes was parked out at the front, and my lights ran across it. I parked. I wouldn't have left my Merc there. Surely she had garages somewhere — there had to be.

Oliver got out and straightened. He looked up at the house, and so did I. All the windows were dark and the curtains were not drawn. Only dimly, from above and somewhere at the side, was there any light.

'Perhaps they've gone to bed.'

'D'you think that's likely, Oliver? The way things are.'

'No.'

I tried the front door. It was locked. So I pressed the bell push. Wherever the bell was, I didn't hear it. There was no reaction. I pressed it again.

'Something's wrong,' I said.

'It doesn't have to mean that.' His voice was reassuring. 'Surely, though, we said we'd be back.'

Then a light came on, way down the hall. I could see it through the stained glass panel in the door. Hesitant footsteps approached the door, but nothing happened. Then a voice cried out, 'Who is it? Who is it?'

Kathie's voice, it was, and close to hysteria.

'It's me, Kathie,' I called out. 'Philipa and Oliver. Let us in.'

Faintly I heard a distant shout. 'Tell them to go away.' That was Heather's voice, shrill and penetrating.

'Kathie!' I called, my face close to the door. 'This is ridiculous. Open the door. If there's something wrong . . .'

There was no response. Then I heard her feet retreating.

'Kathie!' I shouted.

'Oh, for heaven's sake!' said Oliver. 'Everybody's gone mad.'

I put my finger on the button and held it there. There was shortly a returning bustle of hurrying feet. Kathie called out, 'Wait! Wait!'

I heard the lock turn over, then a great crashing of withdrawn bolts, and the door opened. 'Quickly!' said Kathie, peering past me into the darkness. Oliver reached beyond me and put a hand against the door, in case there was a change of mind. We got inside. At once she slammed the door, and crash, crash, the bolts went home again.

'This is ridiculous,' I said. 'Where's the light switch?'

Oliver found it. The subdued light seemed

at first to be a blinding glare.

'What's the trouble?' I asked.

Kathie was shaking and her face seemed pinched. She shook her head, drawing in her lower lip. I knew she was trying to stop herself from breaking down, and had been fighting for a while against it. In the sudden release, she was on the verge of tears. The responsibility had been too much for her.

'Kathie?' I asked gently.

She pointed a finger. '*That* came,' she whispered.

We turned to look at the hall table. The package had been sealed, and appeared to have been delivered by post. Now it was open, torn open in a fury. Lying in the paper there was a soiled blouse, soiled green and brown. I knew that smell. I didn't have to look too closely. Now we had the lot, most likely — briefs, bra, skirt, and now blouse. It was all Mandy had probably been wearing — except the shoes.

And I knew where those were.

15

I could feel that Kathie was poised and anxious, and could guess the reason. 'You'd better get back to Heather,' I said quietly.

'Yes . . . I'd better.' But there was no conviction in it.

'Where is she?'

'She's in the loft,' Kathie said hollowly.

'The loft!' I stared at Oliver, who shook his head. He could make no sense of it, either. 'What's she doing there?' he asked.

'I don't know.' But Kathie was agitated because she did.

'Then I'll go up and see. Shall I?'

'Oh yes, yes. You do that. I'll . . . I'll get some tea made.'

She looked from face to face, having passed the stage of making her own decisions. Even this one she couldn't trust.

'You do that,' Oliver told her gently. 'We'll see to Heather.'

We! He meant that I would. But the thought was there.

Once Kathie was gone we were able to give more attention to the package. The wrapping was mangled, but it was possible to discover that it had been posted the day before at Taunton. That was no help. It was addressed to *Martin Reade, c/o Hellyspool Hall.* Care of! That carried a nasty little hint that he might never be able to claim it as his own address. There was no message because the blouse told it all.

And this time there was a definite linking clue. The blouse was of fawn silk, very chic and very expensive. On the left breast there was hand-embroidered *Mandy.* This was possibly why it had been kept until last.

But this final item had been posted the day before. We had not at that time encountered Clive Garner at the mill, where his spicy cedar body spray had not protected him from the odour of guilt. It was he who had stripped Mandy, cleaned her, and perfumed her. So it was he who had used her soiled and odious clothing as a threat to Martin. To Martin, not to Heather, who was only too eager to clasp the tricks of fate to herself. To Heather they would be frightening; to Martin they would stink of threat. You were seen in the district. You visited the mill, and Mandy was there. I know this. The police don't . . . yet. Keep this in mind when we discuss the future of the farm, and they need never know.

So clear, to Martin, would be the threat . . . and he was the one who knew nothing at all about the deliveries of soiled clothing! Wasted, wasted . . . apart from the fact that Heather had been driven nearly out of her mind.

'Aren't you going to see what she's up to?' asked Oliver.

'What? Oh yes — of course. But how the devil do I get to the loft?'

'I suggest we climb, and when there's no climbing left, there'll be the rafters, and there will be Heather.'

'Oh, clever, clever.'

But that was exactly what we did. We climbed the stairs from the hall to the half-balcony, then up the short flight to the floor we already knew. We were now on the first floor. The rooms below had very lofty ceilings. Knowing there was nothing at one end except the bathroom, we tried a side corridor we had neither of us explored. Stairs again, but these were narrow, squeezed between two walls. They took us up to another floor.

Now we could hear sounds above, thumpings and bangings, and the occasional curse. We were nearly there. The final climb was by a fixed ladder, sloping just enough for the rungs to be called steps, but not stairs. At the head of it there was a large gap, beyond that, dim lighting.

I looked at Oliver. 'Me, I think,' I said. 'From what Kathie said, Heather's so fragile she might panic at the sight of a man.'

'Hmm!' He nodded. 'I'll come up quietly after you, and just stick my head through.'

That would perhaps be more frightening then the whole of him, but I made no objection. I was anxious to get to Heather.

The loft was a large expanse, though it was difficult to see its full extent because of the poor lighting and the amount of junk there was scattered around. There were two dim lights. The restless sound came from the far end. Then abruptly it stopped.

'Who's there?' she called out, hysteria in her voice. 'Who is it?'

'It's Philipa. It's me. What the devil are you doing?'

Then, as she straightened, I saw her. For a second I couldn't recognize her, but then I realized it was because she was wearing slacks. Somehow she seemed slimmer, a disorganized and tattered waif, with her hair flying and her face dirty.

'I don't want you,' she said, her voice empty.

'What on earth are you doing, Heather?' The best thing was, I'd decided, to speak to her casually and approach slowly, with caution.

'I can't find it!' she wailed. 'Not anywhere. And we're all alone here . . . '

'Not now you're not. I'm here, and Oliver.'

It seemed not to comfort her. 'I was sure it was in this trunk. It's taken me ages . . . oh, Phil, go away please. Give me room. I'll have to find it. Just have to.'

'Find what?'

She turned away and bent over an old-fashioned travelling trunk, its curved and banded lid thrown back. She bent over it, then fell to her knees and rummaged frantically, like a squirrel searching for last season's nuts.

'Here it is!' she cried out, suddenly happy now, relieved. 'I *knew* we hadn't thrown it away.'

Then she stood up, and she was waving around a huge revolver, complete with lanyard through the ring in the butt.

'For God's sake . . . ' The thing must've weighed well over two pounds, and she had difficulty handling it.

'Grandfather's,' she told me. '*Now* we're all right. Just let anybody try anything now!'

Oh no, we weren't all right. She'd now discovered that the gun needed two hands. She was clutching at it awkwardly. I flinched.

'Is the damned thing loaded?' I asked.

'How do I know?' She tossed her head. 'I expect it is.'

'Then give it to me.' I advanced a couple of paces, but she jerked it up, her two hands fumbling for a grip, and for all I knew there could have been a finger or two around the trigger. The thing was probably corroded beyond operation. Its ammunition, I'd heard, if any was present in the cylinder, was most likely to be useless by now. A plop and a fizz, that was what you'd be likely to get now. Maybe not. Perhaps it was capable of firing, but the odds were that it would blow up in her hands if it did. Nevertheless, I stood very still. I repeated, 'Give it to me, Heather,' but I waited for her to come meekly to me. I certainly wasn't going to make any movement she might interpret as aggressive. I stood. She didn't move.

'This is very foolish,' I told her severely.

'I can defend myself now,' she said, delighted at this ability. 'I don't need you any more. I don't need *anybody*. And all you've done is make it worse. All of it.'

'That is quite untrue.'

She made a derisive noise. Then, 'Get out of my way, Phil. I want to get where I can see what's around me, then I can look after myself.'

'Just put it away, Heather. Please. Put it

back where you found it.'

She gave a high-pitched laugh that sent the blood draining from my cheeks.

What I was afraid of was that Oliver, having heard all this, would decide it was a man's job, and advance to the rescue. His speciality, that was, advancing on weapons controlled by highly tensed and unpredictable people. I wasn't going to allow him to try it again. I took a pace forward, to get in there first, but she cried out, 'No!' It was in a strange, near-tearful voice, but there was determination behind it, even intent.

I opened my mouth to appeal again, and then I became aware of background noise. There was a clatter as Oliver backed down the steps quickly, and then a banging. Someone was hammering at the front door. I hadn't heard the bell. Perhaps Kathie hadn't, either. The banging was now joined by a blast from a car's horn, then more banging.

'Oh, no!' Heather whimpered, then she thrust past me and had rattled down the steps to the corridor below before I could recover my wits. Oliver called, 'Phil!' But I was already there, and on the way down myself.

He caught my arm. 'I couldn't believe my eyes. It looked like a bloody great revolver.'

'It is. Her grandfather's. Of all the stupid . . .'

'If she tries firing it she'll blow her hand off — or at the very least break her wrist.'

We were by now hurrying after Heather, who was shouting, 'What is it? What's all the noise about?'

We came within sight of the half-landing as Heather reached it and ran forward, leaning over the banister. From our position we couldn't see the front door, but the noise was continuing, and now I could hear the bell in the far recesses. And Kathie's voice, 'I'm coming, I'm coming.' She was almost in tears; the words choked her.

Then Martin's voice came through. 'It's me, Heather. Martin. Open the door.'

'Don't let him in!' Heather screamed, but Kathie, confused, was already doing so.

The blast of the horn suddenly ceased, the door swung open, and Martin thrust his way in. 'What the hell . . . '

'Don't come in — stay there!' shouted Heather.

'It's me, lover.' Martin took a stance. The return of the weary warrior. 'They've let me out.'

I heard tyres grating on the gravel outside. More visitors. By that time I was beside Heather at the banister. She didn't see me. I watched as Rupert followed Martin inside, frowning, looking round.

'What's going on here?' he enquired plaintively. Then his eyes lifted to Heather, and he saw what she was holding. 'Oh, good heavens.' His voice was hollow. 'Heather, whatever's going on?' He stared up at the half-landing, standing shoulder to shoulder with Martin, who was obviously baffled, the light and glow of his return gradually dimming as his face stiffened.

I glanced sideways. Tears were streaming down her cheeks, but the pistol was rested on the balcony rail, and aimed downwards. Then her legs slowly gave way, and clumsily she sat, crouched, and for ease she thrust her legs forward between two of the staves. Now she could cradle the gun in her lap, but not for a moment did she relax her grip on it.

She drew a deep breath, and from somewhere managed to produce a reasonably sane voice, which sounded more threatening than her hysteria.

'Don't let him come near me,' she said. 'You stay down there. Keep away from me. Go down and tell him, Phillie. Yes . . . you go down and tell him.'

'Tell who?' I asked softly.

'Martin. Him down there. What've they let him out for?'

As far as it was possible to make sense out of Heather's reasoning, I had to assume that the brooch had done its work only too well. Keep your mouth shut. This, from Martin, whom she'd seen at Fillingley Towers, she now saw as a threat — from her own dear Martin. It was in attempting to reconcile the opposing aspects — his obvious love for her and at the same time a threat — that she'd pushed her poor brain over the edge.

Rupert, however, accepted her question as reasonable and sane. She *would* want to know why they'd let him out. He therefore gave her an answer. 'He's released in my custody, on my surety, Heather. The police have decided that their case isn't yet sound. Now listen to reason . . . '

'And what's *he* doing here?'

Jeff had just eased himself through the door. He looked startled at what he saw.

'Jeff came with his Fiesta,' said Martin. 'The police have let him have it back. He was waiting hours. We drove on ahead of Rupert. Just couldn't wait to get to you, my sweet, and he'd still got a mass of things to clear up.' But Jeff had told us the police still had his Fiesta!

Heather seemed to choke on some remote emotion that I couldn't understand. She tried to put her hands over her face, but this required that she should release her grip on the pistol. It fell between her legs, she forgetting she was wearing slacks, and clattered down to the hall.

Whatever she'd done to it, she had brought it to a critical condition, because the impact fired it. Certainly, it fired, and quite impressively. Martin cried out, grabbing for his left upper arm. Heather howled, and scrambled to her feet, then clattered down to him, throwing herself into his arms and not helping at all.

Then Oliver and I were there. 'Heather, we must see,' I said, prising her free, and Oliver got Martin's jacket off.

'It's nothing,' said Oliver. 'A flesh wound. Kathie, have you got anything to bind it with?'

Poor Kathie was lost, defeated and confused. But instructions she could cling to. 'Yes, yes,' she said, turning and almost managing a run.

'It's all right,' said Martin. 'Don't worry, Heather. Don't fuss, please.'

Rupert fetched a chair from the dining-room and we sat him down. 'I'm all right, damn it,' Martin protested, but he sounded very tired and the chair was gratefully accepted.

When cleaned, it showed that Oliver was correct. A flesh wound. We nearly got a dressing on it, but the final stages were interrupted by an approaching off-beat racket from outside. It was only when it cut out with a thrum that I recognized the sound as belonging to a motor cycle.

'Mr Reade!' The shout came from just outside the door. Then it was thrust open forcefully. 'Mr Reade, sir . . . '

It was the lank-haired youth from the kiosk at Martin's place. Jeff's, rather.

'Mr Reade — there's a man. In the repair shed. He's caught under the hydraulic hoist.'

'Oh Christ!' said Martin.

'Was passin',' said the youth. 'Saw the lights was on, so I checked. A man. His feet was sticking out — '

'All right. All right, Larry. Thanks. We'll have to go and see. Heather, we'll have to — '

'I'll come.'

'No . . . please . . . '

'I'll come, Martin. Don't be silly. I'm not going to let you out of my sight.' Her emotions didn't know what they were supposed to be doing.

So we streamed out into the night. Larry's bike was a sit-up-and-beg, the seat over the rear wheel and the handlebars like a fighting bull's horns. He was off and away in a great burst of exhaust before we had all scrambled into our cars, Oliver and me in the BMW, and Martin with Jeff and Heather in the

Fiesta. Rupert, very silent and very grim, seemed prepared to tail along behind. Nothing was as he would have wished, and he'd barely had time to say a word. I was sure he had plenty waiting for release.

Martin led the way, spurting gravel back at us from his tyres. But the way wasn't clear. When we reached it, the gateway was blocked by the Range Rover, just entering.

We all stopped. Clive Garner jumped down from his seat, advancing on us. He seemed very purposeful.

'I want to talk to you, Martin. Things to discuss.' There was determination in his voice, and a jaunty confidence.

'For God's sake, man, we've got an emergency on here.' Martin had his door open, and was shouting from it. 'Get that damned Range Rover out of the way.'

Garner stared at him blankly for a couple of seconds, then he ran back to his car and clambered inside. It backed out. We streamed past him.

The eight or so miles were covered very briskly. I managed to hold on to Martin's tail, but Rupert lagged behind. Martin was driving, and that arm must have been hurting like hell.

Larry was there before us, his bike on its rest beside the dark pumps. He was waving from the entrance to the repair shed, as though we didn't know where to find it. Martin and Jeff were out together, running and staggering up the rutted path. Heather got out more sedately, and waited for us. But Oliver and I also took it at a run, leaving her to be shepherded by Rupert, who was just turning his car in, followed by Garner's Range Rover.

The roof lights were on again. Jeff had put them off as we'd left him there. But now the yellow Dolomite Sprint was no longer lifted six feet from the ground, as the hoist's metal tracks were almost touching the concrete floor. Its bonnet was raised. It had probably been raised before, but I hadn't noticed it, way up there in the shadows. And I'd stood beneath it!

Larry lurked near the doorway, unable to drag himself from such a hideous scene. There were legs and shoes sticking out sideways from beneath the yellow car. They were a man's shoes and trousers. The toes were pointing downwards. There was no movement.

'Lights!' said Oliver, using his flat and official voice. 'Aren't there any more lights?'

Jeff went and switched on three bench lights, swivelling them to point at the hoist. I glanced at Oliver. He seemed to be hesitant.

'Aren't we going to lift it?' I asked. 'There could be a chance — '

'Not a chance.' He shook his head. 'The police will want to see it as it is.'

'But we ought to be *sure*,' I said. I was impatient, and, my legs not too steady, advanced to the car. The feet were sticking out just behind the front wheels. There was not necessarily no chance at all, I was thinking. With the engine out . . .

The control panel was on one of the stanchions involved with the hydraulic supports. The operation was very clear. There was an 'up' button and a 'down' button, and a red one between them, obviously the 'stop' button.

'I'll do it,' said Oliver at my shoulder. He reached past me and pressed the 'up' button.

There was a gentle hum from the pump. Slowly, smoothly, the car lifted. When the tracks were level with my eyes, Oliver jabbed at the red button. Nothing happened; it continued upwards.

'It doesn't always work,' said Martin from behind us, his voice chill and distant. Heather was making whimpering noises. 'It stops when it's on full lift or when it reaches the ground.'

Before he'd finished speaking, it demonstrated this fact. It stopped in exactly the same position as it had been when I'd stood beneath it.

I had to force myself to look downwards, even then finding my head swimming at the shock. I took several deep breaths, and felt Oliver's hand at my elbow. But there'd been no chance, after all. Absolutely none. I'd assumed that with the engine out . . . but the engine wasn't out. It was there, resting on the cross girder — and sump and girder between them had done the job. The upper abdomen was smashed in. The dead face, twisted frantically sideways, was distorted with terror and pain. Nevertheless, it was recognizable.

Victor Peel's career had come to an abrupt and unpleasant end.

Oliver turned me away. 'Police,' he said, still with his flat voice operating. 'Rupert — are you there?'

'Here,' said Rupert, now out of our sight because of the bench lamps centred blindingly on us. He'd had to clear his throat.

'Get the police, will you? Young Larry's probably got the key to the kiosk. There's a phone in there.'

There was no reply, but I guessed Rupert was already on his way.

'Who is it?' Martin asked. He'd waited a long while to ask it.

'Victor Peel,' I told him, my voice still not

steady. 'You've probably met him.'

There was no reply. I walked through the blinding glare of the three bench lamps. 'He's been everywhere, seen everything, talked to everybody.' Now, beyond the light, I was able to see him, Martin, with Heather clinging weakly to his good arm, Jeff to one side, smoking furiously to steady his nerves. 'Martin, he must have contacted you, some time or other.'

'Not me.'

'Not even to ask for money?' I asked. 'To shut his mouth.'

'He could open it as much as he liked, as far as I was concerned,' Martin claimed.

The side-light was throwing harsh shadows into his features. His face looked cadaverous. I didn't reply, but moved sideways to the bench. I'd noticed a trickle of blood dripping from the fingers of Martin's left hand.

'What is it, Phil?' Oliver asked. 'What're you getting at?'

The engine I'd previously noticed was still there on the bench, its rocker box cover off. I pointed.

'Look at that,' I said quietly, for his ears alone. 'The cover's off, and the word Triumph is proudly displayed. But I know about the Dolomite Sprint, Oliver. Didn't I tell you about my father?'

'You did. Tried to kid himself you were a boy.'

I ignored that. 'But I enjoyed it, you know. When you're that young you're not obsessed with your hands — or your sex. I *liked* working with him. And *this* engine — it's the six cylinder one from that Triumph 2000, over there. I expect work was being done on it, but it's *displayed*, Oliver. To be seen. There was the Dolomite Sprint, up on the hoist, and an engine on the bench indicating it was a Triumph one — it was to create an impression. Deliberately done. An impression that the Dolomite was out of commission — its engine out and on the bench.'

'So?' But his voice was taking on a lilt of interest.

'Its intention was to deceive. I should have realized earlier — you see, you don't take out an engine from beneath, you lift it out, upwards.' I stared up and around. The light wasn't good, up there, but I could just detect them, the overhead rails with the two mobile cranes, chain operated. 'No . . . you lift it out. And I missed it. The Dolomite was up there on the hoist for a vastly different reason.'

I hadn't heard him approach, but Martin now spoke from my shoulder, giving me quite a turn. 'I told you . . . I was doing some work on the brakes.'

'No,' I said flatly, turning on him. 'That was the Fiesta. About the Dolomite, you said you were doing a complete overhaul. But I believe you'd already done that. I believe you'd already given it to Jeff . . . isn't that so, Jeff? Before the wedding day.'

'What, what . . . ?'

One's name always penetrates, and my voice had been the sole sound, if only quiet. Jeff came forward to us.

'What's this about?'

'I was saying — that yellow Dolomite Sprint's yours, isn't it? Didn't Martin give it to you — '

They answered together, interrupting me.

'Not then,' said Martin.

'Well, yes,' said Jeff.

'Which is it?'

Neither answered. There was a short silence, into which Rupert, walking in through the open doorway, said, 'They're coming. An accident, I told them.'

'It was no accident,' I said flatly. 'It was murder.' I said this softly, for Oliver's exclusive benefit. Then I turned back to Martin. 'You two don't have to argue about it, you know. Mr Garner — are you there?'

'Reluctantly,' he said. 'Lord, I never expected this.' His face was bleached by the bench lights as he came forward.

'Just answer a simple question, will you?'

'If it'll help. Can't we have those lights off?'

He meant the lights that so cruelly illuminated the crushed body of Victor Peel. I didn't answer him. We needed light, light, wherever it was aimed, that rather than shadows. The very thought of shadows, at that time, was sending icy shivers up my spine. I went on as though Garner hadn't spoken.

'You said that Martin had been seen in the area of Fillingley Towers, on the day before the wedding.'

'Yes. That's right.' He seemed uneasy, and was choosing his words carefully.

'But . . . *seen?*' I asked. 'By whom? Oh, I know Heather saw him. He was standing in the lay-by near the entrance to the Towers. But it was Mrs Thomas's day out, and she took the gatehouse owner's wife with her. *You* didn't see Martin, Mr Garner, did you? Not in the flesh, with your own eyes, because you didn't drive past that particular lay-by. You mentioned seeing the Mercedes, in a lay-by half a mile back. But Heather was using that. So, what *did* you see?'

He looked around from face to face, wondering what to say, who he might upset. He didn't want to upset Martin. Then, reluctantly, he said, 'It was that yellow car of his I saw, driving out of my own farm entrance just before I reached it. It didn't come past me, but turned away from me, towards the entrance to the Big House.'

Heavens — another point I'd missed! He had said: Martin had been in that area with *that car of his*. I had assumed he'd simply made a mistake, and that he'd seen Martin with the Fiesta, or someone else had. But he had meant the yellow Dolomite Sprint!

'You saw the yellow car, and assumed Martin was driving it?' I asked.

'Yes.'

'Why did you assume that? How did you connect Martin with the yellow car?' I was snapping out the questions sharply because the thoughts were coming like that.

My attitude made him impatient. He was shaking his head and moving restlessly from foot to foot. 'Because I'd seen him in it, that's why. I saw him get out of it — '

'Now wait, wait.' Oliver had detected the direction of my thoughts. 'When was this?'

Garner shrugged, shedding his interest in the whole set-up. 'A week before. He was at The Towers. He'd come to see Mandy, I reckoned.'

There was a shuffling silence around that bench. I turned. Martin had taken one pace forward.

'Martin?' I asked.

'Martin!' cried out Heather, from between her cupped hands.

Martin said unemotionally, 'I went to have a talk with her. That great lout Peel had been to see me. He said Mandy knew about the wedding. No — I'll amend that. The bastard . . . he said Mandy *would* know all about it, the next day, because Peel was going to tell her. Unless I signed a bit of paper promising him a lot of money, which he thought I'd be able to squeeze out of Heather. I nearly killed him there and then. On the spot. Nobody's going to threaten me. So I went to Shropshire and saw Mandy myself.'

'Wait!' said Oliver sharply. 'You nearly killed him *there and then*? Are you telling us you have now? Here?'

'Let's keep to the point,' said Martin flatly. This was a different Martin, no more the posturing and the constant displays — the man covering up for the man beneath. We were seeing the real Martin, who drove in rallies, who bored ahead, regardless. 'Yes, I saw Mandy. I told her flatly that I was going to go through a marriage ceremony with Heather, no matter that it wouldn't be a legal marriage. It'd make Heather happy, and all I wanted was that. I told Mandy I was in love with Heather, and that all I had left for

Mandy was nothing. I told her that, straight out. I also told her I'd kill her if she tried to ruin things for us. That suit you? Is it clear? Do you get the point?'

Heather got it. She choked on a little whimpering scream, then she fumbled her way to Martin and grasped at his bad arm, while he smiled bleakly at her, and patted the hand that clung tightly to his wound.

Oliver touched my arm. It was his signal — leave the next bit to me. 'So he tried it again, I suppose? This evening. Vic Peel, I mean. More blackmail was it?'

Martin gestured with his free hand, dismissing Peel as of no consequence. 'Jeff picked me up in the Fiesta outside the police station, as I told you. He'd hung around for hours, till dear old Rupert had done his stuff. Then we went on ahead — Rupert was going to be some time, he said. We really piled on the speed, 'cause he said Peel had been hanging around here, and hinting. More threats, I reckoned.'

'The rotten swine,' put in Jeff. 'Said he was there — '

'Let me tell it, mate,' cut in Martin. 'Yes . . . he was there, he said, at Fillingley on the day before the wedding. Gone to see Garner, or some such thing . . . '

'That's true,' said Garner. 'His car was at

the farm when I got there. He was walking up from the mill. Great ideas, he had, that Vic Peel. He wanted to tell me how I could land the lot . . . '

'Never mind that,' I said. 'Vic Peel was blackmailing you, Martin, wasn't he?'

'Trying.'

'What hold had he got?'

'He said he'd seen what happened at the mill.'

I took a deep breath. 'So you killed him for that? I suppose he said he could prove you'd killed Mandy?' I felt confident in that, confident of what Peel's attitude would be.

'Hell no!' So I was wrong. 'No,' said Martin. 'What he said was that he'd seen Heather there, at the mill. So I belted him one.'

'Oh? You fought?' My mind was fumbling around, trying to ignore the thought . . . Heather!

'Try fighting a polar bear,' Martin grumbled.

Now that I looked more carefully, there were certainly signs that Martin had been in a fight. Heather was a little late with her choked scream this time. 'He saw . . . ' she choked, and Martin hushed her.

'In the end, I got him with a spanner,' he said. 'One of my own.' He decorated this statement with a flicked smile. 'It sent him down, but I was about finished. Couldn't stand. Peel just turned away, stumbled, and grabbed for something to hold on to. I reckon his hand hit the 'down' button, 'cause that's what the hoist did, and he fell face down on the planking underneath. I think he must've been out, good and proper.'

'You didn't try to help him?'

'No,' he said solemnly. 'I told you — I couldn't get to me feet.'

'And what about you, Jeff?' I asked.

'What . . . me?' Jeff stepped forward. 'Me help? How could I? I'd run down to the kiosk to get to a phone — fetch the police. But I couldn't get in. It was locked. When I got back it was all over, and we thought . . . anyway, we just got back in the Fiesta and I took Martin home to Heather.'

He looked so meekly innocent as he said this that I knew nothing would budge him from it. Martin smiled at him. I think he winked. Heather leaned forward and kissed Jeff's cheek. Jeff turned away abruptly.

I didn't trouble to remind him about the phone in the pre-fab.

But we had met and spoken to Jeff, in this repair shed, not so long ago, and the hoist had been raised at that time — and no dead Peel. So where had Martin been at that time?

Where had Peel? At the pre-fab, probably, in the kitchen at the rear, arguing it out, and finally fighting it out. So maybe Peel had died there, or at least been unconscious when they'd carried him down to the repair shed.

It was only an idea. Maybe they'd intended to drop him in the inspection pit, but hadn't been able to lift the railway sleepers over it. It was no more than an idea. Nothing, though, would ever force either of them into admitting it.

Faintly, but still in the distance, I heard the wail of sirens.

16

There wasn't much time left. I spoke rapidly now.

'So the yellow Dolomite Sprint was there,' I said. 'At The Towers. But it wouldn't have been Martin driving it — he was using the Fiesta. No — Jeff would be driving it. It was his. And Martin, you watched from the lay-by and saw Heather and Mandy arguing on the drive. You saw Mandy turn away. But Martin, could you really have seen the brooch drop from that distance? I don't believe you did. They hadn't come to the scratching and clawing stage by then, anyway. Mandy turned away and hurried off. You would know where she was heading. To the mill. You didn't want to go there yourself, though, and I'd guess that in any event Heather hurried after her. So you sent Jeff round there in the yellow car, to keep an eye on things. You'd want to keep out of it.'

The sirens were now closer. All but Martin, Heather and Jeff had gone outside, to meet the oncoming relief. The authorities would shortly be taking over.

I asked, 'What did Jeff find there, Martin?'

It wasn't really a question. I rushed on with the answer — my guess. 'I would say that Jeff found Mandy lying on the floor. He found the brooch, too. The final dispute between the two women took place there. But there was Mandy, and there was Heather's brooch. So Jeff took it. Keep your mouth shut, that was the message. But Heather, you thought it came from Martin. You thought she'd been alive when you left her, and that Martin had come along and finished her off. For you, Heather. Not for himself — if he did do it. But no . . . Martin didn't leave that lay-by. I think it was Jeff who pushed Mandy's body out of the window and into the pool. I don't know whether or not you struck her with a spanner from that bench, Heather . . . ' I left it hanging in the air.

'No,' she whispered, past her knuckles.

'But if you did, it was for Martin, because you love him, and for yourself, because you couldn't live without him. Or perhaps . . . ' I turned and stared at him. 'Perhaps you, Jeff, killed her. That would be for Martin. I just don't know.'

'I don't . . . ' Heather was groping for words.

Martin said, 'Tell her, lover.'

She looked at him entreatingly, and Martin smiled. Fumbling, trying to unload it all

374

quickly, she said, 'We didn't get to fighting at the front of the house. Only argued — shouted. Then she turned and almost ran away, but I'd got more to say. I went after her and saw where she went. Then I saw her climbing that ladder thing to the mill, so I had to go up it after her. And there she got herself all wound up. Me too, I suppose. We struggled. Scratched . . . ' She bit her lip to silence.

'Tell it all, sweetheart,' Martin said. He seemed unaware of the approaching sirens.

'She grabbed at my brooch. It tore my blouse. She'd got it in her hand. My brooch. She turned away to the window, and I thought she was going to throw it out. So I threw something at her. The first thing that came to hand. It was a spanner, I think. Yes . . . and it hit her in the back. Not her head — I'm sure. She fell down, and she still had my brooch in her hand. I was scared of touching her. Terrified. So I ran away.'

'And Jeff saw the result,' I decided. 'He saw you run off, and probably saw that your blouse was torn.'

Martin sighed. 'He told me later. He collected the brooch, because it was Heather's. He'd seen some of the struggle, coming down from the farm side.'

'Did he say he'd put her body in the pool?'

I looked round. Jeff was now by the open doorway. The sirens were dying, the tone leaping about as the police car ran through the village.

'Did you kill her, Jeff?' I asked him. 'Kill her, then put her body in the pool?'

The sirens were dying to a whimper, then to a growl. There was more than one vehicle, probably an ambulance, too. Jeff's head swivelled frantically, his eyes racing from face to face — from Martin's then back to Heather's.

Then he turned and ran for the darkness outside. My eyes following him, I realized that a dark and bulky shadow stood there, legs apart. It was Clive Garner, but he made no attempt to intercept, though Oliver said, 'Don't let him go.' There'd been no conviction in his voice.

Garner said flatly, advancing on us after a glance after Jeff, 'I found her in the pool. I waded in and got her out and carried her in my arms up to the farm. And I washed her there in the bath — both of us — naked together for the first time. Washed her and sprayed her, and scented her. I'd only got some aftershave — but sweet, she was. And I took her in the Range Rover and left her where I thought she belonged — in Martin's bed. Because I thought . . . the yellow car . . . you know.'

From outside there were disorganized shouts. We hurried out past Garner, Oliver and I. For a second I glanced back. Martin had his arms around Heather, she clinging to him with her head on his shoulder. Garner was hovering in indecision.

I heard an engine start, then the scream of spun tyres. We began to run. A uniformed officer reached for Oliver's arm, but he thrust it aside.

'Hey . . . you . . . ' The shout followed us.

The Fiesta's rear lights were disappearing through the village. I fell into the BMW, behind the wheel, but Oliver was slower. I got the car moving before he'd slammed the door.

'Leave it to the police, Phil, please.'

'No. I want to get there first. One more question for Jeff, Oliver. Only one.'

'For God's sake!'

I slammed my foot down. A dog scuttled across the street and I almost mounted the kerb, missing him.

'I want . . . ' I didn't complete it.

A siren began wailing behind us. Blue light tinted my rear-view mirror. I'd lost Jeff's tail-lights, but his heads flickered through the trees on the rise beyond the village. The corners were sharper than I'd expected.

Oliver muttered something. But Jeff had the advantage of knowing the corners.

'What?' I shouted, though the clamour could have been in my head.

'What question?' He shouted too. The siren was closer.

'Did he realize he'd been spotted when he drove out of the farm entrance?'

'Of course . . . of course he did. Why else did they lift the yellow Dolomite on the hoist? You know that, Phil. It was all they could do, getting back late for the stag party. Minutes, they had, but in that time they created the impression it hadn't been out that day. Wasn't that what you were getting at?'

'I want to hear it from Jeff's own lips.'

'What's the matter with Martin's lips? He'll know the answer. Take it easy, Phil, for heaven's sake!'

But I was ignorant of the road's contortions on the far side of the village. It wound and twisted, dived and plunged. And always the lights ahead played a dodging game, receding from me gradually. He was now further away, in the trees on the slopes. With a whine, and a howl from its horn, a police car overtook us wildly. Oliver shouted, 'Leave it, Phil! Leave it to the police.'

I eased up. There was no heart in it now. Whatever happened, I wasn't going to be able to ask my question.

'Ask Martin,' he repeated.

'And get the truth?' I drew to a halt. 'Never. They lie for each other, they cover for each other. Never the truth, if it's been for a mate — or for Heather.'

Oliver was silent for a while. We sat in the darkness with the lights on park, and the silence stretched out into the night. At last he spoke, and it was very gentle, almost soothing.

'D'you realize something?' he asked. 'Whatever it's been, it's all been for love. Remember that, Phil. And I don't mean they were homos. For love of each other, for love of Heather. And what Heather's done has been for Martin. It's rare, this. No hatred, no jealousy. Just for love. It's a thought to cling to.'

I leaned forward intently. The leading headlights had suddenly disappeared, way out there on the slopes. Ten seconds later, a great flare of light, orange spiked with red, took their place. I listened, listened, but I heard no sound of an explosion. Then I was shaken through and through by a surge of emotion, and buried my face in my hands, the tears pouring, my throat constricted.

'Phil, Phil,' said Oliver softly. He draped his near-useless arm around my shoulders, using more pressure than he could really afford. 'Phil!'

I managed to raise my head. 'But I *liked* him, Oliver,' I sobbed. 'I did.'

Then he was silent, waiting, except for foolish murmurings and inadequate words — and still he waited.

Another police car came howling past. I raised my head.

'And now we'll never know,' I whispered.

'Know what, my love?'

'Whether Heather killed her, and then Jeff put her body in the pool, or he found Mandy unconscious, and finished her off . . . to . . . to clear the way for Martin. Never know. Never.'

'What say we simply turn round and go home? Eh?'

I looked intently at him. We would be leaving little behind, and the police could contact us if they wanted written statements.

'Now?'

'Now. And I'll drive for a little while. Find somewhere to turn her around, and I'll take over.'

'Yes,' I whispered. 'Yes, Oliver, we'll do that.'

A long while later we pulled into an all-night café and ate sandwiches, and soaked ourselves in coffee. We seemed to have been living in cafés lately. Oliver was watching me, his eyes serious and thoughtful.

'But of course,' he said, 'we mustn't forget the death spasm. Cadaveric spasm, they call it. It's a muscular contraction thing.'

'Is it?' I couldn't find any interest in it, couldn't see the connection.

'Yes. In a violent death . . . anything you're gripping can't be released afterwards, unless the fingers are broken. Drowning people clutch at straws.'

'Oh? I often wondered what that meant.'

'And we've heard nothing about Mandy's fingers being broken . . . but it was Jeff who had the brooch.'

'Oh,' I said.

'Think about it.'

I didn't need to think. I knew already about cadaveric spasm — it happened only with drowning. And Mandy hadn't drowned. Had she!

Silently, we proceeded. I knew that Oliver had intended to spare me this knowledge. I didn't let him know I knew; it was these little secrets that bound us.

I touched his hand. No more.

We do hope that you have enjoyed reading this large print book.

Did you know that all of our titles are available for purchase?

We publish a wide range of high quality large print books including:
Romances, Mysteries, Classics
General Fiction
Non Fiction and Westerns

Special interest titles available in large print are:
The Little Oxford Dictionary
Music Book
Song Book
Hymn Book
Service Book

Also available from us courtesy of Oxford University Press:
Young Readers' Dictionary
(large print edition)
Young Readers' Thesaurus
(large print edition)

For further information or a free brochure, please contact us at:
Ulverscroft Large Print Books Ltd.,
The Green, Bradgate Road, Anstey,
Leicester, LE7 7FU, England.
Tel: (00 44) 0116 236 4325
Fax: (00 44) 0116 234 0205